IN DAYLIGHT AND DARKNESS

WORLDWALKERS: BOOK 1

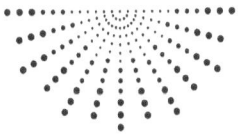

DANA ARDIS

In Daylight and Darkness
Copyright © 2021 Dana Ardis
All rights reserved.

Print edition

ISBN: 978-1-7369899-2-0

PUBLISHER'S CATALOGING-IN-PUBLICATION DATA

Names: Ardis, Dana, author.

Title: In daylight and darkness / by Dana Ardis.

Description: First edition. | Feathered Dog Books, 2021.

Summary: After eighteen-year-old Kate is released from inpatient psychiatric care, her friend Cor returns and she must decide whether he and his warnings are real or a sign that her symptoms have returned.

Identifiers: ISBN 978-1-736-98992-0 (pbk.)

Subjects: Belief and doubt – Fiction. | Ability – Fiction. | Magic – Fiction. | Predation (Biology) – Fiction. | Oaths – Fiction. | BISAC: FICTION / Fantasy / Romance.

To Josh, for giving me my first critique. I promised.

To Shami and John, for being the catalysts.

PROLOGUE

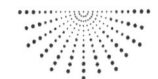

A girl screamed and I ducked down into the chest-high grass, praying no one could see me. I moved forward in a crouch, trying to disturb the grass as little as possible, aiming for the pair of saplings ahead that would give me a little more cover. The stiff stems rustled against my green Bulbasaur pajamas.

The girl's yells kept going, growing louder as she came down the sunlit field. She'd never make it to safety now, but having her as easy prey would at least distract the catchers. I dashed forward, sprinting across a shorter patch of vegetation before diving into the thicker growth around the little trees.

I plowed right into another kid. Coran couldn't quite smother his yelp of surprise. We toppled in a tangle of limbs. The girl's distant yell cut off like someone had flicked a switch. There would be another catcher now, making it even harder for us to get to the safe zone—the hedge at the end of the field.

"Shh, they'll hear us," I hissed under my breath, trying to free myself from my best friend without tumbling out of our hiding place.

Coran scooted over to give me some more room. A grin lit up his narrow face and he had a twig sticking out of his long, candy-orange braid. He whispered, "No, Pizan's playing the chaser on this side of the field and she's short. She'll be playing low to the ground. She won't hear anything over the rustling of the grass."

"But what about the other chaser?" I asked. The field had gone quiet again, nothing but the occasional birdcall and the murmur of the breeze through the grasses. Just enough sound to make it hard to hear someone sneaking up on us.

He rolled his shoulders, making a simple shrug way too dramatic. I smothered a giggle.

"It's just Bir," Coran whispered, then pointed up over the plants sheltering us. "You should check if you see anyone."

"Me?" I mouthed.

Coran tweaked a lock of my chin-length, dark brown hair and mouthed back, "Human."

Fine. I rolled my eyes. He and his Thurei cousins had hair colors that looked like they'd come out of a box of crayons. No wonder no one believed my descriptions of them.

Grabbing one of the tree trunks to steady myself, I rose out of my crouch to peer over the grass.

Six catchers made a loose line along the bottom of the meadow, where the hedge marked the field boundary. They didn't bother to hide. They just had to wait while we came to them. We'd made it most of the way down the meadow, but that had just brought us closer to danger.

I spotted one of the other runners, trying to make it through the catchers to safety. He bolted out of a thick stand of grasses thirty feet away, heading toward a clump of brambles he could sneak around for cover. His pale, yellow hair stood out like a highlighter against the meadow greens. He made it halfway there when a navy-haired girl leaped up from the waist-high grass, landing a quick tag on his side as he tried to twist out of the way.

The boy groaned in frustration, then stood up and ran straight for the bottom of the meadow, yelling his head off. A couple of catchers started moving to cut him off. There'd be seven catchers to sneak past by the time we made it there.

We didn't wait to see it. Coran and I snuck around the left side of the little stand of trees, moving fast while all the yelling would cover our noise. The navy-haired chaser, Pizan, would get us next if we waited any longer.

"Come on," Coran whispered, beckoning me to follow.

He knew this field better than I did. We moved forward, crouched as low as we could. The grass barely reached over our heads.

If anyone saw Coran's traffic-cone-orange hair, we'd both get caught.

Like he could read my thoughts, Coran ducked even lower.

No, he'd stepped down into a little gully that dipped a few inches below the rest of the meadow. No grass grew in it, either, creating a little canyon in the greenery. We didn't have room to stand up all the way, but we could move faster and still not disturb the grass around us. He turned around to give me an I-told-you grin.

I trusted you, didn't I? But I'd have to wait until the game ended to tell him. I joined him in the gully, sidestepping along the narrow passage through the grass. Somewhere behind us, another kid got tagged by a chaser.

Her yelling came closer and closer, cutting off only a few yards ahead of us, with a burst of laughter from the catchers before they went silent again.

We were within sprinting distance of the line of catchers, but that last tag had clustered them right around us.

Coran turned to me, fists clenched in frustration. Then a birdcall rippled over the meadow and Coran's eyes lit up, a grin tugging at his lips. He held up a hand, waggling all five fingers. Then he pointed to me and off to the right, himself, and then the other direction.

Well, we couldn't hide here much longer. The catchers would trip over us by accident. I nodded and started silently counting to five along with him.

On the count of three, Coran let out a whoop at the top of his lungs and leaped out of the gully, veering off to the left. Surprise froze me for a moment, but I didn't waste the opportunity. I ran, half-crouching, toward the safe zone.

No one paid me any attention. I was just a quiet, brown-haired human girl in green pajamas. A handful of catchers ran toward the maniac yelling his emergency-orange head off.

I reached the hedge in time to watch. The half dozen other kids who'd made it safe formed an audience around me.

"They're gonna kill him for sure," one of the girls said.

Coran sprinted for the patch of brambles, but there were catchers on both sides. Sneaking around it wouldn't work. Instead, Coran crossed his arms over his face and dove straight into the brambles.

The world disappeared in a flare of white light. I winced, flinching back against the hedge for a second before forcing my eyes back open. My vision swam, dazzled with bright spots like the aftereffects of a camera flash.

"What was that?" I asked. Around me, kids were laughing, still excited.

"He scared the blazebird off its nest," the girl next to me said, sounding impressed even as she rubbed her eyes. A pigeon-sized bird whirred past overhead, flickering like a distant strobe light.

I dragged my gaze back down and scanned the meadow for Coran, trying to blink past the bird-shaped spots in my eyes, but I couldn't see him. Neither could the catchers, at point blank range for the flash.

I laughed. He might make it out of this, after all.

"You're supposed to be yelling still," one of the catchers complained, squinting at the brambles.

Coran could hardly answer for himself, so I spoke up. "He never got tagged."

A breath later, I caught a flash of orange outside the loose circle of catchers as Coran left the tall grass to duck down into shorter growth. That much closer to the hedge.

The rules lawyer shouted, "Over here!"

Coran gave up on stealth and just sprinted. The closest catcher lunged for him, but Coran whirled away from him. He almost lost his footing, stumbling a couple of steps, and the other catchers gained on him.

"Run!" I yelled. One of the other kids along the hedge echoed me.

Then we were all yelling, cheering, as Coran charged the last few yards to safety, catchers right on his heels.

Coran hit the hedge right beside me and we all exploded into cheers. Even a couple of the catchers joined in. He wrapped his arms around my waist and lifted me in the air, whirling us around in triumph.

I laughed and hugged him back. "What kind of plan was that?"

"It worked, didn't it?" Coran asked. I would not be surprised if his face froze with a smile like that on it.

I just shook my head, giggling, as he set me back on my feet. Around us, the game continued. The runners had taken advantage of all the distraction and the audience at the hedge went back to the show.

"You're all scratched up." I dabbed a spot of blood from his cheek.

"It'll be fine, don't worry. Look." He held out his fist and uncurled his fingers. A feather lay in his palm, dove gray and slightly crumpled. Nothing special, until he tapped it sharply. It flickered, like metal in the sun, then went dark again.

"It's beautiful," I said, delighted by the magic of it.

"You should keep it." Coran tucked it into my hand before we both turned back to the game.

When I got dressed for school the next morning, I checked my pajamas carefully for grass stains or any other sign I'd been outside. I'd gotten in enough trouble for 'sneaking out' at night to play in the yard and 'telling stories' about what had really happened. My dad had said more than once that I was too old for imaginary friends and I needed to stop blaming them for my bad behavior. At school, no one saw anything more than a dove's feather, same as any they could pick up off the sidewalk.

By the time I learned they would never believe me, it was too late.

CHAPTER ONE

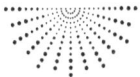

The sun set without any trouble. For the second night in a row, I didn't see anything I wasn't supposed to. I pushed the cold cup of coffee away, relieved.

Then Cor walked through the door of the diner.

After everything I'd gone through, part of me still wanted to rationalize why no one stared as he walked to my table despite his tangerine hair and his long, black coat. Maybe he stood out less in my sketchy neighborhood. Maybe people assumed his impossibly bright hair came out of a bottle.

No. No one else could see Cor because he didn't exist. I couldn't make excuses for him anymore. By now, I knew better than to think imaginary friends were harmless.

I didn't want to see him, but I couldn't quite ignore him, either. He stopped just outside the range of comfortable conversation, his golden eyes not quite meeting mine.

If I'd meant to ignore him, I should have stayed in my apartment, taken my sleeping pill like usual, and been out like a light before the sun had slipped beneath the horizon.

"Cor," I said, his name familiar on my tongue, though I'd sworn

I'd never say it again. His narrow shoulders relaxed just a bit at the fact I didn't say his full name, as a stranger might have.

"Kate." He spoke so softly, the name almost sank beneath the level of diner chatter. Or the sound of the blood pounding in my ears. He slid in to the opposite side of the booth.

He'd never been shy like this as a child.

The last time I'd seen him, five years ago, he'd been hardly more than a kid, spindly with sudden growth, stricken by my disbelief. It unsettled me to see him recast as this nervous stranger. His face was long and lean, his features angular and stark, handsome but subtly inhuman. His alien eyes, yellow-hazel with a vertical pupil like a cat's, had changed the most. I didn't recognize the hardness in them at all.

I was not prepared to have him sitting here, real as real, toying with the salt shaker.

He'd said once that the ever-present salt and pepper shakers were another indication of how bland things were here in my world.

Acknowledging him had been a mistake. Memories I'd tried to shut away for years clamored for my attention, and I felt like I was drowning. I squeezed my eyes shut and tried to slow my stuttering pulse. *It's all in your head, Katherine. Ignore it. Don't give in. Call the doctors.*

"Katen, stop."

'Katen,' like we were still the best friends we'd been as kids. I opened my eyes to find Cor's hand stretched toward mine, but he stopped shy of touching me. I hid my hands in my lap.

"I know it's been hard for you. I saw what happened in...that place." Cor had always held a dim view of human doctors. "I tried to respect your choice."

I opened my mouth to object, but he flicked his fingers, a Thurei gesture of denial.

"Let me finish. I tried to respect your decision, even if it hurt. I stayed out of your way. Shom has left you alone. But that's not enough, Kate. Now that you're older and free of that place, you're not safe. Hunters can find you. You don't have the training to protect yourself and I can't protect you if you don't want me around."

I don't know why I'd expected things to go better, playing into this. I should have ignored the note I'd found outside my door. I'd hoped I could stare my fear in the face and find it unfounded. That I could go out at night—the hallucinations only happened at night—and have no recurrence of symptoms. I'd been wrong. Cor was here, talking to me, feeding me a line of textbook schizophrenic paranoia. I couldn't lose myself to madness again. I looked him squarely in the eye and kept my voice as calm as I could.

"I'm only here to tell you to go away. You're not real."

It had worked before, after months of insistence. Now, Cor just narrowed his eyes. He took a deep breath and started again, in a voice much lighter, much more hopeful. A touch desperate. "You kept the note I left you, didn't you? You must have."

The look on his face denied any possibility I would say *no*.

As much as I wanted to deny it, the thick paper crinkled in my pocket, an accusation. I'd found it on my welcome mat, folded into a precise, abstract shape that had been tip-of-the-tongue familiar. Humans didn't leave notes like that, even if I *had* known someone inclined to leave a note outside my third-floor walk-up. That particular custom belonged to his world, Kuyen. Crazyland. I'd been so surprised to see it that I'd picked it up and unfolded it, read the simple message, 'I need to speak with you. You are in danger.' Then I'd scrunched it up and flung it away, afraid of what it meant—a failure of my medication, and an end to the five years my illness had mostly left me alone.

And then I'd chased after it and picked it up because...

I kept everything. I always had. Cor knew that.

"Here." I pulled the paper from my pocket and thrust it at him, trying to ignore how my hand shook.

He smoothed the crumpled paper with careful fingertips, his only acknowledgment of its wrinkles and creases. The original shape of the folded note had been 'Urgent.' He made no mention of that, either. He placed the salt shaker on top of the sheet, used the paper to tug it back and forth. I knew exactly what he meant by the little display: an object from his world could move one from mine. We'd had this argument before.

"There, see?" he said, like it could be so simple. "They're both real."

"That doesn't prove anything."

Cor leaned forward, the thread of desperation in his voice stronger. "What do you want me to do, Kate? Dance on the table so you can ask people if they see me?"

"No!"

A middle-aged couple from the next table over glanced up at me. I could only imagine what they must have been thinking—nutcase, arguing with herself. And who could blame them? They were right.

I gritted my teeth against the building urge to shout, to throw things. *That's the last thing you need, Katherine.* I'd learned years ago to stay quiet and unnoticed, no matter what I saw. Or thought I saw. I lowered my voice. "What I want is for you to go away."

Cor clenched his fists on the tabletop. I turned away from his anger, stared out the window. We'd argued just like this the last time we'd spoken.

"I know you don't want me here, but things can sense you, even on your side. You can send me away because you don't want to see me, but that doesn't work with Hunters. I will not leave things this way." He paused, a moment where I was meant to face him. I didn't. Couldn't. I stared out at the darkened street.

"You must see this, Katen." A sigh. A squeak of leather on vinyl and he walked away. I waited until I heard the door close behind him. When I turned, the note sat on the table, refolded. This time the form was 'Request.'

CHAPTER TWO

I awoke expecting the fluorescent lights of the ward. Instead, dawn brightened the plain white walls of my bedroom. Although the four months I'd been here wasn't long enough to make my apartment feel like home, the reminder that I'd made it out—that I finally had my freedom—was a comfort.

Until I remembered that last night hadn't been a dream.

I'd built such a fragile form of safety, getting my apartment and my job here in San Jose. I'd moved far from the schoolyards where children pointed and laughed because of the stories I'd tell and believe. Away from my parents, who'd come to see me as something broken that had to be managed if it couldn't be mended. I'd even made it out of the hospital where they'd finally left me, surrounded by enough nurses and doctors to make reality stick.

In the end, it didn't matter how far I ran. I couldn't get away from the problem—my lying, unreliable mind that couldn't tell false from real, no matter what drugs they gave me, no matter what therapy. Cor was back, pushing me one step closer to raving bag lady with an aluminum foil helmet to keep out the alien mind rays.

I rolled over, reached for the phone, and dialed my psychiatrist's office.

"Thank you for calling Bayshore Psychiatric. If you have a medical or psychiatric emergency..."

I hung up.

Dr. Vargas would be delighted to call last night's episode a "psychiatric emergency." Symptom-free patients made poor subjects for journal articles. His interest in studying my case—unusual, on account of my full-blown hallucinations in the absence of so many of the other standard indicators of schizophrenia—had made the six years of inpatient psychiatric care possible. My dad's landscaping nursery could never have funded it otherwise.

I still remembered watching my parents walk out of Bayshore's doors when they'd left me there, a terrified twelve-year-old no one would believe. I hadn't had the freedom to follow until I'd turned eighteen, and even then it had taken a battle. The agreement I'd hammered out with my parents traded some help with my finances for regular outpatient visits with my psychiatrist.

It didn't take an unhinged imagination to picture Vargas' clinical gaze over the top of his bifocals. *I warned you that the stress of a life on your own might cause a relapse, Katherine. You need to be realistic about what you can handle.*

Say goodbye to my apartment, at the very least. In the best case scenario, I'd have to move back in with my parents in Eugene, where everyone knew me as the crazy girl who'd gotten sent away. No one here in San Jose knew me. Here, I could be normal.

If I fought for it.

Calling Vargas' office would mean trying another long list of medications and enduring their inevitable side effects to find the right dosage to snuff the symptoms out. Vomiting, dizziness, cotton-headed zombie-brain feelings. Skin rashes and seizures and muscle twitches. Brain meds were not gentle drugs in my experience.

It was only a matter of time. Schizophrenia had no cure.

But I had come too far to give up.

My other option was to wait this out. I could always hope the symptoms—

A memory flared, a night Shom and Cor had slipped in to see me in the ward. I closed my eyes and repeated my coping sentence out loud.

Coran's puzzled question, "What does that mean, a 'delusion?'"

"They told her we're fake and she believes them, not us." Shom, furious. She shifted out after that, so fast it must have made her sick.

Cor stayed silent then, though he argued with me passionately in the weeks that followed. Uselessly, as it turned out. By then, I'd known I was truly crazy. Even he'd given up, in the end.

—the symptoms might fade on their own, if I were patient. That was riskier, as they might also grow in strength and overwhelm me, maybe even put me back in the hospital if I went too long without updated medication, treatment, and monitoring. Outpatient could become inpatient again with a single misstep.

Not that my parents or Dr. Vargas had wanted me out in the first place.

I clung to the hope that I could get all of this trouble crammed back into my Pandora's box. The medication had been working fine up to this point. Maybe last night had just been a...hiccup.

Schizophrenic episodes could possess a kind of internal logic, following their own rules. Mine always had. Once I'd refused to cross over to Kuyen and forced Cor and Shom to leave me alone, I'd managed to stop the episodes altogether. It had worked for the last five years.

I could do it again.

If I was wrong, I could always call the psychiatrist later.

I locked up my bike behind After Image and let myself in the back door. Rose was there already, counting out the till. She scraped the change off the counter and dumped it into the register tray.

"Good morning, Katherine! I have a favor to ask you."

From what I'd learned of Rose over the past few months, this enthusiasm was typical. My hold on sanity already seemed fragile enough that I wasn't sure I could handle six hours with her.

She flopped the shift calendar down in front of me and hopped up to sit beside it, her pixie features set in a look of melodramatic appeal. She did all of her emotions big. Or maybe it just seemed like it since she was so small.

"I have a show coming up in a couple of days. Frank and Eviana can't cover. I know you don't work evenings, but you'd really be my savior here. Could you swap shifts with me?" She cocked her head like a bird. "I mean, you're not really afraid of the dark."

She said it the way she was supposed to, the way that meant she knew it was a joke. I wasn't afraid of the dark and I never had been, even as a kid. After all, I always had a sun available—when it set here, it rose again in Kuyen, opening the way for me to visit my friends, Earth night paired to Kuyen day. It had seemed like a blessing any child would wish for. Only later had it become a curse.

When I applied for this job, I had marked myself unavailable in the evenings, and I'd dusted off that old joke because I didn't have a normal excuse. No college classes like Rose or Frank or a family to take care of like Eviana. Certainly no extracurricular social activities. I didn't avoid going out at night because I feared the dark, but because I feared the light of a different day.

If I could get this episode under control like I hoped, I wouldn't have to worry about being crazy in public. If I wasn't confident I could make it work on my own, then I should call the doctor's office right now.

"That shouldn't be a problem," I made myself say.

"You're the best!" She flung her arms around me in a startling hug.

"You're welcome," I stammered, but she was already turning away, jingling the keys for the front door and the security grille.

I dug in my messenger bag for my pillbox. The little compartment for today held three tablets. They looked simple enough, but each had an unpronounceable name and a thick packet of warnings when I'd picked up the prescriptions at the pharmacy. Together, they made the perfect chemical cocktail to mend my broken mind.

At least in theory.

I dry-swallowed my medicine with the ease of long practice, then bent to stow my bag under the counter. Something crinkled in my pocket. I fished out Cor's folded note. It felt just as solid as it had last night, the fine paper turned velvety from repeated foldings and crumplings.

I'd spent so long trying to bury my memories of Kuyen that the sudden rush of nostalgia caught me by surprise. Coran and Shom had been my best friends. I hadn't even asked him about her.

Of course I hadn't. What was the point of asking after someone who doesn't exist?

A customer pushed open the door, saving me from that particular downward spiral. The woman pulled a stack of photos out of her purse and fanned them on the counter.

"My daughter is getting married in June and I wanted to do something with these pictures of her and her fiancé." The collection was a motley mix of baby pictures, candid school-age shots, and a couple of formal portraits. I brought out the binder of custom memorabilia and sank into a discussion of DVD slideshows and memory books.

As we spoke, the customer rummaged through her purse. She found a pen and asked, "This is scratch paper, isn't it?"

The woman plucked Cor's note off the counter. I must have been even more tired than I thought to have left it lying around. Before I could answer, she jotted a list of prices on the square of paper, her looping numerals scrawled above his precise Kuyene script.

"Yeah, it's fine," I mumbled, not that she was listening. Of course it was scratch paper. She'd seen scribbles on it—if she'd seen anything at all—because there was no secret, special foreign language written just for me. What would I have done, kept it forever?

I had the only important information already. Cor was back because he wanted something. That gave me room to bargain.

That meant I would have to see him again.

CHAPTER THREE

I paced my tiny living room as the sky shaded from blue to gold to the deepening plum of coming night. I had no way to find Cor. I would have to ask him to come to me and I would need to slip part of the way over to Kuyen to do it.

Crossing without a clear destination in mind was dangerous. Landmarks on the other side shifted unpredictably as claimed and unclaimed lands moved against each other like tectonic plates. While claimed territory was safe enough, my friends always cautioned against traveling in the wildlands.

Cor's family had an enormous, formal home, but I couldn't call to mind much in the way of detail. The places I could remember—the meadow where we'd had picnics and played tag, the huge tree where we'd been pirates and monkeys, the rush-ringed pool where we'd fished in the drowsy Kuyen sun during Oregon's winters—they could be anywhere.

I'd sent messages to my friends often enough as a kid that the method came back to me effortlessly, like recalling your family's first phone number as soon as you started to dial. Plain paper would have to do since I didn't have anything as fine as his note. I tore a sheet from a spiral notebook, trimmed off the ragged edge, and cut it square.

Then I took out a pen and sat there a ridiculously long time trying to decide what to write. I settled on the formal Kuyene phrase 'I will listen.' Not quite an apology, it acknowledged that a disagreement had gotten out of hand and the speaker wanted to resolve it reasonably. It had smoothed over many squabbles between the three of us.

I found the Kuyene characters a little trickier. I'd picked up the spoken tongue with the ease of any child learning a second language from her playmates and Shom had patiently taught me to write it, but the skill was buried under years of deliberate forgetting. I had no choice. English words would not send the message on its way. Both form and intent needed to match, according to some convoluted set of rules Shom had tried to explain to me several times. After a couple of false starts, I worked it out and signed my name at the bottom.

I remembered the correct folds, creasing the paper in just such a way that, combined with the writing and my wish for its delivery, would send this Summons to Cor. When I finished, the shape was bird-like—another culture's origami. I wrote Cor's full name on each wing, Coraven Temarel.

I settled cross-legged on the floor. My hands trembled, making the folded paper shiver. I took several deep breaths, then closed my eyes and reached with my mind toward the sideways edge of this world and the other, searching for the passage between them.

I couldn't find it at first, couldn't make my mind reach in that twisty, edge-on direction. When I did, the margin was slick and my grip feeble. By the time I had a solid grasp, my head pounded. I opened my eyes. Since I had no fixed destination, I would most likely be slipping into wildlands and I wanted to go no farther than necessary to send my message.

Steeling myself, I began to slip across the gap. Like a double-exposed print, my apartment changed as another scene came into focus, overlaying it. While I was still clearly in my living room, I was also, just faintly, elsewhere. A ghostly set of sensations built around me as I pulled that other place closer. I could make out a wooded landscape, filmy against the solid sight of my apartment, a few misty trees plunging up through my ceiling. A whiff of rich loam and growing things breezed through the apartment's still, urban air. The sounds of traffic faded, indistinct, mixing with a fragment of bird song and the rustling of leaves.

This was far enough. Nothing moved in the Kuyene wilds as far as I could tell, but even this hazy version of it felt dangerous. *What might be here is irrelevant. It's the fact that I'm seeing it at all.*

I set my attention on the Summons. The paper stirred in my hands, but nothing more. I inhaled slowly and slipped a bit farther from my own familiar apartment. The forest on the other side grew a little more tangible, as my threadbare carpet, the bare walls, the electric light from the ceiling fixture all grew slightly less. The paper lifted up out of my hands, flapping its folded wings and heading between the trees in the general direction of my half-visible apartment window. Nothing could impede a Summons, once sent. It would reach Cor, wherever he was.

I let go of Kuyen, sliding back into my own world. The real world. A flutter of white caught my eye. My Summons was slipping back, too, right outside my window. There, just visible in the dark once I knew where to look, I could see a shock of vibrant orange hair. Cor himself, standing on my fire escape.

He moved closer to the window, where the light from inside fell across him. His hands moved and stopped in a kind of stutter, as if he were unsure whether to read my note now or tap on the glass and explain what he was doing there. Shocked, I simply stared. Seeing me unmoving, he ducked his head and unfolded the paper. He read the simple message and folded it up again. No fancy shape, then, just a small square for saving, which he slid into an inner pocket of his coat. He splayed the long fingers of one hand against the window.

I dragged myself to my feet, stumbling a little with dizziness and the sharp, pounding pain in my head. When I opened the window for Cor to climb through, I had to steady myself on the sill.

"Katen, are you unwell?" He used the Thurei-style diminutive of my name, the way a close friend might in private. That betrayed his concern louder than the worry in his voice.

"It hurt, slipping over far enough to send that." My voice shook and I cleared my throat. Even without the headache, that glimpse of Kuyen had left me rattled, to say nothing of finding Cor lurking at my window. I closed the window behind him and drew the blinds.

"Perhaps because you haven't crossed in so long." His words held no judgment in them, but only in the too-careful way that meant that he must have scrubbed them clean first. The golden undertones of his skin contrasted starkly with his long, black leather coat, which he wore over a plain, dark shirt and slim trousers. He looked every bit as ill at ease as I felt.

My apartment must have seemed pathetically small and poor to him, only one bedroom, a tiny living room, and a kitchen that could fit in his pocket. I didn't even have real furniture, just a card table and a single folding chair, a couple of yard sale shelves lined with battered paperbacks and a stack of jigsaw puzzles.

I was proud of getting out on my own, considering where I'd started. I'd been proud, anyway, until I'd had Cor here in my living room. His family lived in a mansion.

No, his fake family lives in an imaginary mansion in fantasyland. I could feel myself scowling and tried to dial it back. I needed to stay calm, despite proof of my madness standing here in front of me.

First things first. "Why were you skulking around my fire escape?"

"Skulking?" His English wasn't as rusty as my Kuyene, but being the product of a native speaker's imagination had to have its perks. He continued without waiting for a definition. "I didn't have your permission to be there, and for that, I'm in the wrong. There has been a Bolgen in the area, one of the lesser Hunters. I set some wards here and I wanted to make sure they held. I should have asked first, but you would've refused. It needed to be done."

I pressed a hand against my temple. "You were doing what?"

Cor pulled a strip of something from his pocket. Ribbon, or some type of flat cord woven from off-white fibers, shot through with occasional threads in darker earth tones. "Wards. They help conceal you from Hunters, like a mask, or a shadow."

"Fine. Leave it, whatever you put up. If you think it's so important." The concept of asking for forgiveness rather than permission was more human than Thurei, but he wasn't even doing that. He hadn't said he was sorry and didn't sound like it, either. Waiting for an apology from a Thurei was a waste of time. I let it go. I didn't need his regret.

His brows drew down. "It is important. Tell me what your plan would be when a Bolgen shows up at your door, wanting your blood for her birth-tithe?"

Delusions, I was familiar with—a magical slip-world laying overtop this one, filled with intelligent species, the closest neighbor of an untold number of such worlds, according to Shom. It was only accessible to the rare human with the ability to slip between boring old Earth and fantastic Kuyen.

That was crazy enough, but this talk of Hunters and danger smacked of paranoia, the schizophrenia pushing closer. I pushed back.

"My plan for imaginary monsters is the same now as it was five years ago."

We had enough history behind us that I could see the effort it took Cor to ignore my sarcasm. He let out a slow breath. "There's nothing imaginary about the danger. If you lived on Kuyen, you would have Truce and claimed land and family to protect you. You have none of that on Earth and I can't replace it all."

He said it like he was admitting a personal failure. I shook my head. "Living in Kuyen is not an option."

"Clearly," he said. "You have the means to keep yourself safe. What you need is training in your skill. Each kind of worldwalker has a specific skill that helps keep them safe, just as each type of Hunter has a skill that makes them more dangerous. For Thureis, it's the *zaret*, but—"

"Do you have any idea how stereotypically schizophrenic this sounds?" I interrupted. This was not how I'd meant things to go, but this conversation slipped back into old arguments, waking old fears. Not of Hunters, but of insanity.

"You're out of that place." Cor made it sound ridiculously obvious, like a reminder for a child. "You can think your own way now."

"That's..." He'd never tried that particular angle before. "I was in Bayshore because I'm crazy. Are you trying to send me back?"

"No!" He held up his hands in a gesture of harmlessness. "Please, you must believe I would never risk what you've built here."

I glared at him so hard, he flinched. "Must I?"

"Yes. You must believe that, at least. But I can't do this anymore."

I thought he meant arguing, but as he dragged a hand through his bright hair, I could see he was talking about something more. I refused to think about how tired he looked.

"What do you mean?" I asked. "What is it you're doing?"

He waved a hand at the world outside my window. "I've been keeping you safe while you hide your head under the blankets like a child and refuse to see. Learn to protect yourself and let me go."

"Let's skip to the end and you just go." I meant it to be mean. I couldn't afford to feel bad for him.

"I won't leave while you have no means to defend yourself. Do you think I could walk away and let them kill you?"

I made no effort to hide my skepticism. It worked. He drew himself up. "You said you would listen."

I couldn't let him stalk off in a self-righteous huff. He'd as much as said he wouldn't leave me alone if nothing changed. If I wanted to stop this episode on my own, he had to agree to leave.

He said it himself. I uncrossed my arms and tried to sound reasonable. "Okay, fine. I need to learn this skill so you can leave. Teach me, then."

He hesitated, like my sudden agreement derailed him. "I can't."

"Why not?"

"I could train another Thurei, but humans and Thureis don't have the same skill. I don't know what the human skill is. You must be taught by someone who does. You'll need to come to Kuyen to learn."

"I can't do that." This conversation was already more than I should have been doing.

He braced his hands in his pockets like a jumper at the railing of a bridge, reaching for the courage to leap. "Not to stay. Just long enough to get the training you need to protect yourself. That's all I ask."

"And then what?"

"Nothing," Cor said, his voice just above a whisper. "Just that."

The thought of going back sent a shiver of fear through me. Keeping a firm hold on reality was hard enough to do in my own apartment.

But now I had my bargain, if I had the guts to use it. Sink or swim.

"If I go back and get this training, then I'm done. That's it. We're finished. You leave me alone." In case it wasn't clear, I added, "That means my fire escape, too."

"Agreed." He looked away. "Do this and you'll never have to see me again. You can forget you ever knew me. But you'll be safe."

I nodded, glad I didn't have to meet his gaze. "Okay then, yes. If that's the agreement, I'll do it."

He let out a long breath and held out his hand. "Will you swear to it?"

I could hardly say *no*, since I'd come up with the terms. Would it count as lying if I broke a promise to a hallucination? I swallowed hard and nodded.

"Do not swear it if you do not mean it, Katherine Kjelgaard."

Full names meant something, both on Kuyen in general and among Cor's people in particular.

"I mean it."

I fit my hand into his. His grip strong and his palms unexpectedly calloused. For the first time, I noticed how much taller than me he was. He must have been six feet at least.

"I am sworn to this agreement, Katherine Kjelgaard." He said it in English, but with the cadence of a formal phrase.

"As am I, Coraven Temarel." I pulled my hand back and barreled on before I could lose my momentum. Or come to my senses. "So how are we doing this?"

"Ah, well. There's a Scholar who is said to have an interest in humans. We can start there."

The sketchiness of his answer wasn't lost on me. "And he'll teach me?"

"She," he corrected offhand, but I recognized the stalling. He hadn't changed so much, it seemed. "I wrote to the Scholars. They said we must come in person."

"That seems convenient."

"No, it doesn't," Cor said, his tone brittle. "If I could have brought a tutor here to set before you, I would have."

"But she's said she'll train me?" This was not going to turn into a loophole.

"The Scholars will help us, Kate. They're dedicated to truth. This is what they do."

"And if they don't? What then?"

"They will. I'm not trapping you with this."

No, not like I was doing. Cor had never been a liar. If he thought it would work, I would try it. "All right. Let's go, then."

"Now?" He blinked his amber-colored eyes at the sudden reversal. "I can come tomorrow and bring something to eat for us and we can have a day—"

"This isn't a picnic opportunity, Cor. Now." By tomorrow, I might talk myself out of it. I stepped around him to the kitchen and grabbed a fistful of granola bars and a couple of water bottles. I fetched my jacket and the backpack I used for library trips out of the closet, feeling ridiculous. It wasn't like we were really going anywhere. "There. We won't starve."

He sighed and held out a hand. "Then we go now."

I shook my head. "I'll shift myself."

"You've never been there, and I only have one token."

"Token?" I asked, wary of all these little oh-buts.

He fished in his pocket and pulled out a metal disk about the size of a quarter. "They're for slipping to places you've never seen. We

24

didn't need them as children. You crossed with us, and Shom and I stuck to the places we knew. I didn't think to ask for two."

"But you did happen to have one."

"Yes! I'd hoped—" He stopped. Started over. "I didn't expect things to go this way."

"Wait." There were too many undercurrents here and any one of them could pull me under. "What is it you're not telling me?"

"Everything, Kate." The hardness in his voice cracked, showing something raw underneath. "Tell me that my world is just as real as yours."

I shook my head.

"Then what difference does it make?"

None. None at all. I had his word about our agreement. He could keep his secrets.

I held out my hand. "Are we going or not?"

"Close your eyes," he reminded me so he could guide our travel. He curled his fingers around mine and pulled us across to Kuyen.

CHAPTER FOUR

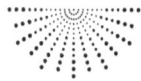

Sound swelled around us in a murmuring, chattering rush. A cold breeze tugged at loose strands of my hair, heavy with humidity, pungent with unfamiliar odors. The ground changed beneath the soles of my sneakers, gritty when I shifted my weight. Dampness worked its way under my coat. I shivered.

"Here we are. Scholar's Hall." Strain rasped through Cor's words.

I opened my eyes. We stood at the base of a steep hill in front of a stout, metal gate, all wrought bars and rivet-work. Beyond, stone steps rose, disappearing into a riot of vegetation. Behind us spread a bustling, bizarre city, the streets crowded with people and creatures of every description.

My gaze snagged on a familiar-looking Lan te Kos girl. Shom? No, of course not. She had the same gray skin and signature, loping gait that came with the faun-like legs, but of course Shom would have aged, as Cor had. *Assuming there're rules for any of this.*

The girl ducked into an archway draped with colorfully-patterned fabric.

I turned away. We hadn't come here to sightsee. I still had Cor's hand clutched in both of mine. I pulled away and frowned at the steps. "This looks more like stairs than a hall."

"The Scholars answer the questions of anyone who needs an answer badly enough to ask. After they climb the stairs." In the bright midmorning sun, he looked unsteady and pale. When I said as much, he forced a chuckle. "I will try to spend less time in night."

Before I could puzzle out that strange phrase, he headed for the gate.

Ancient as it seemed, it swung open at a gentle push. The broad steps allowed us to climb side by side. Lush forest pressed in on either side, a patchwork of green foliage stitched together with grasping vines, embellished here and there with gaudy blooms.

Just the sort of scenery a horticulturist's daughter would imagine for a subtropical climate. I held on to the thought and kept climbing. The higher we got, the less urban it smelled, more earthy, sharp with the scent of growing things, just like my dad's nursery.

After a few minutes, I noticed Cor's labored breathing.

"What's the matter?"

"You make no win building over wildlands," he said, grafting a Kuyene proverb onto English words with no care for making sense out of them. That, more than the tension on his face, told me how much his head hurt. Cor guarded his words like ward keys.

"Stop." The worry in my voice surprised me.

With the same willfulness I remembered from him as a child, he climbed three more steps before swaying to a halt. When I caught up to him, he let me glare him into sitting. His face shone with perspiration, although it wasn't that warm and I hadn't even begun to feel tired. Maybe I had bike riding and the stairs up to my apartment in my favor, but Cor didn't strike me as frail.

"I don't know what you think you need to prove." It came out peevish, but I hated the worry behind it. Not for me and my sanity. For him.

Which was crazy.

He pinched the bridge of his nose and mumbled something into his palm.

"I can't hear you," I said.

He beckoned me closer with a minimal waggle of long fingers and

I lowered myself to sit on the smooth stone next to him, tilting my head near his. His voice was low, brittle with pain. "I am not your enemy, Kate."

No. I'm my own enemy. Arguing with him now would be like kicking a puppy. And he knew it. I switched subjects. "What's wrong?"

"It was very hard to bring you across. Much harder than it should have been."

"I didn't fight it," I said, although he hadn't accused me of anything.

Cor grunted. "I know. I just need a little rest."

I wished I had some aspirin to offer. I pulled out a bottle of water, still cool from the fridge, and handed it over. He leaned his forehead against it and sighed.

I settled back against the next step and gazed at the slice of city I could see from between the walls of wild vegetation that framed the stairs. From this distance, it could almost pass as a city from my side. More organic, its jumble of buildings tended to curve rather than facet. Less glass or metal shone in the morning sun. Traffic filled the streets, people and draft animals, not automobiles. I wished I had brought my phone for pictures instead of leaving it on the charger. Maybe next time.

That thought froze me, shattering the tenuous feeling of wonder. 'Next time' was not part of the plan. The plan involved finishing this as quickly as possible so I could get back to my normal life. Or what passed for normal. The plan did not include building a timeshare in delusion.

Cor's voice brought me back. "Are you ready?"

"Are you?" It came out sharper than I'd intended.

He nodded, careful, as if his head might roll off his shoulders otherwise. At least he didn't seem one step away from collapse. Three or four steps, maybe.

Well, a hallucination didn't need me nagging after his health. I stood up. "Let's go, then."

He raised both orange brows when I offered my hand to help him up, but it put a smile on his face. It surprised me how light he was. Thureis were slender, but he must not have an extra ounce on him under that coat.

It turned out I was right. The noon sun, the humidity, and the climb all took their toll. We stopped to shed our coats. Perfectly tailored, his tunic and dark pants left no doubt that he was strong and well-muscled, but in a lean way, not bulky. His shoulders were narrow and his long torso tapered to even narrower hips. He reminded me of a gymnast I'd met at Bayshore, lithe grace coupled with power.

I dragged my gaze away before he could catch me staring and concentrated on bundling my jacket up to stuff in my bag. Cor suggested we rest again, since we were both out of breath. My calves burned as we lowered ourselves to the steps.

"They had better...have hammocks...after all these stairs," he said between deep draughts of green-scented air.

Kuyen didn't have hammocks. My friends had been surprised and delighted the night I'd shown them the one my dad had put up between two birches in our back yard. The tangle they'd made figuring it out had been epic. I'd laughed so hard, it was a miracle I hadn't woken my parents.

I giggled now, letting the memory blossom inside me. Cor glanced up at the sound, his eyes bright and wide.

"How did you manage to get your braid tangled up in it?" I asked.

That startled a laugh out of him, and we were ten again, laughing so hard, we couldn't even breathe, only curl around our aching sides.

It had been ages since the phrase 'inside joke' had meant anything to me.

The laughter ran its course and left us wiping tears off our cheeks. I reached over and brushed my fingers through Cor's close-cropped hair. "What happened to your braid, anyway?"

He froze, like my touch was a wasp and he feared the sting.

I jerked my hand away and lurched to my feet.

"*Yuvena se*," he stammered, too late and in the wrong language. 'It's okay,' or maybe 'It was better,' in Thurei, but I didn't know if he meant his haircut or whatever faux pas I'd just made. It really didn't matter which. How else could things play out, really, between a crazy girl and her imaginary friend, all grown up and reunited?

All I needed to do was fulfill our agreement and that meant finishing the climb. Reminiscing would get me nowhere. We both saved our breath for the stairs.

∼

My legs had turned to wood, my feet to bricks, and I had no idea how long we'd been climbing. Our lungs labored for air, but neither of us offered to stop and rest again. Cor wasn't the only stubborn one.

Between one aching step and the next, the broad-leaved tunnel around us opened to sunlight and a wide, paved square. A stone building, blindingly white in the afternoon glare, reigned like a temple on the far side, rows of columns disappearing into the heavy gloom beneath its pitched roof. After the green-gold shadows of the overgrown stairway, the sun-washed flagstone square shimmered with the heat of early autumn.

"Here we are," Cor panted.

I set my hands against my hips and arched my back in an attempt to stretch free of the fatigue. Was it past midnight, really? Or later? "So let's go meet your Scholar."

"Hardly my Scholar," he said.

"The one who's going to train me, I mean."

"Well, let's see if we can ask her." Cor strode off across the courtyard before I could get started on the topic of vague answers and endless, possibly pointless stairs.

Just like he'd acted as a kid.

"You don't even know if this Scholar will talk to us?"

He kept going.

"I'm not going to run to catch up with you!"

He stopped. When I caught up, he said, "The Sheverns value knowledge above all else and the Scholars here are the most important among their people. They don't answer to any Thurei, no matter how polite his letter. We will simply have to ask."

We walked in silence a moment more, both of us tense with more than just fatigue.

"You're right," I started. I needed his help to make this work. Just because this situation was imaginary didn't mean it would be easy. And that didn't make it Cor's fault. If the concept of 'fault' made any sense here, anyway.

The rest of what I'd planned to say to smooth things over fell apart as we stepped into the deep shadow of the portico. Momentarily blinded, I stumbled over my tired feet and Cor caught my elbow to steady me. He pulled his hand away as soon as I had my balance back.

It took a minute for me to put my thoughts back in order. "I know you're doing the best you can. I just don't want to draw this thing out any longer than I need to."

"Speaking of that," he said, hesitant. "It would be best if you let me talk with the Scholars. They value the truth above everything else."

It shouldn't have stung, but it did. "So I'm a liar now?"

"That's not what I meant," Cor said. I couldn't read his expression in the dimness, but I could imagine it as sharp as his voice. "If you're ready to be honest with yourself, then talk with the Scholars as you like."

I glared at him, a useless expression in the dark. "I tell the truth when I can tell truth from delusion to start with."

Cor tilted his face up at the shadow-swallowed ceiling for a long moment. With his slit-pupiled eyes, he could probably pick out every detail in the faint light that filtered between the columns. Which meant he could probably see my glare. I didn't like the advantage that gave him when I could hardly see his face at all.

He sighed and ran a hand though his short hair. He answered much more gently than I'd expected. "I will listen, Kate."

Willing or not, it was pointless to make peace over an issue that couldn't be resolved between us. "I have nothing to say."

"And nothing I can say will convince you."

I shook my head and told myself that as long as I didn't jeopardize my goal, none of this mattered. How I felt about it made no difference.

We walked deeper into the colonnade. Double doors loomed ahead, twice my height, a deeper black in the darkness. This far from the sunlight, I couldn't make much out, but there must have been some kind of carving or decoration, because Cor reached out to trace a pattern across the wood.

Once the silence stretched too far, I commented, "Well, we're here."

"I knocked." His answer was light, ignoring the tension between us.

It had been too long of a day for me to do the same. "I didn't hear anything."

"You doubt me?"

Then the great doors swung open.

CHAPTER FIVE

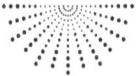

In the doorway stood a copper-skinned, gray-robed Shevern. He had an expression of confident authority on his prominent features, though the top of his smooth, bald head didn't even reach my shoulder. Cor bowed deeply.

"Good day to you, Scholar," he said, switching over to Kuyene, the common tongue. "I am Coraven Temarel, and I make known to you Katherine Kjelgaard."

The Scholar made a complicated motion with his stubby hands. I didn't know anything about Sheverns, to guess at the meaning. He turned wide, dark eyes to look at me. "You are the human?"

He said it just like a state-paid psychiatrist might ask, "And you're the juvenile-onset schizophrenic?"

Into my pause, Cor said, "Yes, honored one. I've heard that a Scholar among your number has taken a special interest in human lore. We've made the journey here with questions for Scholar Issai. May we speak with her?"

The Shevern stepped aside and motioned for us to enter. "Welcome, Temarel and your companion."

We followed him through another colonnade, this one lit by high windows. Shelves filled with books and papers divided the space into semi-private areas arranged with benches and tables. Many were empty, but a dozen or so other Sheverns sat talking or reading. They noted our passage with glances or stares, pauses in conversation, or sudden whispers.

We went through a central courtyard to a row of open doorways on the far side. Our guide led us through one into what looked like a study room, holding a table with a couple of chairs and a pair of shelves, empty and waiting.

"Sit," the Scholar told us. "Someone will be here to speak with you soon." Then he left.

"Someone?" I repeated. "That was an awful lot of stairs to climb, if Issai isn't going to see us."

The chairs, built for Sheverns, made me feel like I was trapped in a grade school classroom. Cor couldn't be comfortable with his knees drawn up that high, either, but he didn't mention it.

"It wasn't easy to track down information about Issai," Cor said. "If there're more stones we have to step on before the river's crossed, isn't it worth it in the end?"

I shook my head at his choice of metaphor but conceded his point. It didn't make my aching feet any happier. "A minimal number of steps from here on out would be great, that's all I'm saying."

The first Scholar we'd met returned before Cor could reply, three others trailing after him. All Sheverns tended to be short, but they had a broadness that gave them heft. With four of them and the two of us, the small room felt claustrophobic.

Cor rose to bow and I expected his height would make him loom reassuringly, but their bulk just made him seem even thinner, a twig among boulders. If they made Cor uneasy, he didn't show any sign. They went through a round of introductions. On the Scholars' part, this included areas of expertise and lists of accolades, most of which were technical beyond my Kuyene vocab.

One of the Sheverns finally came around to the purpose of our visit. "Issai is no longer at the Hall. Her memories are lost to us."

"She's dead?" I blurted out. In English, too, judging by the fact that the Sheverns all looked at me blankly.

Cor glanced at me in a way that said 'damage control.' "It's an expression, perhaps…" He switched back to the common tongue and asked, more delicately, "The Scholar's life has come to an end?"

"Issai is no longer counted among the Scholars," said a Shevern with ink stains on her stubby fingers. "She's been expelled from the Hall. Her memories will not be passed on to future Sheverns."

I forced down a groan. We could have started with that and saved ourselves some time. In fact, if Cor had managed to find that out beforehand, we could have skipped this whole day.

He must have seen this on my face, because he spread his hand out flat on the table between us, a wordless plea for patience. "Honored ones, may I ask what Schol—ah, what Issai might have done to be sent away?"

He gave the words an odd emphasis as he said them, like being sent away was a fate much crueler than simple death. Maybe it was, for Sheverns. In any case, it wasn't my puzzle to worry about.

"This is a private matter," the spokes-Shevern answered.

Cor accepted this with outward grace, but I knew him well enough to pick out the slight signs of growing frustration, the extra care he took when he spoke. "When Issai did have a place among the Scholars, she devoted herself to the study of human lore, didn't she? Surely, that knowledge hasn't been lost. We seek to learn more about the unique human skill. Kjelgaard needs training. Perhaps another Scholar can help us?"

The group of Sheverns had mostly let the first one do the talking, but this question brought them all chattering into the conversation.

"Humans can't use *jeira*," said the one closest to me, leaning in to blink at me in a way that pinned me in the chair, though she was scarcely taller than me sitting.

"It's well known," put in another, "that Earth is an empty world and lacks the resonance to support *jeira* at all."

The Kuyene word that the Sheverns used had no English equivalent, although as a child, I'd thought of it as 'magic.' Shom had informed me, reproachfully, that Kuyen had no cartoon wizards, after I'd made one too many comparisons to my favorite movies. Some mix of training and inborn ability, *jeira* was what animated the Summons, what allowed me to worldwalk. All Kuyenes had it in some measure and it was common on most other worlds as well. Not Earth. So far as I knew, I was the only one from Earth who could use it.

"The Runval study indicated that worlds empty of *jeira* can only support blind populations," said the one hovering near the door.

"Kjelgaard can see us. She is right here." Cor actually pointed at me, a gesture that barely shifted the Sheverns off their growing debate.

"Seeing what is and using *jeira* skills are two entirely different matters, Temarel," said the one who had met us at the doors. "You prove nothing."

"Scholars, please." Cor sounded like he was hanging on to his manners by his fingernails. "You can see how bright Kjelgaard is. She's a worldwalker. All worldwalkers have skills to protect themselves against Hunters. She's in danger."

"All Kuyene worldwalkers," said the Scholar beside me. "But that merely means all Kuyenes. It doesn't apply to an empty world. Only a fool would spin a single fact into an entire theory."

Cor did not seem to appreciate being called a fool by a stumpy, bug-eyed toadstool. It occurred to me that today had been a long and exhausting day for him, too. With his formality fraying, Cor said, "It's not just Kuyen. Among the peoples of Emere, Paulik, and Cryge, worldwalkers can protect themselves. Even where most of the population is worldbound, those with *jeira* each have their own defensive skills."

"It's the popular example of the predator-prey hypothesis," said the Scholar closest to the door, but it didn't sound like his heart was in it. "From ages even before Sheverns learned to gather their memories, Hunters have preyed on those with *jeira* and, in balance, the worldwalkers developed skills to protect themselves from predation. Even with the rise of Truce and the civilization of most of the Hunter clans, the echoes of old battles remain."

"But Earth has no Hunters," the spokes-Shevern said, spacing the words out like bars across a window.

Cor's eyes narrowed and he dropped the guise of supplicant entirely. "The references I've found to Issai's studies indicate that humans have a primary skill they can use to protect themselves. Is this true or not?"

The Scholars traded glances. Reluctance translated just fine across species barriers. I realized that in this flood of information, no one had given Cor a straight answer. Instead, they'd passed generalities back and forth, like a game of keep away. We weren't getting anywhere. I rubbed my temples, trying to ease the headache I could feel thumping to life.

"It won't do her any good," said the spokes-Shevern. "Humans don't belong here. There's a reason the worldbound on empty worlds are left alone. She doesn't belong here."

"Great," I snapped. "Even my hallucinations think this is a bad idea. Classic paranoia."

I spoke in English, but of course Cor understood me. He turned, temper slipping. "Stop. That's not what this is."

He turned back to the Scholars but paused, like he was only just now considering for himself what, exactly, this was. "When I sent my request, you said you had answers for me. Why are you not helping us?"

"Sometimes the answer is *no*," the Shevern's leader said. He adjusted the drape of his robe and straightened his shoulders. "Earth has no Hunters for this to be an issue in any case."

"None of its own," Cor agreed, his voice edged. "But ones from Kuyen and other worlds can still find her."

That spark flared into another debate among the Scholars. "Empty worlds have no Truce to dissuade status seekers."

"And no *jeira* to draw them in the first place," the Shevern nearest me objected. "Even for the most savage of the Hunters, pitting themselves against the blind would give them no more satisfaction than slaughtering *kittu* in their pen."

"There are reports of empty worlds being used by Hunters," said the one almost hiding by the door. "They could use it as a slip anchor or a simple retreat in case of ambush or attack."

"And with an ignorant population, there would be no opposition to a Hunter," said the Scholar near me.

"She is more than bright enough, if a Hunter crossed her path," the one by the door replied.

The lead Shevern tilted his head toward Cor. "What about yourself? You have earned a certain reputation. You may well draw them."

That struck a nerve with him. His fingers flashed, that flick-away Thurei gesture as eloquent as any angry head shake. "I would have no reputation at all if not for the Hunters I met on her side. They came long before I would be a worthy trophy."

My fatigue blurred some of these Shevern voices together, but this last point was something that I couldn't afford to ignore.

"What are they talking about?" I asked, straightening up as much as the cramped chair would allow.

Cor hesitated under my glare. The Scholars watched us, a robed gallery. In English, Cor whispered, "They're wrong about this. I don't bring danger to you."

I shook my head and switched to Kuyene. "I thought you said Sheverns swore to tell the truth. Even I know that, and I'm just a dumb human."

The spokes-Shevern drew himself up, indignant. "It is more than an oath, human. Our memories pass directly from one generation to the next. Dishonesty pollutes the very foundation of what we are."

The quiet one by the door spoke up, his voice carrying in a way that surprised me. "Send them to Issai and let her give them answers."

It silenced the other Sheverns for a moment, but Cor jumped at the chance. "I would be in your debt, honored ones."

The outspoken Shevern put his hand out in a gesture of refusal. "We have no need for your debt. Consider it paid, if you bring the human to Issai."

"My thanks." Cor offered them a bow, gracious now that he'd gotten his way. "I request a token."

"Issai gives no tokens," the Scholar said. "She doesn't care for visitors."

"May I have her full name, then, so I can write to her?"

"If she wished to arrange audiences, she wouldn't be living alone in the wilds." The Scholar crossed his thick arms. "If you insist on this path, you'll have to take your chances."

The Scholar with the ink-stained fingers cleared her throat. "You must make the journey overland above Firrel. It will be a long one, if the wilds are uncooperative."

"Dangerous country," the one next to me added. They all quieted, peering at us, waiting for an answer.

Cor flicked his fingers, brushing away their concern. "Not that dangerous, honored ones. An ally of my House lives a short distance from Firrel. The wilds there are unexceptional."

Another set of traded glances. Suddenly solicitous, the leader Shevern asked, "You will begin at House Pareshol, then?"

Cor looked at me. "Most likely."

"Then you will wish to begin as soon as possible," said the writer Shevern, starting a general group movement toward the door.

The idea of shuttling off to yet another place tonight hammered home the late hour and the long climb. How late was it, really? I yawned and caught Cor studying me sidelong.

"Perhaps tomorrow will be early enough," he offered. "We can start just after sunrise. No need to disturb any in the House, and you can have time to rest."

I nodded and stood, my stiff joints creaking.

The group of Sheverns parted, leaving an unambiguous path to the door. The Scholar nearest the door bowed, a clunky version of the Thurei gesture, and waved us out. "Our most earnest wishes go with you on your journey."

CHAPTER SIX

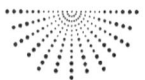

It was an altogether more encouraging group of Sheverns who ushered us out of the Scholars' Hall. Cor seemed to think so, too. He wore a bemused expression as the massive doors closed us into shadows.

"It would've been nice if they had mentioned this when I wrote to them," he said, with the slow precision that meant his mood still shaded to frustration.

"I thought this trip was supposed to be the end of it," I said, following him back through the colonnade. I had the premonition of our agreement spiraling out of control, like a dropped spool of ribbon.

"One day?" When he turned to look at me, his eyes flashed like a cat's, catching the faint afternoon rays from the distant courtyard. "That's what you'd give me—a single day? You promised, Kate."

I spun to face him, a shadowy shape in the dimness. "I didn't say—"

He grabbed my wrists and I yelped in surprise. Surely, Cor would never hurt me. He tugged me toward him and hissed in my ear for silence. "Hunter."

Before us, silhouetted against the sun-drenched courtyard,

someone—something—moved toward us. It was tall and broad-shouldered, long-headed, the other details hidden beneath the flowing lines of a robe or cloak. Something about the way it moved cut straight through to a primitive part of me, a quivering hare frozen at the soft padding footfalls of a wolf.

I pushed his name up through a fear-parched throat. "Coran."

"Here," he murmured. "Come, Katen. You always trusted my eyes for this."

He slid his hands down my wrists to lace his fingers with mine, as he had for dozens of night games we'd played with Shom. Hunter-and-House, a kind of hide-and-seek that seemed innocent enough at nine or ten years old and terrifying now. His keener vision had made him a valuable asset for Shom and me to ally with or quarrel over, but it gave cold comfort now.

"This isn't a game," I breathed.

The creature kept walking, but its path curved toward us now, close enough for me to pick out the shape of its rounded shoulders and unnaturally long arms in the swirls of its smoke-colored cloak. Its steps clicked, not quite like hard-soled shoes on the flagstones.

"I know." Cor turned to track the Hunter as it passed us. I stayed at his side, hypocritical, given my own lack of faith, but it meant not being alone to face the nightmare by myself.

A couple rows of columns away, I lost track of the form in the gloom. The clatter of its steps grew fainter.

"There," Cor said, barely more than a whisper, close enough to tickle my ear. "Nothing to worry you."

Then the footsteps wound around behind us and headed back. It circled like a shark, cutting between us and the lengthening rays of afternoon sun out in the courtyard. Cor stepped forward, angling himself in front of me.

"You're under Truce," Cor said.

"On these grounds," the creature answered. His voice held death in its depths, oily and chill. "I'm not breaking the Truce. Yet."

He circled closer and Cor shifted us to compensate. I caught the glint of teeth beneath the cowl. I glanced down, away from the long jaw outlined against the bright sky, to discover the clicking footsteps came from claws, not boot heels. I caught my breath against a sudden start of fear and the thing rumbled a perverse sort of purr.

"Who is it you have here, little Thurei? It doesn't smell like she's from the sort of world to have a Truce at all."

"Your business is with the Scholars. Nothing else here concerns you."

I fervently hoped Cor was as bold as he sounded.

The creature let out a rolling, broken sound that may have been laughter or a snarl. "Brave threat, Houseling! I'm not the one concerned. You draw on me in this place and you will be the Truce-breaker." The Hunter tilted his head, shifting his gaze to me. "I am Tharkesh. I look forward to it if we meet again. All honor to the Hunt."

That last was said over his shoulder as he turned and walked away, swallowed by the shadows of the colonnade.

Cor hissed a Thurei curse and spun to me, clasping his right hand over mine where our fingers twined together. I'd clung to him this whole time without realizing. I tugged my hand and after a moment, Cor let go.

"What was that thing?" I wrapped my arms around myself, chilled.

"A Hirach. One of the Greater Hunters." He scanned over my shoulder in the direction the monster had gone.

"They can come here, too?"

"Yes." As we continued toward the bright courtyard, he added, "Public places are open to all peoples, as long as they hold to the Truce."

"Monsters who prey on people can come here." I'd talked myself into this. Why was I surprised that it had turned out to be a bad idea?

"Ah. As the Scholars mentioned, Hunters used to choose intelligent targets, for the challenge of it, or status, or as part of their tradition." Cor shaded his eyes as we stepped out of the shadows into the slanting rays of sunlight. "But that was generations ago. All the peoples of Kuyen have agreed to the Truce, and those who break it are considered rogue by their own kind as well as everyone else."

"You're telling me that thing that threatened us was stopped by some truce." Even with the late afternoon heat radiating up from the flagstones, I couldn't banish the chill left on my skin by that encounter.

"No," Cor said. "Those who break the Truce answer to their own councils. In theory, he would have gone before the Hirach leaders if he had attacked us. I would never have let it go that far, I promise, but I couldn't draw on him simply for his words."

"I just want to be done with this." I pressed my palms over my eyes, which felt gritty with lack of sleep. Then I opened them again so I didn't trip and break my neck on the flagstones.

"We're one step...ah, we're closer to it." Cor put on his most persuasive look, his bright eyes warm with encouragement, his mouth softened into a hopeful smile. It was easy to remember why he'd gotten his way so often before. "Now we know where to find Issai. She can teach you to defend yourself against any Hunters—all the monsters, Katen. In the time between, you have me to keep you safe."

All these statements seemed optimistic to the point of absurdity, but right now, I just wanted to leave. "Fine. But right now, I'm going home."

He glanced back over his shoulder. I didn't know if he could pick out the Hirach in the blackness and he didn't say. "Come to the edge of the courtyard and I can take you."

When he reached out a hand to lead me, I tucked my own in my pockets. "Why? I can take myself."

He let his hand drop with a sigh. "Hiraches aren't great trackers, in general, but why take the risk that he might follow in the wake of our travel? I can take you back a little ways away from your apartment so we can walk the rest of the way and not lead him back to your home. If you'd like."

The Kuyene sun had a few degrees yet to reach the horizon, but if

I concentrated, I could feel the tug of sunset. If I wasn't gone by then, it would rip me back to my own world, perhaps fatally.

According to what I'd been told.

"Fine, I'll be careful, I promise. Go home." We stood at the edge of the stairs now, on the far side of the courtyard from the Scholars' Hall.

"I can't walk to the House from here." He peered meaningfully down the stairs. "I have to cross over to your world in order to slip back home in any case. We can go together or I'll follow you, but I *will* see you home safe."

I hadn't given it any thought. Worldwalking didn't work between locations on a single world, only between worlds themselves. He'd need to go somewhere else before he made it home. It might as well be my neighborhood. I just wanted tonight to be over. Go home, crawl in bed, and be unconscious for a precious hour or two before my alarm clock went off.

"Okay, okay." I held out my hand. "But I'll take us. You won't have enough time to rest before you cross again. You'll hurt yourself."

"Thank you." He sounded so surprised by this small favor that I felt guilty. He slid his hand into mine. "Pick somewhere far enough away—"

"That we don't lead him back to my apartment. I was listening." I squeezed his hand. Then I added, "I know this is going to take longer than a day."

We slipped from the sun-drenched courtyard to the clammy pre-dawn fog in San Jose. Vertigo clawed up from my belly. A headache hammered behind my eyes and I swayed. Cor caught me. I gritted my teeth against what the jolt did to my head.

"Katen! What happened?"

I leaned against him for another ragged breath, wishing I could take comfort in his support. Instead, I straightened back up, care of my balance. "I'm okay. Just tired."

This isn't real, I reminded myself. Kuyen made that surprisingly easy to forget, but the neon glow of the minimart signs drove the point home. *And now I'm stranded by myself at the gas station six blocks from home at some ungodly hour of the morning.*

I stopped by this place all the time when I didn't want to make the full grocery store trek. "Safe and familiar" at four in the afternoon became something else when you rotated the clock by twelve hours. The fog pressed in close around the streetlamps, making the shadowed, cracked pavement and distant traffic that much darker.

Cor still hovered like he expected me to collapse at any moment. "Did you sleep today? I mean, your day. Before I came."

"No. I was planning on sleeping tonight. Well, last night, now."

"You'll exhaust yourself." He frowned. "And you haven't eaten anything besides that grain bar hours ago."

"Neither have you," I said, which was ridiculous, since his metabolism only existed in my head. My stomach growled, asserting its existence in no uncertain terms.

All I got for that was a flick of his fingers and, "Wait here."

He ducked into the Mini-Mart. I sat down on a concrete planter near the door, pulling my jacket tighter against the chilly damp. I couldn't see past the beer posters, but he returned in less than a minute with a candy bar.

It took longer for the wheels to turn in my head than it had taken him to get the thing. "Did you just steal that?"

His expression soured. "He took my money. Kuyene marks, but what else could I do?"

Had the cashier seen Cor? Or was this just another granola bar from my backpack? Or was it all in my imagination? Maybe I'd sleepwalked in there myself to buy it. I was too tired for this. "I just want to get home."

He helped me up, then tucked my hand in the crook of his elbow. I let myself lean against him as we headed down the street.

"May I come back tomorrow so we can begin searching for Issai?" He asked it like he expected me to say *no*.

But I couldn't, for multiple reasons. "I promised, didn't I?"

"Yes, you did."

I tilted my forehead against his shoulder for a step or two. "I intend to keep my promise. If you do."

It made no sense, keeping a promise to a figment of my own imagination, but that rationalization felt far flimsier than the warmth of Cor beside me. The concern I knew I would see in his eyes if I looked up at him. Maybe it wouldn't matter, as long as this bargain worked.

"I'll do as you asked," he murmured.

We walked a block in silence. I let my eyes drift closed. I hadn't felt this worn out since I'd been on doxepin in the ward.

He steered us around a corner. "You might want to open your eyes for this part."

Ugh. My stairs. The three flights looked like Everest.

"I could carry you," he offered. "My toothpick days are over."

"You have got to be kidding. No." I reached for the railing and started trudging up the steps. Then his comment caught up with me. "Tiny Titanium Toothpick."

I'd been eight and just learned about alliteration. And thesauri.

The streetlight caught the curve of his grin. "Shom had so much fun translating that for my cousins."

I untwined my arm from his, then dug my key out of my pocket and unlocked the door. The east glowed with a false dawn filtering through the morning fog. "The sun's almost up. You need to go home."

"Tomorrow, then." He didn't turn to check, but I knew he must have felt it pulling at him. If he lingered, the sunrise would wrench him brutally back to his own world. Even Cor couldn't fight that. He faded away before I closed the door. I flipped the lock and rested my head against the cool wood.

If the first thing from Kuyen I'd seen yesterday had been the Hirach, I would have called the doctor's office right away. Even if Shom had come back first, as hurt and hurtful as I'd last seen her at Bayshore, I wouldn't have agreed to this, new drugs or no.

Anything from Kuyen would have been easier to deny than Cor.

CHAPTER SEVEN

E ither my alarm clock hadn't gone off, or I'd slept through it. I groaned, still exhausted after—what, an hour and a half of sleep? If I hurried, I could make it to work on time. Pushing back the covers, I rolled out of bed, then traded pajamas for jeans and a long-sleeved shirt. I dragged a brush through stubborn tangles and scraped my long, brown hair back into a ponytail. No time for breakfast. I stamped into sneakers and grabbed up my bag.

The sore muscles in my legs didn't raise any warning flags right away. I felt every bit of the exhaustion that went along with my muddled memories of endless stairs and unhelpful Scholars. It was the candy wrapper on my card table that caught my eye and dragged me to a full stop.

I'd been out walking all night. That was indisputable. Not on Kuyen, obviously. The thought that I'd spent all night alone on the streets of my cheap-rent-and-liquor-store neighborhood chilled me. I hoped I'd bought the candy bar and not stolen it. Vaguely, I recalled Cor saying he'd left money. Did that mean I had? I had no clue how closely my hallucinations mapped to reality. I'd had complete belief in them as a kid and in the ward the plan had been to end them, not figure them out.

My weekly appointment with Dr. Vargas was scheduled for this afternoon. Maybe I should tell him.

Maybe this was more than I could handle on my own.

A glance at the clock told me I'd have more to worry about if I didn't get to work.

"You feeling okay?" Rose didn't even say 'hi' first.

I tried to make my smile reassuring. "Do I look that bad?"

"I didn't mean it like that." She didn't offer an alternative, though.

"I'm okay, just tired. I didn't sleep well." I loaded a package of paper into the photo printer and queued up the first order of digital prints. The machine hummed to life, settling into a rhythmic purr as it sent prints trundling down the conveyor. A child's birthday party, all chubby cheeks and giggles and smears of frosting.

"Insomnia?" She mimed a leer. "Or something way more fun?"

Even insomnia sounded more fun than climbing stairs or wandering the city all night, so I picked that.

Rose nodded. "I feel your pain. I'm a mess with this show coming up. I feel like I haven't slept in a week."

"Do you take anything for it?"

She lifted a perfect black eyebrow. "Like sleeping pills? No. It's just a few days of being stressed out. After the show, I'll be fine."

"That must be nice." I usually guarded my tongue better, but I was too tired to pay attention to what I was saying or how I was saying it.

"Katherine, what's wrong?" She looked worried, but nowhere near as worried as she'd look if I told her I was insane. I didn't want to lie to her, but I had no choice, so I stayed as close to the truth as I could.

"I've been thinking maybe things aren't working out that well for me here. Maybe I need to move back home."

"Oh, no, you can't!" Maybe she would have taken it better if I'd told her I was crazy. "Is it bills? We could talk to Mr. Parker about getting some more shifts if you need them."

"No, it's not that. I just think maybe I'm in over my head." *Out of my head*, to be honest.

"This is all pretty new for you, isn't it? You've only been away from home for, what, a few months?"

"Four." I hadn't lived at my parents' home since I'd been twelve, but it had been only four months since getting out of Bayshore.

She patted my hand. "Give it some time. It's hard at first, but you can't give up when you've only just gotten out."

The way she said it sounded eerily like how I thought of getting out of the ward. I wanted to ask why, but I was hardly in a position to pry.

Dr. Vargas' office sat two blocks from the bus stop, a single, straight jaunt from my apartment. It had been a selling point for my parents. If I wanted to try living on my own, it was only sensible to make sure I had direct access to psychiatric care.

"How have you been this week, Katherine?" Dr. Vargas delivered the standard line as he tapped at his keyboard. His glasses glowed with the reflection of his computer monitor.

"Okay." My standard response. If I'd gotten hit by a bus on the way here, I would still have said, 'Okay.' We both knew it.

He finally finished whatever he'd been doing on the computer and looked up. "You seem tired. How are your sleep patterns?"

"I didn't sleep well last night." Not a lie, but blatantly untrue all the same. If I was going to say something about the hallucinations coming back, now would be the time.

He reached for the prescription pad, as quick as ever. "Are you still taking your zaleplon? If it's stopped controlling your insomnia, we should try something else."

"No," I admitted. I'd stopped taking the tranquilizer shortly after being discharged. I found it much easier to sleep in my own bed in my own apartment after a day of work and errands than it had ever been in the shared space of the ward. It also occurred to me that I probably never had insomnia—I'd just been awake at night because I could see my friends then.

Dr. Vargas gave me a professional frown. "You need to take your medication, Katherine. We've talked about how delicate your situation is. The pressures you're facing in this attempt at independence might easily overwhelm your ability to cope. Stress is a trigger, and you've taken on a lot trying to do this by yourself. You need all the support you can get. Even that might not be enough."

Leaning back in his chair, Dr. Vargas tapped the prescription pad with his pen. "You should evaluate your goals, Katherine. And you need to be honest with yourself about what you can handle."

Just then, it didn't matter that Cor was back and I might or might not have wandered the streets of San Jose in a schizophrenic fit. I would make this work.

I got through my appointment without any further prescriptions, in return for a promise to consider resuming the tranquilizers. I dutifully thought about it on the bus ride home.

For now, I suspected I wouldn't have any problem falling asleep when I finally got the chance, which was exactly what I did when I got home.

My grumbling stomach reminded me that I had put off grocery shopping long enough. I dragged myself out of bed and headed back to the bus stop. Habit led me to the freezer section. I stood before the glass doors, studying the tidy packages of microwave meals. I'd never learned to cook, but I could remember my mom cooking when I'd been little. Before things had gotten...crazy. I remembered her sautéing onions and garlic, making the whole house smell divine. I'd helped sometimes, grating cheese or measuring flour. I'd sneaked from-scratch cookies sometimes for Cor and Shom.

"Convenience" foods came later, once things had started to

unravel. Meals at Bayshore hadn't been much better. But now, I was out and had a home of my own. If I wanted something homecooked, I could make it myself. Like a normal person.

I left the freezer aisle and gathered a selection of ingredients from the produce section. Normal people cooked all the time, so it couldn't have been that hard. I'd seen people do it on TV.

When I got home, I unloaded the bounty on my kitchen counter. My pots and pans lived in a cupboard beside the stove, proudly purchased the day I'd moved in, never touched since. I pulled out the largest pot, for soup. Or stew. I didn't know the difference. I could get a cookbook the next time I went to the library. For now, I'd just have find a recipe online.

Of course, I should have thought of getting the recipe first. Nothing matched the ingredients I'd bought at the grocery store. I had a potato, a carrot, a zucchini, and an onion. I'd just have to improvise. By the time I'd chopped everything, I realized I hadn't put the pot on the stove yet. I didn't have any broth. How much water should go into soup? None of the recipes agreed. I filled the pot mostly full and dropped the vegetables in.

Things didn't look promising, but maybe that was how soup always looked at first. It just needed to boil for a while. Dinner didn't have to be delicious, but at least it would be mine, something real I made myself.

I pulled out a jigsaw puzzle to start while I waited. I hoped soup making wasn't an all-day project. Sunset would be here in an hour or so.

And Cor, along with it. I pressed my palms over my eyes and sighed. Dr. Vargas was right about one thing. If I was going to get through this episode on my own, using the bargain I'd made with Cor, I needed to stay focused on my goal. Scholars' Hall had been a disaster. I'd been drifting along like Cor would sort it all out. He was part of the problem, not the solution. Then there was all the hammock-toothpick-let's-be-friends nonsense.

I couldn't afford that.

If I wanted things to go better from here on out, I needed to concentrate on finishing this without getting sucked back in. I just had to remember that this was all imaginary, one big metaphor for getting symptom-free again.

That was a fine line to walk, but I could do it.

Famous last words.

When I went back to check on the soup, it had come to a frothy boil. The bright colors of the vegetables had turned a murky, grayish green. A piece of potato floated up and I scooped it out with a spoon. It crunched between my teeth, almost raw. The piece of carrot I managed to find was mushy. I tried a sip of the liquid, which didn't taste like anything at all.

What a complete waste of an afternoon. I turned off the burner, unsure if I wanted to laugh or throw something.

A knock at the door caught me leaning against the counter, staring at the lousy soup.

Cor waited outside. He had a large bag slung over one shoulder and carried a small, brightly-colored package in his hands. I let him in.

"What's all that?" I asked.

"These are things I'll need for the trip to Issai's." He hitched his shoulder, jostling the leather bag. He held out the little, wrapped bundle in his hands. "This is a guesting gift for you."

It felt light, fragile. I unwrapped the silky, patterned cloth with care. Guesting gifts were very formal. Following my friends' advice, I had brought one the first time I had been to their homes. They were little, trinkety things meant to make a good impression, to offer thanks for letting in a stranger.

At least, that was what a child's guesting gift was. The cloth wrapping of Cor's gift parted to reveal an exquisite hair comb, made of some type of striped wood banded with honey brown and a darker chocolate color that matched my hair. The top was carved into a flock of birds, their pointed wings and tails stretched out to become the tines.

"It's beautiful," I said, rubbing the satiny finish with my thumb.

"I am glad you like it." He folded his hands in front of him, his posture stiff. "Your hair is lovely grown so long."

His compliment sounded practiced. Of course, guesting gifts were meant for near-strangers. Cor wasn't a friend, he was...

A problem. Anyone sane would be able to tell me he was a problem.

It would be easier to remember that if he decided to keep his distance, too.

I still needed his cooperation, though. I set the gift aside on the table. "Thank you, Coraven."

Judging by the widening of his amber eyes, he didn't expect his full name. "Did I offend you?"

"No, it's not that. Sit down. There're some things we need to cover before we go any further with this."

He set his rucksack on the floor and took a seat in my folding chair as if it were the best seat in the house. Which it was, technically. "If I can mend this, Kate, I will," he offered, sticking stubbornly to the more familiar form of my name. "Last night, we parted as friends."

I felt more in control standing while he sat. The opposite of how things had gone at the Scholars' Hall. "I just need to know what's going on."

Cor's gaze strayed to the wooden comb in front of him. "Ask, then."

"When the Scholars were talking about me, they said I was bright. What does that mean?"

Suddenly, Cor was impossible to ignore. I was already looking at him, but not hard enough. Something about him demanded more attention, like something flickering at the edge of sight, or a familiar song playing too low to make out the words.

Then he was simply himself again, lanky body held with perfect posture, a wary expression on his narrow features. "In Kuyene, the word isn't 'bright' like a light is bright. My English doesn't have the reach. You have *jeira*...power? Energy? And so you...glow. That's what the Hunters sense in you. They're much more sensitive than we are."

"Why now? Why is it a problem all of a sudden?"

His fingers flicked, then he caught himself and shook his head. "It's not sudden. Children do not have strong *jeira*. After you refused to see me anymore, I still came sometimes. You remember. I hoped you might decide...well. Then I found a Wogra outside your building. Maybe if I could have warned you then, you would still have believed me, but your world was heading into summer and you were always asleep by the time the sun set."

The medication that had controlled my insomnia did its job thoroughly.

He laced his long fingers together in his lap. "By fall, you forbade me to visit you again. That was your thirteenth winter and you were becoming brighter. All worldwalkers do as they grow up. The misery of that sham healer's masked it somewhat, but now that you're grown and free of that place, you're quite bright. Those Hunters who still take trophies can't resist a target like that."

"The Scholars seemed to think it's your reputation that's attracting them. Don't they have to tell the truth?"

"They're famous for it." He hesitated. "But they're wrong. You heard what they said. Hunters sometimes use worlds like Earth for travel, where no law or power binds them. If they happen to come close enough to sense you, they have no reason to leave you alone. It's dangerous." He added, like a secret, "You are precious, Katen. There is no one like you on all the worlds. Even the Hunters can sense it."

"Yeah, the crazy always think they're special." The Hirach had been a shock, but boogeymen weren't my biggest worry. I pointed at the world beyond the door. The real world. "It's dangerous for me to be wandering around on my own all night in this neighborhood. There are plenty of bad things that could happen without involving monsters from another world."

"Wandering...?" he echoed, then he scowled as he put it together. "Is that what you do? You remake everything in your mind to wipe

Kuyen out, so that...so...I can't guess why. You tell yourself you spent the night walking around the city here. And me?"

I didn't say it. I'd made that point often enough in the past.

"Ah. Of course. You said you were alone." He pushed the chair back and stood. "You promised."

"I promised to get training," I started, wound up in an anger of my own.

"No, before. At the very beginning, when your parents left you there. Remember? You said when you were old enough to leave that place, you would never let anyone tell you we weren't real again."

From some long-buried box in my mind came a snippet of memory: Katie, who preferred to be called 'Katen,' crying and abandoned by her parents, trying to hold herself together until the sun set and her two best friends could come comfort her.

Look how that had turned out. "If I end up back in a mental hospital, it'll be because of things like last night. I can't do this if it's not safe."

"I swear to you, Kate, I'll—" His expression shifted from earnest to something sharper. "Nothing I say is much of a reassurance, though, I imagine."

I clamped down on the rush of guilt. *None of this is real. Just get it over with.* "We just need to find Issai, right?"

He glanced at the window. It was fully dark outside, masked by the city's glow. "It's later than I expected, but that doesn't make much difference. Let me slip us over to House Pareshol, and we'll be well on our way."

CHAPTER EIGHT

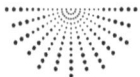

My eyes snapped open as Cor dropped my hand. He staggered toward one of the ornate gateposts in front of us, letting the bag slip from his shoulder. He sagged against the post, resting his forehead on the carved stone.

I touched his shoulder. "Are you okay?"

It was obvious he wasn't. He turned to lean his back against the pillar, wincing his eyes closed against the morning sunlight. He looked even paler than usual.

"That was much too hard." The words came out ragged.

"Here, hold on." I worked my arm between his back and the gatepost and helped him inch the rest of the way down to the ground. He rested his head on his drawn-up knees.

Seeing him like this, I couldn't think of him as part of the problem. I settled on the ground next to him. "Is there anything I can do to help?"

"A minute only," he murmured. "Then we can go."

"Take all the time you need. We're not in that big of a hurry." If he felt as bad as I had crossing last night, he could use the rest.

He sighed. "I think you are."

Not in so big a hurry that I want to see you hurt, was what I wanted to say, but if that were true, why did I keep acting the way I did? I'd been pushing him from the moment he'd come back. "I'm sorry. I'm just scared."

He lifted his head. "Forgiven. We're not at our best right now."

He didn't get his minute of rest. From out of sight along the gravel road came faint yips and growls. It kicked my heart into a higher gear, but Cor only groaned. A wagon swung into view where the road left distant woods. He muttered something in Thurei. Profanity, if I had to guess. He switched to English to ask for a hand up.

"It won't do to alarm the delivery drivers," he muttered, eying the approaching wagon. He stood straight enough, but I thought it was more from willpower than wellness. "Just as well. We can let them pass and then get started on our way."

The horses hitched to the full wagon turned out to not be horses at all, but *morsais*. I'd seen them, once or twice, but they hadn't made much of an impression on me as a child beyond how huge they were. About the size of horses, they had stocky necks and narrow, hound-like heads. They could be Clydesdales crossed with German Shepherds. Their coats were dark and shaggy, striped with browns, grays, and black. They lifted their fringed tails like flags when they caught our scent on the light breeze.

Two people sat in front. Thureis, judging by their colorful hair. Beside me, Cor cursed under his breath.

"That's the Pareshols' father," he said, gesturing discreetly to the passenger. The one driving was a woman with sky blue hair and plainer clothing. "I know this is fake to you, but the Pareshols are important allies of my House. A mistake here would go badly for me. I won't ask you to believe, only...can you pretend? As a favor, please."

This was exactly the sort of complication I needed to avoid, but I couldn't make myself refuse. "Okay. What exactly am I supposed to be pretending?"

"Act like this matters. To me. And, if you can, pretend I matter, too."

He did matter, and he shouldn't have, and I shouldn't have cared. "I won't embarrass you in front of your friends."

"I have no friends here."

I bit my tongue on that one, too, and we watched the wagon draw closer in silence.

The driver called the pair to a halt right in front of us. The *morsais* fidgeted in their harnesses, flaring their nostrils and swiveling pointed ears. One growled, deep in its chest, but it quieted at the driver's curt command.

Cor's ally, the passenger, was a middle-aged man, broadly built for a Thurei, so about the size of an average human man. Cor would probably top him in height. He had square, forceful features and wore his long, emerald green hair drawn back into a ponytail at the nape of his neck.

He boomed out a cascade of Thurei syllables. A greeting, maybe, but not the simple ones I'd learned.

Cor bowed stiffly and made his answer in Kuyene. "And a morning sun's welcome to you, Father Pareshol."

Father Pareshol followed Cor into the common tongue. "If I had known you were coming, boy, I would have prepared something for your arrival. Why didn't you slip over right to the front door? At the very least, I can spare you the walk."

"My thanks, but we're just about to leave. We only needed a slip anchor. I would hate to disturb the House."

"What would your father say about my manners, Temarel, if I let you leave without hospitality?"

That didn't sound like an offer. From the little I remembered about Cor's forbidding father, I wouldn't want to explain my manners to him, either. Cor glanced at me. Did he expect me to stamp my foot and insist we turn the man down? Maybe he did.

In English, I whispered, "It's okay."

Cor heaved his bag up into the wagon and helped me clamber aboard. We found places to sit among the crates and sacks. Once we got settled, the driver called to the *morsais*. The animals leaned into their harnesses and the wagon lurched into motion.

Our host twisted around on the bench seat so he could see us. There was a haughtiness to him, the same air of superiority as

Bayshore's director on his annual patient review. He had the same blatant scrutiny, too, and I wondered if he was seeing the *crazy* I could feel stamped on my forehead. Whatever he saw, he looked pleased in a cat-and-canary way.

"Who's my other guest, Temarel?"

Cor sat up straighter on his makeshift seat. "Father Pareshol, I make known to you Katherine Kjelgaard."

"Pleased to meet you," I added. It seemed wise to be polite.

"Not as pleased as I am to meet you." The Thurei smiled, but it wasn't a nice one. "Tell me, what brings the two of you to my gate this morning?"

"We needed a slip anchor," Cor said. "From here, we'll go overland."

"I should have guessed you came on personal business and not a House errand. Planned to be in and through without waking anyone, did you? I'm so glad I had early errands. If you'll excuse the observation, you look ill-equipped for a journey into the wildlands. Do you mean to go on foot?"

Cor sighed, so slightly I only noticed because we sat pressed against each other in the small coach. "The situation requires it."

"I know you are bold when 'the situation requires it,' but tackling the wilds on foot is impressive on an entirely different scale. Then again, you do spend so much time out of the House." Father Pareshol said the words like a compliment, but I didn't believe it.

I bit my lip and kept quiet. Whether this guy got on my nerves or not, I'd told Cor I wouldn't cause problems. This was Cor's ally; he could deal with the man however he saw fit.

The driver called to the *morsais*, slowing them. Father Pareshol jumped down from the bench seat and waved for us to follow.

Experience had prepared me for the grand mansion before us. I'd seen the Temarel version. Even so, I was impressed. The facade of shimmering, tinted stone had been designed so that the entire public face of the building displayed the House name in complex, looping calligraphy four stories high.

Cor stepped to my side, asking in English, "How're you doing?"

It was a simple enough question, but his voice held an intensity that went deeper than the words. I answered by habit. "Okay. You?"

"Just...keep your ears up."

Then our host strode between us, urging us toward the opening manor door, his hands unwelcome on our backs. Four Thureis in plain workers' garb hurried out, I assumed to unload the wagon's goods. We swept past them, up the wide entryway steps and into a large foyer. Frosted glass windows let in muted sunlight. The floor was a polished mosaic of green and white stone, the walls and ceiling carved plaster. Two stairways rose dramatically on the far side of the room and closed doors hinted at halls beyond.

"Now," Father Pareshol said, donning smugness like a cloak, "no need to measure your manners in my House, Kjelgaard. I know you're unfamiliar with Thurei ways."

My manners on this side might have been skewed through the lens of a child's understanding, and dusty besides, but I was sick of this man talking down to us. "Actually—"

"That is very kind of you," Cor said, interrupting, giving him a slight bow that seemed to be just enough to start his head pounding again. He kept most of it out of his expression, but I caught the tightness in his jaw.

Our host must have, too. "Is there something wrong, Temarel?"

"No, nothing, Father."

"Come now." He spread his hands, his smile generous. I wondered if he'd be asking for our tax-free donations at the end of the visit. "You would not count me short as a host, would you? I insist you see our healer."

Cor hesitated, flicking a glance at me. "Thank you, Father Pareshol. You are right, of course. In fact, I think Kjelgaard has never met a healer before." He turned to me, that odd intensity back in his eyes. "Have you?"

I recalled hearing about Lewrils, at least. Another of Kuyen's many peoples, Lewrils had a unique skill for healing, able to mend injuries and cure sickness. We'd invoked them in our childhood games, but I'd never met one. The most dangerous of our misadventures had ended in simple scrapes or torn clothes, nothing that had needed serious intervention.

Of course, in the morning, I'd gotten in trouble for playing when I should have been in bed asleep. Even worse if I lied about it, once they decided I'd gotten too old to pretend my dreams were real. I learned early to 'admit' I'd snuck out to play in the garden and take whatever punishment that had earned me. I'd learned to hide any sign of my visits.

Cor cleared his throat, the slightest of sounds, pulling me back into the present.

"Um," I said. *Brilliant.* Cor had asked me to act like this mattered and I was blowing it already. No wonder he didn't trust me to mind my manners in front of his allies. "No, I've never met a healer."

"You have no healers in your world?" Our host raised his eyebrows, a caricature of astonishment.

"Oh, we have *doctors.*" I used the English word and suppressed a shiver, pretty sure I knew what mine would say if I told him about this conversation.

"Excellent, then you must come with me." Cor smiled, a thin thing that looked tailored for formal occasions. He turned to our host. "I would hate for Kjelgaard to miss this opportunity. Where can we find your healer?"

A sudden sharpness marred the Thurei's expression, although he answered politely enough. "The atrium is in the east wing. I believe you know the way, wind chaser."

When Cor shifted his weight, the man stopped him. "Do not bow, if the courtesy is beyond you."

"And be counted short as a guest?" He bent smoothly from the waist and straightened. "Come, Kjelgaard. Let us meet the Pareshols' healer."

I followed him through the left-hand door and down a long hallway, glad to be rid of our host, at least.

Once we were out of his sight, Cor's shoulders sagged as he massaged his temples. In English, he said, "That last one hurt."

"Your stubbornness always did, didn't it?"

"Yes, it always does."

Careful of his tenses, that Cor.

"So what's all this healer stuff about?"

"Ah. Nothing, really," he said. I thought he would leave it at that, as the *tum tum* of our footsteps marked his pause. Then he added, "I think Father Pareshol hoped to separate us and get you alone."

When I turned to him in alarm, he backpedaled. "No, nothing like that. You're not in any danger here. He'd only want to...make trouble. To put you on edge, or embarrass you. Or me."

"Why? I haven't done anything to him." It was stupid to feel offended over a hypothetical slight from an imaginary stranger, but there it was.

"You've done nothing against House Pareshol." He said it with care, like he expected a sound byte later. He pushed on before I could pick the statement apart. "But you're here with me, so he's paying you criticism owed to my account. The fault is mine, Kate."

"I thought he was supposed to be your ally."

"Ah, no." Cor gave a dry laugh, bitter as a pill. "Ally of the House. House business didn't bring me here."

No, I did. Skirting that issue, I asked, "Why did you call him 'Father'?"

"Father?"

"Yeah." I pronounced the Thurei term he'd used, "*Denet*."

"*Denet* is not *father*." He looked puzzled for another couple of steps, then his brow cleared. "No, *doset* is a father, as in the mate of the one who birthed you. *Denet* is more like...let me think. A leader, perhaps, or a king."

I stopped in my tracks. "That man is the Thurei king?"

"No, no, no." He flicked his fingers. "King of his own people. All Pareshols answer to him and he's the head of the House. Not my king. Certainly never yours."

As Cor led me up a flight of stairs, I tried to track down how I'd scrambled up such a basic word. When I came up with a pretty good idea, I scowled and stopped in the middle of the hallway. "Cor. Why didn't you tell me your father is a king?"

"I never hid it. Truly, until just now, I thought you knew and didn't care." He turned, catching his balance with a hand against the wall. "Would it have changed anything whether you refused to see a *denet*'s son or a shopkeeper's? Could I have bought—" He pulled up short, making a visible effort to edit his tongue. "Would it have mattered?"

"No." We'd spent little time with anyone's parents, in Kuyen or my world. Cor had never played up a difference between us. How would I have known?

"Well, then." He strode off down the hallway. "None of this exists for you, anyway."

We reached the healer's door in silence. He'd refused my attempts to restart the conversation the rest of the way, except for insisting, "Leave it alone, Kate," when I asked what a 'wind chaser' might be.

Cor rapped on the door and slumped against the frame while we waited for an answer. His eyelids drifted shut. When the door swung open, he winced. Behind it stood a shapely woman in a simple, cream-colored dress. She had a flat, pink-tipped nose that reminded me of a rabbit's, the impression heighted by the velvety brown fur that covered her skin, from the backs of her delicate hands to the crown of her head. She greeted us with a shallow bow and introduced herself as Whisrit Lache, healer in service to House Pareshol.

Cor made our introductions in turn, swaying when he bowed. He dragged himself upright with fingers pressed to his temple.

"Kindly leave off making it worse if you plan to ask for my help." Whisrit caught his arm. "Needs before forms. By all accounts, you know that already. Help him, Kjelgaard."

I ducked under his other arm and we half-carried him inside.

"I can walk," he insisted, but his voice wavered. We lowered him onto a cushioned cot.

"No pride here, child." The healer tugged over a stool to perch on, then placed her hand on his forehead, pressing her bare palm flush against his skin. Her jaw clenched and she narrowed her wide-set, dark eyes, the pain in her expression an echo of his. She glanced over at me. "Thank you for your assistance."

She made it businesslike, but still a dismissal.

"I prefer for her to stay," Cor murmured, his voice slurred with sleep.

"Of course you do. My mistake." Whisrit's expression softened, but she still had the air of someone used to having her orders followed. "Settle yourself for your wait, please, Kjelgaard."

While she turned back to Cor, I wandered over to the windows that ran the length of the room. Gauzy curtains covered them, letting in diffuse sunlight. I pulled one aside just enough for a glimpse of the landscaped grounds. Framing the windows, open shelves filled with exuberant potted plants gave the impression that the distant outdoors had spilled inside.

Behind me, the healer asked, "What brings you to me, Temarel?"

"Crossing with Kjelgaard has been difficult. Headaches, pain in my muscles. It makes me dizzy, sick. It pains Kjelgaard as well."

"Always, or is this new?"

"New, only in the last couple of days."

I noticed he didn't mention that we hadn't worldwalked together for years before that. I tried to ignore their conversation and concentrate on the gardens.

"Can you think of anything different since the last time you traveled together easily?"

A pause. More quietly, he said, "Everything is different since I last brought Kjelgaard here."

They fell silent and I glanced over my shoulder to see that Cor had his eyes closed and the healer held her head bowed over his, her hand still resting on his brow. Strain showed on her features and I wondered how much effort it had taken for Cor to hide it.

He'll be fine now. I turned back to the windows.

Whatever the healer did, it didn't take long. Behind me, Cor cleared his throat. He looked better, like a plant finally moved into the sun. On the other hand, the healer's features looked pinched.

Despite that, Whisrit bowed to me, Thurei-style, and I mirrored it as best I could in an effort to be polite, knowing I didn't do the gesture justice. She held out a hand. "Katherine Kjelgaard, I would be honored to know you more deeply."

Shaking hands wasn't a Thurei custom, but maybe she knew something about humans. Before I could reach out my hand, Cor touched my shoulder. In English, he said, "Only if you want to."

I nodded, on principle. Very little of this trip made sense so far, so I didn't give his comment much thought. I clasped the healer's hand. It was warm and comforting. Whisrit held my gaze and the pupils of her eyes expanded until the dark green irises were whisper-thin rims around black pits.

Then she was in my head.

Fear flared, a jarring twist of panic—this was *crazy*—then sputtered out like a doused match. Calm spread through me, dampening the urge to flinch and pull away. I could still sense an echo of terror crouching underneath, blanketed by this false quiet.

Whisrit pulled her hand from mine, I swayed, off-balance and hollow, like something in me had been drawn out by the roots. Ice crawled up my spine, but I shoved the sensation down. I would not lose it here. I rubbed sweaty palms on my jeans and tried my best for polite-but-firm. "Don't do that again."

Cor glanced at me, but the healer didn't seem offended. She said, "Temarel, wait outside while I speak with Kjelgaard. I trust you will consider her safe here with me."

I shrugged at his questioning look, projecting what I hoped was nonchalance.

"As you like," he said, then bowed, the movement fluid and easy once more, and let himself out.

"The problem is in your blood," she said as soon as the door closed.

"My blood?" I braced myself for a recap of the Scholars' argument. "Because I'm human?"

Whisrit brushed that possibility aside. "It's not an injury, illness, or infection. The problem is closer to poison, but not like any poison I've seen."

"You mean my *medication*." I had to use the English word, since I didn't know one in Kuyene or Thurei for chemicals used to treat an illness.

Trying to sidestep the translation didn't do me any good. The healer just tilted her head and asked for a definition.

"The healers among my people give me drugs to keep me well."

In Kuyene, the word held the same connotation as heroin with dirty needles.

"They do not make you well." Whisrit pursed her small mouth in a frown. "They cloud your mind and interfere with worldwalking. It affects what you're able to do here. Your young Temarel will harm himself, shuttling you back and forth with your mind fighting him every step of the way. I couldn't take all the strain from him. No healer can completely mend such a thing."

The discussion of my medication belonged to another world—the real world—and I wasn't going to tackle that with some rabbit lady.

To her second point, I shook my head, belatedly switching to the Thurei gesture. "I never asked him to do that. He insists."

"The wind never asks." The healer gave me an odd look. "Is this how you take care of him?"

"I need my *medication*. Temarel can take care of himself." True or not, I felt guilty saying it. I started for the door.

"If you won't give them up, they will do you the same harm!" she called after me, but I kept walking.

Cor waited in the hallway. I couldn't meet his eyes. Since I had no idea which way to head in this labyrinthine mansion, that left me staring at my shoes.

"What will harm you?" he asked, then he blushed, like he realized he'd admitted to eavesdropping. "She was quite loud, at the end."

I shook my head, not wanting to start another argument. "Which way are we headed?"

"Nowhere yet. Please tell me."

Going back the way we'd come made sense to me, so I set off in that direction. Cor caught up in a couple of long-legged strides.

"Please, I care about your safety. She said something would harm you. She's a healer. Tell me."

"She's also the one who told you to wait outside, wasn't she?"

That shut him up. For a moment.

"Yes. Healers are strong-willed like that. Kate. Tell me."

No wonder we argued so much. Too stubborn, both of us. I stopped. "What does wind chaser mean?"

Cor weighed the bargain briefly, but he answered. I knew he would.

"It means that I'm not, in fact, the *denet*'s heir any longer," he said, his calm so obvious that it had to be false. "You see? It doesn't make a difference that I never bragged on my father's title to you. My sister will be the next *denet*, not me. She'll make a fine one."

I didn't know what to say. Into my silence, he amended his definition. "It means spending your life—wasting it, maybe—on something others think is foolish. You're not the only one to call me stubborn."

"And this has something to do with me." I crossed my arms, as if that would somehow shield me from the responsibility.

"Is that what she said? Gossip, nothing more." He brushed the suggestion away with a flick of his fingers. When I waited, unsatisfied with this dismissal, he sighed. "You refused to know me any longer, Katen, but I could not stop being your friend."

"And being friends with a human is enough to get you disinherited? No." Fragments fell together, things he'd said that I'd never considered. "It's because you you made yourself my bodyguard."

Even my imaginary friend didn't think I could make it on my own.

"Stop it." He looked offended, if anything. "I set my own circle with my *denet*. I bear the marks of my own decisions. I don't want to be your bodyguard. Stop digging into this." Cor gave me a sharp look. "Unless you can tell me I'm just as real as you are."

I bit my lip and stayed silent.

"Then how could you care what happened, or what the gossip is? You're ticking off the time on your fingers until you're finished here." He turned and walked away.

Cor the boy could have been pushed, our friendship able to

weather many childhood squabbles. But this man had a breaking point. I found I didn't want to reach it.

I hurried to catch up. "I didn't mean to cause you trouble."

It counted as an apology, if you were talking to a Thurei.

"I know," he said gently, then he sighed. "And here I've dropped you into a nest of Pareshols. We're even."

That counted, too.

On impulse, I asked, "Do you have any paper with you?"

He cocked an eyebrow at me and fished a square from an inner pocket of his coat. I started folding. When I caught him watching from the corner of his eye, I glared. "No peeking."

He took to studying the smooth plaster of the wall beside him as we walked.

In his world, paper folding took prescribed, abstract forms, each one with a set purpose. Request, Summons, Promise. The first time Shom had given me a folded get-well-soon card, I'd checked out every origami book on my local library's shelves. My fingers remembered the folds.

When I finished, I hid my small creation in my cupped hands. "Are you ready?"

"Yes."

We'd played this game as kids, the others putting names to the paper sculptures I'd shown them. Clever Shom had been quickest, Cor most imaginative. I opened my hands to reveal an origami butterfly.

The corner of his mouth quirked up. He lifted the tiny paper insect from my palm, balancing it on his fingertips. "Hope. My thanks, Kate."

It felt good to see that look on his face.

"Now," he said, his eyes bright, "what did I win?"

As children, we'd wagered baubles or dares, but our adult bargains all carried edges. When I hesitated, he shook his head. "Let me show you something, then. For hope."

"Okay," I said, curious despite myself.

He had the same grin now he'd had at ten. "Watch."

He pulled out his stub of pencil and sketched a quick, mirrored pattern on both small wings, then he lifted the folded paper butterfly and stared at it. At first, nothing happened. He took a tense breath, another, then a crimson butterfly struggled free of the paper and fluttered into the air. Behind it, a sunflower-yellow one flexed its wings and found its way aloft. A sapphire butterfly followed, then one the color of sunset, another that shimmered like opal. Soon a small swarm drifted through the air, circling us, alighting on our shoulders, in our hair.

"You never knew how to do this as a kid," I breathed, tracking the flight of an indigo butterfly with gilt-edged wings. "They're beautiful."

"I learned it later. It's just a bit of minor skillwork. Anyone could do it if they took the time to practice."

I grinned at him, lifting an eyebrow. "Oh, everyone does it, I'm sure."

"I'm glad you like it." Cor mimed a formal Thurei tone and swept an elegant bow, conjuring a host of scarlet and orange wings to chase after his hair like a trailing flame. He held the posture like a courtier, tilting his face to look up at me. "Sometimes, you're just how I remember you."

Footsteps sounded at the corner behind him. Cor winked at me and straightened back up. As he caught sight of the slim, rose-haired woman turning into the hallway, his butterflies vanished.

CHAPTER NINE

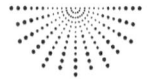

"Turavi." He stumbled over her name, as if he didn't know quite how to address her, but the bow he gave was even deeper than the one he'd given the *denet*.

She was the most beautiful Thurei I'd ever seen, a slender young woman about my age with a fine-boned, oval face, her long hair coiled into a braided crown atop her head. The cast of her features, like Cor's, was subtly inhuman, but striking as a runway model. Her mauve brows arched over a pair of large, golden eyes and her perfect lips were tinted a shade deeper than her hair. She wore a violet blouse with belled sleeves that emphasized her elegant hands and a long skirt that hugged her hips and fell loose around her slippered feet.

The only thing that spoiled her overall perfection was the chilly expression on her face. She bowed to Cor, as precise as if she'd measured the angle beforehand. "Coraven Temarel."

Her use of his full name didn't seem to faze him. He took hold of my hand and drew me beside him. "I make known to you Katherine Kjelgaard. Katherine, this is daughter of the House Turavi Pareshol."

She frowned, eying our joined hands. I squeezed his hand in

support. He'd said he didn't want to offend these people, but so far, they seemed awful.

The silence grew brittle. Ever the diplomat, Cor opened his mouth to break it, but the woman spoke first. "House Pareshol welcomes you, Kjelgaard, but take care that you do not overstep your bounds. I will not accept your offworlder ignorance as an excuse."

It seemed safest to say, "Of course."

She returned her attention to Cor, whose expression had gone hard. "My *denet* asks you both to the noon meal."

"My thanks, but we're in haste. I intend to leave as soon as possible."

"So soon, Temarel?" She widened her eyes in mock surprise. "You do your social duty so seldom, one would think—"

"My House debt falls far beyond the scope of your interest." The edge in Cor's voice sharpened.

"We can stay for lunch," I said before they could take another swing at each other.

Cor looked at me, brows raised. "Are you sure?"

"It's important." Important to Cor, to make a good impression on these people, at least. Even if he wasn't his *denet*'s heir any longer.

He didn't smile. Maybe he didn't want to in front of an audience as hostile as Turavi, but I could see thanks in his eyes. He turned back to her. "House Temarel and House Kjelgaard are pleased to accept the well-known hospitality of your *denet*. We would only wish to add to the honor of this House when we relate our experience. "

"Do you want to refresh yourselves first?" Her gaze swept across me again and her nostrils flared a bit, as if she'd caught a stench in the air.

"How kind." Cor's voice clung to the bottom edges of civil.

"Kjelgaard?" She made my name a challenge.

Oh, goody. I went ahead and smiled since neither of them would do it. "Wonderful."

She brushed between us and down the hallway. Cor and I fell into step behind her. He glanced at me and rolled his eyes. I bit my lip to stifle a nervous laugh. The one good thing about this situation was remembering she wasn't real.

Turavi stopped finally and swung open a door to reveal a lovely suite of rooms, with a sitting area, bed, wardrobe, and washroom.

Cor bowed stiffly to her. No depth this time. None of their exchange had been friendly, but he was positively glacial now. "Be assured that House Temarel makes careful note of the courtesy offered on behalf of your *denet*."

Turavi took her leave with a hurried bow. Even stalking off in a huff, she was beautiful, her full skirts swirling about her ankles.

The gist of this conversation had passed me by so completely that they might as well have been speaking Thurei.

Cor closed the door and leaned back against it, letting out a great sigh. "She's always such a joy."

I glared at him. "Temarel, what's going on?"

"Not between friends, Kate. Not in private. Unless you're that mad at me?"

"Fine. Cor. 'Overstepping my bounds'? What's going on?"

"Word duels. They want to rattle us, if they can." That sigh again.

"But why?"

"Because they're inner House. Because they want to see who will break first." Cor rippled his fingers in a Thurei-style shrug. "Because they're Thurei."

"You're Thurei," I pointed out. I wondered if he was considered inner House anymore, or if he'd lost that status, too.

"Ah, well." Cor offered me a sardonic smile. "And I can be a two-edged handful, sometimes. I'm sure you've noticed."

Despite his smile, tension kept his posture stiff, alert for any new threat. From his 'House allies'? Or from me? *A mistake here would go badly for me*, he'd said.

"I think you're a joy," I told him, making the compliment sincere. I would always remember the butterflies in the hallway, no matter what else happened.

"My thanks." His smile eased into something more comfortable. "And thanks, again, for your patience. I'd thought the road would be clear, but we came too late. If it had been any other Pareshol—but even I can't afford to insult the *denet*. I haven't lost my sense of priorities that thoroughly."

That last sentence came out bitterly, clearly parroting someone else's words.

"Why do they want you here if"—I stopped before I said, 'they don't like you,' which seemed obvious but too unkind—"if they're going to be so mean?"

"These are the sort of House games I'd have to get very good at, in order to be *denet*." He wandered toward the sitting-room chairs. "They can't afford to insult me outright, where I can call it against them. I might not be the *denet*-heir, but I still stand inner House, and I'm brother to the next *denet*. But that leaves a lot of ground to patrol."

I followed him through the sunny, well-appointed room. "What about that Turavi woman?"

"She walks the edge of being openly insulting, but she's done nothing I can answer formally. As I recall, she's always been excellent at that. Truly, only she has cause." He shook himself out of those thoughts. "May I ask a favor?"

I recognized the troublemaker's grin he wore. Things seemed complicated enough already. I was supposed to be getting our agreement over so I could get out of here, not dabbling in Thurei politics. *Pretend I matter.* I would probably regret it, but I said, "Depends on the favor."

"Will you help me answer the insult of this room?"

The suite seemed lovely to me, with graceful wooden furniture, thick, colorful carpets, a wide bed with a clutch of bright pillows, and walls covered in swirling designs painted cream on white.

"Not this." He nodded toward the sitting area. "Not the bathing room, either. Those are appropriate to offer two...unpaired...guests time to prepare for a formal meal."

Oh. The bed, then. I doubled my embarrassment by blushing.

"Exactly. She implies the highest insult. If you'd like, we can turn it back on her."

"How?"

"Turavi is quite vain and would hate to see you outshine her."

"Fat chance of that." Even thinking about her made me feel dumpy. Plain-Jane brown hair and brown eyes and chubby figure, compared with my mind's perfect image of svelte, graceful beauty, personified in that woman.

Cor gave me a stern look. "You outshine her now. The Pareshols, though...you may have noticed a certain lack of depth. It never hurts to have the right armor for the battle."

I rolled my eyes, which he ignored. "And where's this 'armor' supposed to come from?"

He went to the massive wardrobe and pulled open its doors. Garments in every hue and fabric hung inside. "There must be something here you like."

Well, why not? How much more of a fantasy could a girl hope for than playing dress up with an imaginary wardrobe? It wasn't like I'd ever gone to a high school prom. I gathered a likely assortment and headed for the bathroom.

I tried to keep my mind on the clothing. Whatever was going on with Cor, he was right. It wasn't my place to dig. I needed to focus on getting him to leave, not worry about what happened to his reputation. I sighed, drawing a length of embroidered fabric from the pile, knowing full well I had no real desire to march out there and insist we head off to find that ex-Scholar right this instant. No, I was going to keep looking for an outfit to show up a woman who'd insulted my friend. *Pretending* like it mattered.

I wondered if I was fooling Cor any better than I was fooling myself.

Most of the clothing had been made for Thurei-sized women, which made me feel like a whale, but I finally found an outfit that both matched and fit. Thurei favored bright, crayon colors like their hair, but this was...not drab. Subtle. The long skirt, made from crisp, black fabric, belted snugly at my waist and fell, pleated and loose, to the floor. The blouse was a soft, shiny cream, with a low scoop neck and loose sleeves gathered at the cuffs. A long vest in forest green went over it all. Sleeveless, it skimmed my curves, splitting at my hips into panels that shifted as I moved to reveal the darker skirt underneath. Embroidery ringed the hems with tiny leaves and ivory flowers.

I opened the bathroom door to find Cor shrugging into a short blue jacket, which he wore over a crisp white shirt and navy trousers. He did up the jacket's clasps, his gaze never leaving me.

I raised an eyebrow as he finished. "You missed one."

He glanced down and gave an embarrassed little laugh as he fixed his jacket.

I'd never been admired. It felt good, even if I was just imagining it.

"These clothes are pretty nice," I admitted. Certainly worlds above my usual jeans and T-shirts. But clothes only counted for so much. "I'm still no Turavi Pareshol."

"And my thanks for that, I assure you. There is only one thing missing."

"What's that?"

"You are dressed so formally. May I extend the same honor to your hair?"

I must have looked surprised. He spread his hands between us. "I meant no insult."

I almost laughed, that he thought I would be offended. I had little patience for styling my hair on the best of days, and the bun I'd scraped it up into after changing was the fanciest hairdo in my repertoire. It probably did clash with my 'armor,' but it seemed like we'd taken a while here already. "We'll be late to lunch, won't we?"

His fingers rippled in a shrug. "Impossible. We're guests of the House. They wait on us."

Absurd, considering how they'd treated him.

He gave me something like a grin, only without the humor. "Yes, life indoors is full of these little ironies. This is part of our answer. We won't be rushed into presenting ourselves at any disadvantage."

While he picked through a drawer in the wardrobe, I sank into one of the sitting room chairs. Back home, it would be near midnight and it felt good to be off my feet. The nap I'd taken didn't stretch far enough to cover the growing deficit.

Cor carried over a brush and a handful of something that glittered in the sunlight streaming through the tall windows. He kept the brush and passed the crystal-headed hairpins to me.

He unwound my hair from the bun with gentle fingers. As he began to draw the brush through it, my eyes drifted closed.

"When did you learn to do women's hair?"

"You may not remember my sisters. They would have been rather young, back when you visited, so they didn't join us for games." He was quiet a moment, working through a tangle. "My mother returned to her House when Netari was in her second summer."

"Wait, your mom left you?"

"*Helons*...wives? Husbands and wives. They often part ways. She had done her duty in marriage, by the trade agreements she brought and the three heirs she gave the House. My parents were not like yours, with each other and with you."

"Huh." Cor had rarely spoken of his parents when we'd been young, but I remembered how things had been in my house.

"I mean before they stopped believing you," he said softly. "I envied you. Two parents who spent time with you every day and read you stories at night, not just a *denet* and nursemaids. So my sisters and I grew up closer than we would have, otherwise. I asked their maids to teach me to do their hair. It was a joke between the three of us, but it made them smile."

He fell silent, twining two locks of my hair with deft fingers. "Hand me a pin?"

I held one up and he seated it securely in whatever pattern he was creating. Another slight twist, a shift of his fingers. "Pin."

I soon had the rhythm of it. The sensation soothed me as he worked. My mind wandered. "So how long have you known Turavi?"

"Forever. Or maybe it just seems like it. Our Houses have been allies for many years." He reached down, took another pin. Seated it. I handed him another.

I couldn't imagine Cor had done anything to earn her obvious enmity. I could come up with another explanation. "How long ago did she fall in love with you?"

A pin tinged as it hit the floor and skittered under my chair. I started to reach for it, but he stopped me. "There are plenty left. And no, she's never loved me. Nowhere close to it, to my knowledge."

"Oh. Well, what happened to make her so angry with you? You're generally pretty nice."

"Thank you for such great praise." He chuckled and gathered up another lock of hair. "In English, I think you would say she is my fiancée."

"What?" I yelped. I would have turned to look up at him, only he was holding my hair.

"Pin." Like it was nothing.

Scowling, I held one up. "Why didn't you tell me that she was your girlfriend in the hallway? That would have explained a lot."

"Perhaps you misunderstand. I thought 'girlfriend' is the English for *nochel*. A *nochel* is for...ah, company? For fun. Turavi was to be my *helon*. We were never *nochels*."

"Semantics," I said. The blunted tips and faceted crystals of the hairpins dug into my palms. I relaxed my fists. "You said she 'was to be'?"

"Then I did have the wrong word. Hm." Cor let the quiet stretch for a moment. "What is the English for the future wife of an ally marriage, now called off?"

"Ex-fiancée, Coraven! And it's French," I added, which was petty.

"My thanks for your instruction." He sounded smug. "As to your other question, I never told you because I didn't think it was relevant."

"It's not," I said, because it shouldn't have been. At least now I knew where Turavi's enmity had come from, no matter how off base she was. "Marry whoever you want."

He chuckled. "That's kind of you, but I can't take a *helon*."

"Why not?" Surely, he had other, better options than that woman. Any Thurei lady should thank her lucky stars to snag Cor.

"Ah." He worked another pin into my hair. "I swore a *dacha* oath, so no alliance can be made through me and I will give the House no heirs. That's why my *denet* chose my sister Damoret as the heir instead."

"You made a...a vow of celibacy so you wouldn't have to marry Turavi?"

"I don't know that word, but yes, I made a vow before my *denet*. It can't be undone." Rescuing me from what would surely have been an embarrassing explanation of 'celibacy,' he continued. "When my *denet* saw he couldn't force me, he set my sister a marriage pledge instead. Now Turavi's brother will wed my *denet*'s heir and Turavi will have to settle for being sister to one *denet* and marriage-kin to another. No great surprise that she blames me for it. Well, there it is. That's why she detests me."

"Not because you're a sneak?" I held up another pin. "Anything else you need to tell me?"

"There's a whole world, Katen."

Unspoken beneath that was, *Tell me it's real.*

But I couldn't.

His hands moved through my hair, gathering up stray tendrils. "Please, let things be well between us. What does it matter, about Turavi? I had thought...it matters little, what I thought. I didn't mean to annoy you."

"I'm not annoyed." Well, maybe. Mostly, I felt...played. And tired.

Finished with whatever elaborate thing he'd done with my hair, Cor came around and knelt in front of me. The light caught his eyes and they glowed like lit amber. "I put myself in your debt by a thing unfairly said, Katherine Kjelgaard. What would you have from me, to mend this?"

It was another way to ask forgiveness without saying *sorry*. There were so many ways to do that here, as there were so many ways to be insulting without offering insult. Like Turavi, so precise with her 'House Pareshol welcomes you,' which only made it clear that she herself did not.

I squeezed my eyes shut. I had never made another close friend, not after they were gone. Typical negative symptom of schizophrenia, the psychologists said. At the time, I'd refused to betray my friends by making new ones, just to please my parents and convince the doctors I was normal. I'd had no idea, then, that our indivisible trio could in fact be divided. That I could come to agree with the rest of the world that I was crazy and they didn't exist.

"Kate? Katen?"

I opened my eyes to find Cor watching me, worry shadowing his face. His hand faltered on its trip to my cheek. As children, we'd thought nothing of wiping away tears or throwing our arms around each other in a show of sympathy, but that had been a long time ago.

My life would be better off once this was over and maybe Cor's would be, too. I couldn't let myself want him to be real, but I couldn't ignore how it would hurt to make him leave again.

I shook my head. "Let's just get this over with. How's my hair?"

He rose and went to the window, sweeping aside the thick, drawn-back curtains so he could trace his fingers along the carved frame. The glass flashed. When the colors settled, it showed our reflections, solid against the view of gardens outside. I got up to stand beside him, studying the images of us in our borrowed finery. He smiled, a polite expression he wore like a mask.

"A Seeming, like the butterflies," he explained. "Skillwork is carved into the frame, so it becomes a mirror."

"Not quite a mirror. Where's the rest of the room?" None of the guest suite showed in the glass, just the two of us and the garden beyond the window. It could be a photo of us in a park.

"It shows what I want it to." He waved his hand at my reflection. "What do you think? Turavi will regret being rude."

"Yeah, I'm sure she's really worried," I said, but I had to admit I looked good. No way I could be confused for Thurei, but the clothes made me look sophisticated. Cor had woven my hair into something like an upswept French braid, the crystal-headed pins winking among the plaits strands like stars. Beside me, Cor looked like a character from some quirky period movie, the cobalt blue of his short jacket setting off his blazing orange hair, his posture precise enough for a soldier. "We both look pretty good."

"I agree." He tucked my hand into the crook of his elbow. "Are you ready?"

I nodded, stifling a yawn with my free hand.

Our image faded from the window as he looked down at me. "You must be tired. Perhaps you should go home. The Pareshols aren't your allies, so this isn't your duty."

"And let you go alone, after all this work? I don't think so."

The sudden smile on his face, like the wonder of the butterflies he'd conjured in the hallway, would stay with me long after he disappeared again. Blessing or curse, I didn't have to decide yet.

"You don't need to stay long," he said, leading me down the hallway. "Perhaps just long enough to eat a little."

I fervently hoped Cor wasn't thinking of the inedible pot of vegetable-and-murk soup that waited on my stove. He continued. "Then I can slip you home. We can try again tomorrow, if you'd rather not head out this afternoon."

"It's okay. I can take myself back."

Cor shook his head. "No need for you to bear the effort yourself. You're only here because I asked it of you."

"But it'll harm you," I said without thinking. "At least, that's what the healer said."

"Ah. Did she say it wouldn't harm you?"

There seemed no point in hiding it now. "No."

"Did she say why it was so difficult for you to cross, when you did it so easily as a child?"

"She blamed my medicine."

"You mean what they gave you at...at Bayshore."

"Yes." I braced myself for the inevitable argument, but Cor didn't object.

He shrugged his shoulders, making the gesture deliberate in its humanness. "You don't need to worry about me coming to harm. When you close your eyes, I disappear."

"If it's all in my imagination, then I don't need to worry about it hurting me, either," I countered.

Another turn in the hall brought us to an ornate pair of doors. He frowned at them like he blamed them for interrupting, but he seemed to think better of continuing this particular discussion while his so-called allies waited on the other side. When he looked back at me, he'd reclaimed his polite mask. "Remember, you don't need to bow here. You're human, not Thurei."

As if I could forget.

CHAPTER TEN

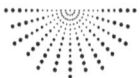

T he doors opened to an immense banquet room scattered with tables. Strands of crystals and light globes crisscrossed the high ceiling. I'd called those flameless lamps 'fairy lights' as a kid, which always made Shom roll her eyes.

At the far end, a huge fireplace sent a wash of warmth into the chilly room. Several people stood near it, chatting and sipping from delicate glasses. Otherwise, the room was empty. The group turned as the doors closed behind us to give us their full attention.

I was glad for the outfit and the fancy hairdo.

While we were still too far away for eavesdropping, Cor whispered, "They have a smaller room for casual meals. They're trying to intimidate us."

I forced a smile to my face. It couldn't have been any less convincing than the ones the Pareshols wore. There were six of them, the *denet* and Turavi, as well as a regal middle-aged woman, two younger men, and a boy of ten or eleven, all dressed in fine clothing. The *denet* confirmed my guess when he introduced his *helon* and sons. The eldest, a pleasant-looking man in his early thirties, was the *denet's* heir. Turavi's elegant brows twitched in a brief scowl at hearing her brother's title.

"Everyone, welcome Coraven Temarel," the *denet* continued, his smile edged like a blade. "He's brought a guest of his own. The lady... could you refresh my memory? It's not a House name."

Cor took over. "*Denet*-heir Katherine Kjelgaard."

I thought I saw a few flickers of surprise at the trumped-up title, hidden quickly as the Thureis made their bows. Technically, Cor hadn't lied. I was an only child. Someday, I would be the final Kjelgaard of my family line.

"How wonderful to finally meet you," said the heir, my theoretical equal. While he kept his expression polite, I hadn't missed the once-over glance he'd given me as we walked up.

Maybe I'd been here too long, but I found myself turning the phrase over in search of a hidden slight. "The pleasure is mine."

As soon as we were all seated at the table, servants with platters filed into the room. Cor sat across from me, and Turavi claimed the seat to his right. I sat sandwiched between the oldest and youngest brothers.

Nalores, the *denet's helon*, looked up from her side of the table. With her every movement, tiny golden chains shivered among the lemon-yellow curls of her hair. She asked me, "How is it that you've never made the courtesy of a visit to allies of Temarel before, Kjelgaard?"

What was the right answer to that? "I don't worldwalk often. I usually stay on my side of the gap."

A servant offering a tray of sliced fruit gave me a brief reprieve. I speared a piece with the two-pronged Thurei equivalent of a fork.

Cor spoke up. "In fact, the Kjelgaards do no business in Kuyen. As you know, they have no formal ties to Temarel."

"And what business does House Kjelgaard concern itself with?" Turavi packed so much condescension into her voice, I was surprised I could make out the words.

My father's landscaping nursery didn't seem like something that would impress these people, with their fancy clothes and ostentatious dining hall, ridiculous for an eight-person lunch. But there had to be some way I could wipe the smirk off that girl's face. I would not be condescended to by my own hallucinations.

Trying for casual, I asked, "Have you ever heard of a *camera*?"

The older Pareshols gave me blank looks, but young Chadef gasped. I saw the smallest sliver of an appreciative smile play across Cor's mouth, hidden before our hosts could see.

"A picture-maker, *denet*." The boy grinned at his father. He turned to me, oblivious to his sister's warning glare. "Yomala's *nochel* had one! He could capture sights in the window of it, but then it stopped working and no matter how he concentrated, he could not make it go again."

I nodded. "The *batteries* probably died."

The boy's turquoise brows leaped. "Something lived inside?"

"Not exactly." I considered how to explain batteries and how they contrasted with the prepared skillwork of the window-mirror, but the *denet* cleared his throat in Chadef's general direction and I returned to Turavi's question before I could get the boy in any more trouble. "I make the *photographs*."

That got more blank looks. The term apparently hadn't made it to even Chadef's savvy ears. My Kuyene wasn't quite up to the task, but I shuffled through my vocabulary and tried again. "We take the images out of the window and put them on paper so you can save them."

"Amazing!" Chadef's enthusiasm held no hint of guile. The rest of his family just stared. I doubted if I could have made a better impression saying 'rocket scientist.'

"No skillwork on our side can do that, not permanently," said the middle brother. Thegal, I thought, the one who would marry Cor's sister. "Seemings come close, but those disappear once you stop concentrating."

"Yes, quite impressive." Turavi feigned disinterest, but her composure wasn't what it had been.

Cor took a slow drink of his wine. By the glint in his eye, I suspected it kept him from laughing.

"*Cameras*, as you call them, are very rare here," said the heir. "There is little trade with your world. I thought it was because human workings are ineffective here, as Kuyene skills are weaker there, but you say something inside dies?"

"I'm so—I mean, I misspoke." I stumbled over the automatic apology. I would embarrass myself—maybe even Cor, as his guest—with such a simple sorry here, no matter how impressed they'd been over digital photo printing. "It was just an expression. There's nothing alive inside a *camera*, but a better explanation is beyond my Kuyene."

Cor stepped into the silence. "The *camera* isn't a working like we would craft. It's entirely mechanical, but far more complex than anything we make here. Humans' lack of *jeira* has led them to create all manner of ingenious things." He appeared to realize how emphatic he'd gotten and finished with an offhand, "Besides, it's just river babble that our *jeira* doesn't work as well in their world."

"Surely, some things don't work as well," Turavi observed, laying on innocence with a trowel. Whatever rise she'd wanted out of Cor, she failed.

"If you stop reaching, you'll find everything is beyond you," Cor said, repeating a proverb even I'd heard before. He played their game better than I'd expected, after his claims to hate it. He beckoned for a particular platter. "Your kitchen must be complimented on the *kittu*. Would you care for some, Turavi?"

She narrowed her eyes. "No."

He turned to me. "Kjelgaard?"

"I'd love some, thank you."

I welcomed the diversion of the servant and his platter, and I kept my attention on my plate. The *kittu* was good, tender meat with a subtle, spicy flavor that played off the tangy, sautéed greens served alongside.

"Tell me, Temarel, how is your House faring?" The *denet* turned the conversation blessedly away from me for the moment.

"Very well at present." Cor cut a slice of some type of pastry and popped it into his mouth.

"Is Netari enjoying her new *morsai*?" Sajora asked.

Cor swallowed, hard. He reached for his wine, his face suddenly as expressive as flat steel. "She's elated, I'm sure."

"You mean to say you missed it?" Turavi's eyes went wide. *Not a model*, I decided. *An actress.* "It was only yesterday."

I caught the narrowing of Cor's eyes before he smoothed his expression back to a mask. "I had other business, as it happens. I had no official place there, as you know. Damoret would have offered the saddle."

Turavi threw an obvious glance my way at the mention of 'business.' I ignored her as loudly as I could.

The conversation drifted on to other things, but Cor's shoulders held a tension he couldn't poker-face his way out of for the rest of the meal. I stayed as quiet as possible, only speaking when I had to.

Yesterday, we'd been at Scholars' Hall and I didn't even know what event he'd missed to be there.

After a maliciously long time, the servants removed our plates. The food had been delicious, but the company had made it sit like a pound of gravel in my stomach. I tried not to make things worse by recalling it might be the failed soup.

The *denet* offered fruit and iced wine. Before I could think of a polite refusal, Cor pushed back his chair and rose. He shot me a nudging glance, so I followed his lead.

"We intend to set out from here in search of a Shevern solitaire. You must excuse us, but the day grows late."

"You want to leave now?" Nalores did a tolerable impression of concern. "You'll scarcely make it off our grounds before sundown."

The *denet* added, "Tell me you've reconsidered your plan to go on foot. I know you think highly of your abilities, Temarel, but I'd expect more consideration on the part of your—"

Cor interrupted. "My thanks, but time is my main concern."

"On foot?" Our hostess flicked her fingers in disbelief. "Kjelgaard, you're sending him into the wildlands alone and on foot? How does that save you any time?"

All the Pareshols turned to stare at me and my cheeks burned. We'd be leaving this house together, but after sunset, Cor would be carrying on alone.

"He's very capable. If he says he can do it, I would never doubt him." It was probably true, but not much of an answer. I hadn't planned this quest, but I was the reason he was going.

"Circumstances limit our options," Cor said. "I made arrangements I deemed acceptable and Kjelgaard accompanies me out of kindness. Now, if you will excuse us, we don't wish to trouble the House any further with our personal concerns."

The *denet* crossed his arms. "I will not explain to your *denet* why I allowed a pair of my guests to leave my House with so little protection, no matter how skillful you are. You will take a pair of my *morsais*. You can travel faster that way, in any case."

I couldn't decide whether it was a real agreement or just a way to end this, but Cor gave a slight bow. "My thanks, *Denet* Pareshol. I will take Kjelgaard home this afternoon and we can set out from here tomorrow."

"I can take myself back," I said quickly. "There's no need for you to go through all that trouble." I hated all these implications the Pareshols were making that I was using Cor as some sort of high-risk fetch and carry service. They weren't wrong, and that made it worse.

"Excellent." Turavi spoke into the pause as Cor searched for something to say. "Temarel, you can stay here overnight and save yourself the travel." She turned to me with a poisonous smile. "No hurry now, Temarel. Have a pleasant evening, Kjelgaard."

"Your concern does you credit, but I have to excuse myself." He surprised me by smiling back at her just as sharply before turning to me. "Allow me to escort you back to your room, Kjelgaard."

Before someone could rope him back into staying at the table, I gave him another excuse. "Maybe you can help me with my hair."

I could probably get the pins out, but he could do it without making a mess.

Turavi and her mother exchanged a quick glance and a blush touched Cor's cheeks, although his expression said nothing beyond polite courtesy. "Of course."

I'd said something wrong, but asking would only make it worse. I gave up trying to figure it out. "Thank you. Shall we?"

Farewells were given with varying degrees of enthusiasm and I found myself grateful once again to be spared all the bowing. When the banquet room doors closed behind us, we sighed in unison.

"Let's not do that again." I hadn't spoken that much Kuyene in ages. Switching to English was a relief.

"Yes. Once was too many." Cor gave me a wan smile as we headed back toward the guesting room where I'd left my clothes. "You were wonderful, Kate. Thank you for your company. I've always hated this type of thing. Not a great quality in an heir." He chuckled, but his attempt at lightheartedness rang thin. "It was brilliant, telling them about the photos. Is that really what you do?"

"It's simpler than it sounds." I grinned at the idea of a family rich enough to own this mansion being impressed by a minimum-wage store clerk. "I didn't think my dad's landscaping nursery would have gotten the same reaction."

"No, I imagine not." He fell silent, sinking into his thoughts.

I cleared my throat. "I'm not in that big a hurry. I would have gone to Scholars' Hall another day."

"Netari's ceremony, you mean?" He rippled his fingers in a shrug. "Damen's presentation was held in the evening, by her request. Either the *denet* refused Netten the same freedom, or she chose the timing for herself. If anyone had told me about it, we would've gone to the Hall another day."

"I'm messing everything up for you," I said. What was the phrase he'd used before? "I've put myself in your debt."

"You can't be in my debt." He flicked the concern aside. "Did you know about Netten's presentation?"

"No." I frowned at him, guessing where this would lead.

"And would you have kept me from it, if you'd known?"

"No. That's not really the point, Cor."

"It's exactly the point." He stopped at one of the doors and held it open for me. "It wasn't your choice."

Stepping into the room, I changed the subject. A little. "What was it about, anyway? *Morsais* were those things pulling the carriage, right?"

"And for riding, too, yes. Having her first trained *morsai* shows that Netten has gained the right of some independence. Remember how you talked about one day getting your first car?"

That made sense. I didn't mention that I'd never gotten a car or my license. I'd never had the chance. He continued. "A well-trained *morsai* also makes a strong defender, so it's like a car and a bodyguard, crossed together."

He dropped into one of the sitting room chairs and I went to the other room to change. Someone had come in and taken away the pile of clothes from earlier, leaving my own clothes folded on the washstand. When I picked up my jeans, I saw they'd been mended, too. The left cuff had been frayed, but someone had cleaned up the loose threads and done something clever with stitches to weave it together again.

Great, even my hallucinations thought I couldn't dress myself properly. I'd never felt so scruffy. Well, my clothes might have been rags compared to Thureis', but at least they were mine. My image in the mirror was nearly familiar when I was dressed again, except for my hair, which was still wrapped and pinned in Cor's fairytale creation. I lifted my hands to the first pin, then stopped.

Whatever the Pareshol women had found funny about the idea of Cor doing my hair, he hadn't minded. Neither had I.

Cor sat with his foot up on the chair cushion, his fingers laced atop his raised knee, resting his chin on his hands. The casual, unselfconscious pose made him look more like the boy I'd known.

"Would you mind taking my hair down?" There was a pause before he answered, long enough that I added, "You don't have to."

Then Cor shook himself out of wherever his thoughts had taken him and rose. "It's my pleasure. Come, sit down."

He worked quickly, his hands gentle. I was so tired, I started to drift, like a petted cat, and almost missed when he said, "Thank you."

"For what?"

"What you said to the Pareshols, when they were pretending to be so concerned." He set the last of the pins onto a side table and drew a brush through my hair.

"They acted like I'm using you."

"They acted insufferable. Ignore them. I do." He set the brush aside. "There. Now I can take you home."

I took a deep breath. I'd made up my mind on this. He'd told the healer it didn't hurt him to cross alone, just if he took me with him. "You said you'd follow me if I wouldn't let you take me."

Cor nodded, wary.

"Don't the Pareshols expect you to stay?"

"I'll come back here, before your sun rises. They'll have me all evening." He gave me a tragic look. "Then we can leave as soon as you slip here tomorrow."

"Here, here?" I looked around the room, fixing it in my mind so I could remember in the morning.

"You can meet me in the stables." He fished something from his pocket, uncurling his fingers to reveal a small carving of a bird, about the size of an acorn. The style and wood matched that of the comb he'd given me. He placed it in my hand, the tips of his fingers brushing lightly over my palm. "This will bring you to me, like a place token. Just hold it and think of me as you cross. Perhaps Issai will know a way to make the crossing easier for you."

"Maybe so." After I saw this Scholar and learned whatever Cor thought she could teach me, I didn't plan on setting foot here again. My life could go back to normal and so could Cor's, if he had one.

I closed my eyes, focused my tired mind on my apartment, dark and empty in the lonely hours of the night. Card table there, with the partially completed jigsaw puzzle. Folding chair there. Window on that wall. Door there, and the dent in the wall that the doorknob had left sometime before I'd moved in.

I felt for the edges of the mental snapshot and pulled.

CHAPTER ELEVEN

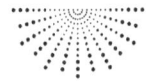

The headache hit like I'd slammed into a wall. I staggered, and a hand caught my elbow. In the dim glow of the streetlights outside, Cor was a shadowy shape at my side.

"I'm okay," I said, steadying myself. My head pounded and my stomach twisted with nausea, but I still felt better than Cor had looked, bringing me to the Pareshols. I was so tired. *And I have to work in the morning.* "I just need to get some sleep."

"Let me help," he said as I started toward my bedroom, but I waved him off. There were some things I could do on my own.

I fell asleep before I had time to wonder what he would do with the rest of the night by himself in a dark apartment, but when I woke it was like he'd never been there at all.

Of course.

The headache was real enough, but I could hardly expect any different after only three hours of sleep. A couple of aspirins made me feel a little better, on the principle that it was something taken care of. A shower cleared some of the grogginess.

Before I left, I dumped my failed soup and set the pot in the sink. I dropped a couple of granola bars, an orange, and a can of soda into my bag and headed downstairs to my bike.

So much for home-cooked.

The crisp air helped, or maybe the aspirins were taking effect. At least I felt awake by the time I reached work. When I pulled my keys out of my pocket, something else fell out and tumbled to the pavement. The little wooden bird Cor had given me. I dusted it off, frowning at the scratch in its smooth finish. It had a hole in its back, like a pendant. I could string it on something when I got back home.

I set the carving aside on the counter and focused on getting the till ready. Tired as I was, the task dragged on. This wasn't even math, just counting, but I was still fidgeting with it when Rose came in.

"Good morning!" She stowed her purse and sketchbook under the counter. "What's this?"

I slid the cash drawer shut and looked up to find her studying Cor's token. So she could see something there, at least. I could hardly say, *Well, what does it look like?* Rude, for one. And also...crazy. Normal people would all see the same thing.

Normal people didn't have to double-check reality.

I cleared my throat. "A friend gave it to me."

"Do you know where she got it? It's really cool."

"He didn't say." It woke a tremor of nerves, to be standing here talking about Cor and something from Kuyen. Maybe I was dreaming. What did she see? I couldn't stop myself from asking, but I tried to be subtle about it. "So, what do you think it's made of?"

"Definitely oak." She shook a wooden-bead bracelet free from her sleeve and held the bird token against it. "See?"

My growing hope fizzled. The honey-and-chocolate wood of the bird looked nothing like the sand-pale, finely grained oak beads. At least she didn't say it looked like something out of a grocery store quarter machine.

She hadn't seen what I saw, so what did that prove? Nothing. No prize for partial matches. I'd tried all those little tests when I'd been a kid and I knew how they turned out. Our brains simply would not perceive the same things.

That wasn't called magic, but hallucination.

She set the token in front of me. "Here, you don't want to lose it."

"Thanks." I had a feeling I was losing it already, whatever that meant anymore.

When I got home after work, I set my alarm clock and crawled into bed. I had to sleep sometime and I obviously wouldn't get to do so tonight. When I woke, the sun hovered just a touch over the horizon. A few minutes more, and I could slip across. Cor expected me early.

Think of me, he'd said, so I did. I imagined his expressive mouth curved in a smile, his clever hands dancing through the air as he spoke. Holding the little wooden token in my hand and the image of him in my mind, I reached for Kuyen.

A musky animal smell and a sudden pounding in my head told me I'd made it. I flung out a hand, dizzy and disoriented in the shadowy space after the fluorescent light of my kitchen, and knocked into a wooden barrier. Something near me growled and I pressed back against the wall, willing my eyes to adjust.

"Quiet, you," someone chided the growler.

Cor. I could see him now, as my eyes got used to the dimness. The stable was a long, wooden building with a single center aisle flanked by a series of high-walled stalls with barred windows. I leaned on the safe side of one. Cor stood inside with a rangy, black *morsai*, buckling on some sort of saddle, scarcely more than a leather pad with stirrups. He had his back to me. The animal perked its wide, pointed ears in my direction and scraped its clawed feet on the floor. Cor followed its attention and looked over his shoulder.

"Kate." He smiled and his face lit up just like I'd imagined. "The crossing went well?"

"Well enough." I forced myself upright, vowing to bring painkillers with me next time. "I see you survived the night."

He widened his eyes in a look of mock innocence that rivaled Turavi's. "Are you implying they'd be rude to a guest?"

I shook my head. Carefully, so it wouldn't hurt. "I don't under-stand you Thureis."

"We're not all Pareshols."

"Thank you for that, Coran."

He paused in the act of letting down a stirrup. It was the nick-name, I guessed, more than the thanks that surprised him. "For not being House Pareshol?"

"Thanks for helping me. The Pareshols don't seem like the type of people who would help a friend."

"Ah. You have that right. Even lending the *morsais* is a counter they will use with my *denet*." He lifted one of the leather bags off the floor of the stall and began lacing it to the saddle. "Thureis don't have many friends outside of their Houses." He weighted the statement with the same intensity he'd used warning me about the Pareshols yesterday.

Small wonder. There'd been three of us, once, and I'd never even mentioned her. "Whatever happened to Shom?"

Maybe that hadn't been what he was talking about because he didn't have a ready answer. "It's been years since I last saw her. I believe she took service with her *tol*. You should send to her and ask."

"Maybe so," I said, but I didn't mean it. Things were difficult enough with just Cor.

He didn't look fooled, but he changed the subject, dipping into the pocket of his coat. He held out one of the wards, a strip five or so inches long. "Here, take this. It will help hide your *jeira*—make you less bright—while we travel."

"What am I supposed to do, tie it around my wrist?"

"I could braid it into your hair, " he offered, grinning. He turned back to mess with the saddle some more, businesslike again before I could tease him back. "Just keep it with you. Tonchu's ready. All we need to do is pick one for you."

I eyed the *morsai*. I'd never ridden a horse, much less something that looked like it could eat me. I glanced up and down the double row of stalls. From some of the slatted windows, curious *morsais* poked out their heads, swiveling their ears in our direction, sniffing the air. They had lots of teeth.

"Um, I don't know how to ride."

"They're well-trained. You'll learn quickly, I'm sure. In fact—" He stopped and took a closer look at my expression. "Ah. How about this? I need to stay on this side of the gap, since the wildlands shift. We'll end up going in circles, otherwise. Tonchu can easily carry us both, if we give her time to rest in between. Or we can walk, if you'd rather."

I sighed. "Walking sounds slow. I'll try riding double."

"In a hurry, but not such a hurry," he said softly. He swung open the stall door. "You need to meet her first or she won't let you on."

The *morsai* looked a lot bigger with no barrier between us. I edged away and she followed, laying back her ears.

"No frightening the guest," Cor scolded her. He drew me closer, his fingers light on mine, as he murmured to her in Thurei. She ducked her head and gave me a thorough sniffing.

"There, now." He kept his voice soft, his fingers curled around mine. The *morsai* followed us out into the aisle. At a word from Cor, she folded into a graceful lying down position, like a sphinx. He pointed to the wide leather band holding the packs. "You sit here, behind the saddle."

The *morsai* made a more comfortable seat than I'd imagined. Cor lowered himself to the saddle in front of me. Tonchu thumped her fringed tail on the ground behind us.

"You need to hold on for this part."

"Hold on to what?" I didn't see straps or anything.

"Me."

Oh. I reached around his waist and laced my fingers together.

Cor clicked his tongue and the *morsai* surged to her feet with a bound that nearly sent me tumbling. Once up, she stood still, waiting for further direction.

"It'll go more smoothly now," Cor said, while I tried to get my breath back and calm my racing heart. He patted my hands where they crossed his stomach. "You don't need to hold on quite so hard."

"Sorry!" I was clutching at him like my life depended on it. I snatched my hands back and sat up, which had me almost falling off again. Tonchu shifted about, making my balance even worse.

Cor chuckled and tapped my knee where it pressed against his thigh. "Relax here, too. Pressing with your legs tells her to walk."

It took willpower, since I was convinced I'd fall off, but I loosened my death grip. Tonchu stopped.

"Now, give me your hands."

I reached forward and Cor brought my hands together to loosely clasp his waist. "There. Are you ready? I'll ask her to walk again."

"I'm ready."

His legs shifted against mine and the *morsai* headed toward the stable door, her gait level and steady. She paused in the slanted patch of sunlight at the entrance, lifting her long snout to test the air. After allowing her a moment to sniff, Cor urged her forward.

The *morsai*'s long strides carried us down the gravel drive to the Pareshols' gate. Manicured gardens and lawns stretched out to the sides, like manor grounds in the vacation magazines in a doctor's office. Beyond the gate, scattered trees marked the rolling grassland, collecting into thicker stands as the valley climbed toward forested slopes. When Cor directed Tonchu to leave the road and head into the wildlands, our mount hesitated, shifting her weight from foot to foot while he cajoled her in Thurei. With a whine and much flicking of her ears, she finally stepped off the gravel.

The long grasses reached high enough to brush my shoes. If she followed a trail, it was too faint for me to see. A steady insect buzz filled the air. I hoped it meant something benign, like cicadas.

Riding turned out to be pleasant. As promised, Tonchu's movement was smooth, a gentle, rhythmic rocking. Cor rode easily, his posture straight but not stiff, his legs relaxed against mine, except when he shifted to direct the *morsai*.

"How dangerous is it out here, really?" I asked. The Pareshols had made it sound like there was a Hunter waiting behind every bush, but it looked beautiful to me. Peaceful.

"Well, there's no Truce in the wilds to stop Hunters from preying on others. But they don't sit waiting at the gates, either." He gave a human-style shrug. Riding this close together, I could feel it in the way his body moved. "Of course, beyond lands that have been claimed and shaped, everything is more dangerous."

"How does that work, claiming?" As a kid, I'd thought it meant people lived there, but it turned out I'd misunderstood a lot of things.

"Claiming takes a lot of *jeira*. Many people together can shape a large area. All the Thureis in House Pareshol and all their guests know the House and the grounds. Their certainty holds the land stable against the wilds. When a House is first founded, the grounds are smaller because there are fewer who know it."

"You mean claimed lands exist because you all agree on it?"

"Agree?" He drew the word out, considering it. His fingers pattered against my knee. He was making the gesture for 'no,' I realized, turning it into a touch because he had his back to me. Surely, not as personal as it felt. Probably common. But it made me wonder whom else he might have been so casual with, to answer a question with a simple touch.

And whatever he'd been saying, I missed it. "What was that?"

"Not agreement the way I think you meant. We know our ground, so we have the ground we know." After a moment's pause, he added, "Tell me it's different on Earth. You all have to agree to see the same things."

I glared at his back. "We just see what's there. Most of us, anyway."

"What you see is there, Kate," he said. I could feel the tension in the long muscles of his back, impossible to ignore pressed this close together.

"Please don't. I said I would do this and here I am, just like I promised. Just like you asked. If you're right, I'll still be safe."

"Not 'if I'm right.' You mean 'if I am' at all."

I had to force my hands to stay flat, not to clench my fists against Cor's belly. This close, there was no filter between us. This was beginning to look like a very, very long day. "What do you want me to say?"

"I want you to *see*. That's all." He took a deep breath. Whatever he was holding so tight to, I felt him let the tension go with his sigh and he returned to his explanation. "Well. That is how land is claimed. Many minds, much *jeira*, all work together against the shifting of the wilds. I can use that to find Issai. Claiming land makes a...a current, since claimed land is stable and wildlands shift."

"Friction, you mean? Like they rub against each other," I offered, glad for any neutral topic.

"Um..." That seemed to derail him again for a moment. "Yes. A skilled tracker can trace the friction a person makes, by claiming a piece of the world."

I started to ask how, but Tonchu froze beneath us and he fell silent. His hands found mine and tightened, pulling me closer. The trees loomed over us and the shadows seemed darker than they had only a moment ago.

"What's wrong?" I kept my voice to a whisper, afraid of what might hear us. Beneath me, I felt the rumble of the *morsai*'s growl.

"She hears something," Cor whispered back.

Tonchu sidled, scratching her claws in the fallen leaves every time she shifted her feet. The trees seemed to reach for us and the *morsai* flinched every time a twig brushed against her. He murmured to her in Thurei, so quiet, I could hardly hear him. Her ears flicked back to listen, then out, scanning the forest around us.

"What's going on?" I hissed at him.

"Gorvas. We just need to find the chaser."

'Gorvas' was a Kuyen game, like tag. We'd played it as kids up and down the rows of shrubs and saplings in the nursery or with the other Thurei kids in the meadow. Tall grass for ambushes. Lots of runners. Lots of catchers.

I'd never thought what the name meant or where it had come from, but I had a feeling there wouldn't just be a shuffling of roles if a catcher found us first.

The forest felt very full.

"This isn't a game. What's going on?"

"They're hunting us." He worked the words into a calming litany for the *morsai*. Maybe for me, too. "Stay calm. The fear you feel is sent out from the chaser toward the catchers. Once we find the chaser, it will fade."

Adrenaline kicked its way through my system. It felt pretty convincingly like my own fear. "Find it? We don't have to play. Let's just get out of here."

"This is the only way. The catchers will be ready and waiting to bring us all down together if we run. But between Tonchu and myself, a single chaser isn't much of a threat. Gorvas rely on their skill, the fear, to control their prey."

He might have said more, but a twig snapped off to our left and the *morsai* leaped sideways. I clutched at Cor and he grabbed my wrists. After a single, sickening movement, he had her back under control, though her ribs swelled like bellows against my legs. He let my arms go to lean forward and rub her neck. Her muscles stayed tight beneath her thick fur. Even Cor was tense against me, despite acting like nothing was wrong.

When Cor nudged her back into motion, I still hadn't managed to slow my heartbeat or get my lungs to work like they should have. Tonchu picked her way through the trees like she expected land-mines, ears on constant alert, nose high to catch the fitful breeze. I couldn't help scanning our surroundings, too, trying to look in every direction at once. Not that there was anything I could do if something jumped out at us. I wasn't a fighter. Trapped up here on Tonchu's back, stuck behind Cor, I couldn't even run. Helpless. I'd be as good as dead if something charged out of the undergrowth.

"Hold on." Cor locked his fingers around my wrists and that was all the warning I got before the *morsai* sprang into motion. She bucked and twisted beneath us, leaping and dodging through the trees. If Cor had any control over her, I couldn't tell. The wind stole the air I needed for breathing, let alone questions.

I buried my face against Cor's shoulder and squeezed my eyes shut, too terrified to watch. We were headed into an ambush, a trap, a massacre. There was no way we could make it out of this alive, stranded in the middle of the hungry wilds with no hope of rescue.

I felt the *morsai*'s snarl before I heard it, a rumbling thunder that built beneath her ribs. Cor yelled, wild and wordless. Panic wrenched my eyes open, just in time to see something dark and spindly in our path. I screamed, bracing for an attack.

It scrambled out of our way, flailing like a startled spider.

In a flash, we were past it and away, pelting through the trees.

CHAPTER TWELVE

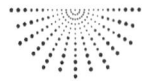

The terror broke.

Cor whooped and the wind whipped his triumph into streamers behind us. My heart still pounded like it might rattle loose and I held tightly to Cor, but it wasn't a death grip any longer. Even Tonchu's stride seemed easier, more even.

Nothing had killed us. We were fine. I tried to remember how to breathe normally.

The pace slowed sometime later. It felt like hours but couldn't have been more than a couple of minutes. The *morsai* dropped out of her canter into a trot, then settled into a walk. Cor loosened the hold he had on my arms and I found I had his shirt clenched in my fists, my knuckles digging into his ribs. I let go and sat up a bit. I probably had the stitching from his coat embossed on my face.

"Are you okay?" His voice came out rough, like the wind had scraped all the polish off it.

I had to clear my throat twice to get an answer out. "Yeah. Fine."

He said something to Tonchu and the *morsai* stopped. To me, he added, "Wait a moment."

He pulled my arms loose and swung off Tonchu's back, a complicated maneuver since I sat behind him. I grabbed for the edge of the saddle, worried for my balance up there alone.

"Let me help you down." Cor tilted his gaze up to mine. "Tonchu needs rest."

The *morsai* seemed taller suddenly.

There was a scratch on his cheek, blood bright against his pale skin. I reached down to wipe it away. My hand was shaking.

He held still until I took my hand away. "One of the branches."

One of them? I hadn't felt any branches, but then I'd been riding behind him.

Cor helped me down and my knees buckled as soon as my feet touched the earth.

"Kate!" His hands tightened on my waist as he caught my weight. "Are you hurt?"

"No, I'm fine." I forced my legs to work. The terror was gone, but it had kicked its way through me with steel-toed boots, leaving everything shaky and scattered in its wake. When I had some hint of self-control back, I pulled away. "That's all it was, that skinny, baboon-looking thing?"

"It's the ambush and their *jeira*-fueled fear that make them a threat. You don't need to worry with me here. And Tonchu." Cor started working at the laces on Tonchu's saddle.

"I thought Hunters didn't hunt people much anymore." I wrapped my arms around myself, trying to chafe some warmth back into my arms.

"Gorvas are lesser Hunters. They simply set an ambush and take whatever prey the Chaser's fear can push into the waiting Catchers. They would've been just as happy with a pair of meadow...ah, deer?" Cor lifted off the saddle and bags. Freed, the *morsai* lowered herself to the ground and rolled on her back. She twisted back and forth, her legs thrown up in the air like a dog's. "But remember, the Truce doesn't reach out into the wildlands."

"Why didn't their fear work on you?"

He looked up from digging in one of the packs. "It did."

"Yeah, right." I snorted and held up my hand, fingers spread, to show him how much it still shook.

Cor reached up and set his palm on mine. His long, slender fingers trembled against my short, stubby ones. "I just knew not to trust it."

"Of course." I pulled my hand away, feeling like an idiot. How much more of a metaphor did I need? "It was all in my head."

I didn't realize how relaxed he'd been until he wasn't, going as tight and edgy as he'd been under the Gorvas' fear. Carefully, he said, "I protected you. Count the *morsai* for some of it if you like. Would you want to face the Gorvas on your own?"

I'd admitted my fears about wandering around my neighborhood in the middle of the night when we'd "visited" Scholar's Hall. Part of me knew this was no different. I wasn't really riding through the woods on the back of a giant dog with my imaginary friend and having them with me didn't make me any safer.

But that wasn't the part of me that had spoken up.

"I meant the fear, Cor. The fear was all in my head. You said so yourself."

What if I could hold on to Cor and let the fear go? I shivered. *No. Been there, done that.*

Cor stared a long moment into the saddlebag in his hands. Finally, he pulled out a blanket and spread it on a reasonably level patch of ground. "Here. You should sleep. It's night on your side."

"On the ground?" Maybe I wasn't that tired.

"It's all I have."

"I'm sorry. It's fine." My cheeks flushed. This is what Cor had brought for himself to sleep on. I sat down on the blanket and drew up my knees, careful to keep my shoes off of it, and tried to think of something to say. "I thought Gorvas was a game."

"It's like your cops and Indians."

"You mean cops and robbers. Or cowboys and Indians." I couldn't stop my smile. Sometimes he could be so familiar.

He smiled back, just a little. "Those ones, yes. True battles become games for children. The danger isn't any less real, for all that we played Gorvas in the meadow."

I leaned forward to rest my chin on my knees. Sitting up straight was an overrated waste of energy.

"Sleep, Kate. I need to send word to the Pareshols. They should know a pack of Gorvas is so close and in such a strange place." He dug in the inside pocket of his coat and pulled out a square of paper.

"In the wildlands? I thought that's where Hunters usually live."

"Wilds, yes, but not here. This is too open. They prefer valleys, or canyons so they can control where the prey goes." He finished writing his note and folded it up.

"Hmm," was all I could manage. I, for one, was glad they'd picked a lousy spot for an ambush.

Cor held up the folded Summons, requesting a bit of silence so he could concentrate on sending it. I nodded and closed my eyes.

"Kate?"

I jerked awake. Cor still stood a couple of feet away. I rubbed my eyes.

"Sorry. I'm just tired."

"I know." He gestured at the blanket. "Lie down and stop being stubborn. Tonchu needs rest. We can't go any farther today."

I grumbled but stretched out and found it didn't matter that it was on the ground. I was too tired to care. I pillowed my head awkwardly on my arm. "What'll you do while I sleep?"

"Keep watch." I heard his coat rustle, then he sat down at the edge of the blanket. He held out his coat, folded into a pillow. "What else?"

I tucked it under my cheek. His coat smelled like leather and *morsai* and forest and Cor, just like I imagined it would.

CHAPTER THIRTEEN

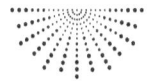

The alarm clock didn't go off to wake me up. I lurched out of bed, certain I'd be late to work, and scrambled for my phone to call in.

No, I wasn't late. I'd switched shifts with Rose. I'd completely forgotten. At least I could go back to bed. I crawled back under the covers, trying to ignore the hammering in my head.

When I got to work at two, Rose's boyfriend, Troy, lounged against the counter, making the place feel about as big as an Altoids tin. He was huge. Not just tall, but big, like a football player. Rose always teased that he should have gone for a sports scholarship, and not into engineering.

"Howdy, Katherine." He grinned at me as I came in and Rose flashed me a smile.

"Hey." I dropped my bag beneath the counter. "How's work going?"

"Fine," Rose said, but she looked concerned as she filled me in on the pending orders and she finished up with, "and how are you?"

"Okay." The extra sleep had helped catch me up, but the headache hung on as a dull pressure behind my eyes. Aspirin knocked the edge off but couldn't get rid of it.

"Well, any news? Did you decide about moving back?"

Moving? Oh, yeah. "No, no. I'm staying here. If I can, anyway."

"Good," she said, but her expression said the discussion wasn't over.

Troy must have recognized that look of hers, because he jumped into the conversation. "See, that's what I'm talking about. If there's no wave function collapse, then in another world, Katherine does decide to move back."

My head snapped around. "What?"

"It's DeWitt's many-worlds theory—"

Rose reached up to whack him on the shoulder. "He means physics. He was trying to explain it before you got here, but all I remember is the cat in the box."

"Hey, you told me you wanted to hear it." He ducked down to kiss her neck and she pushed him away, blushing.

"You're confusing me with alternate-Rose who wanted to be distracted from her show tonight."

He grabbed her waist and plopped her up on the counter. "I don't need quantum mechanics to do that. Newtonian physics will work just fine."

This was the point where I should have gone to work on the poster order, but there was no way I could leave an opening like that. "No, really, I want to know. What did you mean about other worlds?"

"See, Rosie? Some people like physics." Troy swiveled to face me, making sure he stayed in Rose's way so she couldn't hop down. After a half-hearted shove, she just leaned on his shoulder and listened in. "According to the many worlds theory, every alternative exists simultaneously. Every event makes reality branch off so that versions of each possibility continue on. Basically, an infinite number of universes, where everything that could happen has happened."

Rose kicked him—not too hard—and said, "You made it seem a lot more complicated when you explained it to me."

"I was trying to impress you." He grinned at her and I felt a flash of jealousy, that their affection was so easy and unselfconscious. He looked at me. "No offense."

"What? No, none taken." I straightened a stack of photo paper. "But that just means other versions of Earth, right? Not...like, other worlds."

Troy finally let Rose hop off the counter. He wrapped an arm around her waist. "Not just us. The whole universe. And if you figure there are infinite versions of a universe, even if only a small percentage of extra-solar planets are inhabited, that number would also be infinite."

With an infinite number of inhabited worlds, would there be room for Kuyen?

"Ooh, talk nerdy to me." Rose pinched his cheek and laughed. "I didn't know you were into science, Katherine."

I'd never really gotten the chance, but I could hardly say that. With my thoughts as tangled as they were, I tossed out on equally incautious comment. "Well, I have this friend..."

Great. How was I going to finish this sentence? 'From another planet'? I flailed for something vaguely normal. "You know, from a long time ago. I hadn't seen him in ages. He just kind of showed up out of the blue, and..."

I still couldn't figure out how to tie this into quantum physics.

It turned out I didn't have to. Rose was more than capable. "And maybe in another world, things went differently between you."

Not what I'd meant, but it struck me all the same. I'd spent years thinking Cor and Shom had ruined my life, but when Rose said that, it wasn't Bayshore that came to mind first. It was the way Cor had looked when he'd missed his sister's presentation.

"Maybe in another universe," Rose continued, "the two of you are together?"

"No, no." That was highest insult, according to Cor. Was that because of his *dacha* vow, or would that bedroom stunt of Turavi's have been an insult no matter what? I wasn't Thurei, after all.

"Is that why you're blushing?" Rose's gaze was sharp and now I had Troy's full attention, too.

"No! It's not like that. Actually, I think I messed up his life."

Troy frowned. It made his height a lot more imposing. "He said that? What a tool. I'll kick the—"

"Stop it," Rose said, smacking his arm. "He didn't actually say that, right?"

"No, of course not." I shook my head. "He would never say something like that. It's just...I think there's a lot of stuff that we made more complicated for each other. You know how it is."

"No," said Rose, at the same time her boyfriend said, "Yes."

She gave him a look. He shrugged. "That was before you."

"Wait," Rose said, turning back to me. "You said this was a long time ago. How old were you?"

"Twelve. Almost thirteen."

"That's so young," she said, like that excused me. "How badly could you have messed up his life at twelve? You were kids. Anyway," she continued, pushing Troy toward the door, "we've gotta get going. Thanks again for trading shifts with me."

The afternoon shift was busier than my usual morning one, but not busy enough to distract me. Once I'd said it out loud, I couldn't get the thought out of my head. *We just make things worse for each other.*

I couldn't brush it off as being unimportant. Kuyen was a product of my illness, I knew that. Or I should have known that. It was getting harder and harder to think of things that way.

If I really was schizophrenic like all the specialists said, I would be better off finishing this agreement and never seeing Cor or Kuyen again. If Kuyen was real...it would still be better to see out the terms of our agreement. Cor was wasting his own life because he thought I couldn't look after myself. If the Shevern Scholar could train me to defend myself, he would be free to do whatever he wanted. Maybe he could make peace with his *denet*. I could get back to having reasonable amounts of sleep and stop having to lie about what was going on. We could both make normal lives for ourselves.

Business slowed down as afternoon grew into evening. Cor had said it wasn't safe for me to be alone, but it hadn't meant much to me at the time. Safe, to me, meant not-so-crazy-it-showed. Spending all that time with Cor, though, had blurred the line I'd spent so long carving. If Cor was real, I would have to believe in his warnings, too.

The night seemed endless, unfurling beyond the walls of the print shop. I throttled the surge of paranoia and concentrated on the family vacation album I was supposed to be creating. I set one of the snapshots in place. Two children stood in the surf, the rolled cuffs of their jeans dark with seawater and dusted with sand. They had pink cheeks and noses after too much sun, their image preserved forever in the light.

No monsters jumped out of the shadows when I rolled down the security grille at the front of the shop. No ambushes waited on my bike ride home through the night fog. I felt like a fool for having taken the danger seriously.

As I tugged my keys out of my pocket to unlock the door, a streamer of ribbon snaked out with them, snagged on the teeth. Cor's ward.

If, in fact, that was what it was and not just a scrap of fabric I'd picked up somewhere. *If.*

I couldn't let it go. I knew this was all in my head and I knew Cor was real. Those statements couldn't both be true.

Without a doubt, I knew if I showed this 'ward' to anyone, they wouldn't see what I saw. But I couldn't make myself throw it away.

Even if I weren't crazy to start with, this would drive me to it eventually. I dropped my bag down on the card table among the scattered pieces of my jigsaw puzzle and tugged the bird token out from under my sweatshirt. Curling my fingers around it, I thought of Cor. The image that came to mind was Cor squinting in the bright morning sunlight at the Pareshols' front gate, asking for a favor.

Soon, I'd be able to put this behind me, for good this time. It'd be better for everyone, no matter what turned out to be true.

Until then, I could let Cor matter. I tucked the token back under my collar and picked up my bag. I had one more quick stop I needed to make before I went to see him.

Clammy air wrapped around me, an instant before the drizzle hit. My feet skidded and I yelped, almost dropping the bags I carried. Eyes flying open, I caught my balance. Lucky that I did.

I stood on a thin, broken trail across a boulder-strewn hillside, the surface slick in miserable wet weather halfway between heavy fog and light drizzle.

"Katen!" Cor, who'd been riding up ahead, urged the *morsai* over to me, sliding from her back before she'd even stopped. "Where have you been?"

"At work," I said, surprised for a moment. But I hadn't told him I'd be late. He'd probably worried. I lifted the bags a little. "And shopping. I should have let you know."

He hesitated then, looking at the plastic bags I carried in each hand. "What's all this?"

"Lunch. Or time slot of your choice." I suppressed a shiver as the damp crept into my clothes. The familiar headache stomped around between my temples, too, but that didn't give me much room to complain, comparatively.

The rain had darkened Cor's bright orange hair to copper, and he stood close enough that I could see the droplets caught in his lashes. Behind him, Tonchu shook like a dog, catching us in the spray.

"Here, let me carry those," Cor said, taking the bags. "There might be a dry spot a bit up the trail."

"Your hands are like ice. How long has it been raining?" I paid much better attention to my feet as I followed him. It seemed like the perfect place to sprain an ankle.

"Last night there was just the fog, thinking of being rain. The clouds have still not made up their minds."

"Well, hopefully, they'll be friendly," I said as water dripped down the back of my neck, trying to sneak past my collar. Even with his long leather coat, Cor must have been soaked.

Mist curled around the rocky outcroppings flanking the trail, turning the view into a series of blocky shadows.

"There." He pointed off to our left, where a trailer-sized pile of stone sprawled some yards off the path. Leaving the bags and the *morsai* with me, Cor made a quick survey of the jumble.

He returned with a relieved grin and led me to a spot where one tall boulder tilted against a couple of smaller ones, creating a lean-to about five feet tall, shielded from the rain. I took the food bags and ducked into the shelter. Cor unbuckled Tonchu's saddle and bags and brought them as well, tucking them out of the way against the stone.

He paused, looking down at the takeout containers I had lain out on the ground, then came around to sit next to me. "You must have known I was getting tired of travelcake."

"Well, I was pretty sure you didn't have dim sum." I handed him a plastic fork, trying not to shiver. Almost sacrilege, but this didn't seem like a good time to teach him to use chopsticks.

Ignoring the food for a moment, Cor stood, shrugged out of his coat, and draped it over my shoulders. It carried an echo of his warmth.

"You're cold, too," I protested. Dampness ringed the collar of his tunic. "Don't pretend you're not."

"But I can fix that." He dug into one of the saddlebags and came back a moment later with the blanket. He sat down again, tucking himself against my side, and flipped the blanket around us both. Warmth spread through me every place we touched. "Better?"

"Better," I agreed.

The dim sum had gotten cold by then and, in hindsight, it might not have been the most practical choice for a wilderness picnic on another world. At least I'd thought ahead and brought a trash bag so I could cram all the empty boxes into my backpack without spilling sauce all over the place.

Once we'd eaten every last piece of food—an impressive amount of which went into Cor, despite his slender frame—and laughed at the dubious cookie fortunes, I tucked the edge of the blanket tighter around myself.

"Are you still cold?" Cor asked, though he sat close enough to know I'd stopped shivering a long time ago.

Though the drizzle had let up, the humidity kept my clothes from drying. It didn't make a difference. The little space between Cor and me held all the warmth I needed. Going back out into the cold and wet to hunt for a rogue Shevern held less appeal, however much we needed to do it.

"No," I admitted. "I'm not cold anymore."

Cor seemed just as eager to get going. In a voice bordering on hopeful, he said, "It might start raining again."

I chuckled. "Yeah, I'm tempted to stay, too."

He turned to look at me, his face close to mine. His golden eyes always seemed the brightest in low light like this. "Would you stay, if you could? Not right here," he amended quickly. "But on Kuyen?"

That brought reality back like a bucket of cold water. I looked away, focused on the edge of the blanket I twisted between my fingers.

"I can't."

After a breath of silence, he said, "Not past sunset, and we've wasted enough light already."

The rain held off for the rest of the day and the cloud cover captured an award-worthy sunset. Between riding double and sharing the blanket, we stayed tolerably warm, but some of the chill stayed with us, impossible to banish.

CHAPTER FOURTEEN

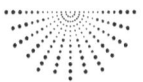

The apartment was dark and empty when I got back to it. I'd never realized how quiet it was, with only one person in it. Crossing home brought the headache back, a familiar hammer trying to demolish my forehead. I went to the medicine cabinet for aspirin and found my three prescription bottles sitting there on the shelf, insistent. With my crazy schedule the last few days, I hadn't been keeping up with my doses as well as I should have. One bottle was turned, almost accusingly, so that the bright warning stickers caught my eye. The pharmacy had provided a thick packet of information on side effects and the signs of accidental poisoning every time I'd refilled the prescriptions. I had to get blood tests periodically to check for liver and kidney problems.

Long-term use of these medications would take its toll. I thought it was worth it, if the medicine kept me sane and out of the psych ward, able to hold a job and take care of myself. Now, though, it didn't seem like such a great tradeoff. Especially since chemistry had shirked its side of the bargain. I rolled the bottle of quetiapine fumarate between my palms, listening to the pills rattle inside, like the staccato patter of rain on stone.

Kuyen seemed insubstantial and far away under the bright, antiseptic lights of the bathroom.

If the meds made worldwalking difficult, then I should wean myself off of them. At least for right now. On the other hand, if these were legitimate psychoses for them to keep away, they weren't doing much for me in that department at the moment. I'd put my bet on my agreement with Cor to get my life back to normal. Completing it meant more worldwalking.

I might as well go all in and stop making it harder for myself.

I left the bottle on the counter.

The next evening, I crossed as soon as the sun set, toting my backpack with granola bars, bottles of water, and a collapsible umbrella. Better than no help at all. At least it turned out to be a clear morning on Kuyen.

I had expected to find Cor on the trail already. Instead, he sat on a boulder overlooking the narrow path, absorbed with something in his hands. Tonchu waited at the base of his lookout, saddled and ready to go. They both focused their attention on me as Kuyen solidified around me.

"I didn't want to be late again." I pulled my coat tighter around me against the dawn chill. I tugged at the strap of my backpack. "I brought some snacks."

Cor slid down from his perch, dropping lightly beside me. "My thanks. I...worried, yesterday, when dawn passed and you didn't come."

I rested my hand on his shoulder for a moment in wordless apology, then I nodded toward Tonchu. "What's going on?"

"Ah. Well. Let me show you the problem."

From the top of the boulder, I could see the rocky ground slope down to a canyon. The far side was wooded. A slim bridge arched across the chasm, a solid span, like it had grown that way.

"How is that a problem? There's a bridge."

"And something else. Someone's down there."

"Is it Issai?"

Cor settled cross-legged on the boulder, tapping his fingers on his knee. "A Shevern, here? I doubt it. And the bridge isn't a good sign. "

"Why not? It's a bridge."

"But a stone bridge, not a made one. This is part of the land. A travel route might have a bridge like this, not claimed by anyone but used often by many. But this isn't a travel route."

"So...what? I don't understand."

"Someone wants it there. This is the only place to cross, unless we go days out of our way. I don't trust it."

"You mean there's a troll under the bridge, huh?" I nudged his shoulder with mine and laughed.

He didn't. "Maybe."

"Oh." That wasn't good. "So it's like the Gorvas?"

"We can hope it's that easy."

That was his idea of easy?

"Why don't we just skip it?" I asked. "Slip over to my side, then back on the other side of the canyon and just keep going from there?"

"There's a lot to be said for that and perhaps it's what we'll do, in the end. But we can't slip Tonchu across with us. Animals without *jeira* can't be taken from one world to another. Not alive, anyway." He glanced at the brindled mount waiting for us. Her tail swept the air in a slow wag. "She could get back to the Pareshols on her own, I'm sure, but we would be without her for the rest of the journey. I don't like to admit *Denet* Pareshol might be right in anything he says about me, but I do find myself wanting the extra protection of a *morsai* on this trip. If we need to, we can do as you say. What do you think?"

I nodded. "Let's try the bridge with Tonchu."

"Good. Now, if a Hunter is in the area and gets close enough to us, the wards won't be enough to hide how bright your *jeira* is." Cor's fingers rippled in a shrug. "Perhaps I can show you how to hide it."

I sat back and stared at him. "Why didn't we try that before? We could have skipped all of this."

"Hiding is not the same as being able to protect yourself." He flicked the suggestion away. "Even if this works, you will still need to learn to use *jeira* for the human skill to defend yourself. I don't even know what that skill is."

"And that's why we're chasing the Scholar," I finished. "I'm sorry. I just wish we had an easier way."

Cor motioned me to scoot around to face him. "Imagine the same energy you use for worldwalking. Only gather it together and make it sharper. Thinner."

I concentrated, trying to feel the same focus I had when I reached for Kuyen. I had to be doing something right because the pounding in my head clamored for my attention. 'Sharper' and 'thinner' didn't make any sense to me, though. I let the focus go. "How am I supposed to make it sharper?"

"It... You must hone your *jeira* and then you..." He mimed sliding a knife into a sheath. "You put it away."

"Okay, let me try again." I closed my eyes and tried to picture what he was talking about. I couldn't think of a way to make my hand-grasping effort at worldwalking into something sharp or honed or thin or keen or... Pain stabbed at my temples and I let the effort go in frustration. "No luck."

His brows creased in concern. "Does it hurt you?"

At least as bad as the crossing between worlds. I rubbed the bridge of my nose. "Yeah, a bit. Give me a minute."

"No, stop. We can try something else." He rummaged in his pocket and pulled out another ward ribbon. "Here, take this."

"I still have the other one you gave me," I said, but I took it anyway. "And I thought you said it wouldn't be enough."

"Now you have two. I just made that one, so it'll be stronger. The wards aren't the whole plan." He stared back at the narrow span linking the two cliffs, then turned back to me with a slight smile. "You can laugh at me if it turns out to be nothing."

The 'whole plan' also involved me riding in front on the *morsai*. Cor wore my backpack.

"How am I supposed to steer?" I asked. Tonchu didn't have reins or a bridle or anything.

"You sit. I steer. Now move your foot so I can use the stirrup."

Cor was the better rider, I'd never doubted that, but I didn't know how bad I'd been until we'd headed down the trail together. I'd held on to Cor like a shipwreck survivor. Even without the stirrups, Cor rode lightly, no matter how rough the trail got. If not for his hands resting on my hips and the occasional light brush of his legs against mine, I wouldn't have even known he was there.

As we reached the halfway point, Cor slowed Tonchu. The trail had traveled through a low spot for the last few minutes, but a few more yards would bring us to a crest, where we should be able to see the bridge.

"We might have to ride hard. I should have better hold of you." A simple enough statement, but he said it like a question.

"Whatever you need to do," I said.

He slid closer, wrapping his arms around me, fitting his legs against mine. I could feel his heartbeat against my back. Close to my ear, he murmured, "Just to make sure."

"I get it," I said, glad he couldn't see my face. This was a stupid time to be blushing.

He nudged Tonchu back into a walk and we crested the rise above the bridge. I couldn't see anything, despite Cor's suspicion. The bridge and the trail did seem to be part of the land more than something planned and built. The path—or what I'd been thinking of as a path—was more like a linked series of spaces between boulders and slabs of rock, not the kind of trail worn into place by dozens or hundreds of feet. Other would-be trails snaked along the slope, maze-like and purposeless.

Fifty yards or so from the cliff's edge, Tonchu stopped again.

"A Wogra," Cor whispered, ducking his head so close to mine that his breath fanned my cheek. "Do you see it?"

A shadow moved among the broken stones in the distance,

resolving into a hulking, blocky shape at least as large as a grizzly bear. It lumbered over the broken ground, the power in its movements obvious even from this far away.

"Now what do we do?" I whispered, glad of his solid presence at my back.

"Wogras aren't very smart and their skill lies in great strength. They pull it from the *jeira* of their prey. We'll be safe if we can stay out of its reach." I didn't have to see him to know his brows would be drawn in thought. I could hear it in his voice. "They have poor vision and it's best for things in motion. A Seeming might be enough, if we only had something to link it to, but I don't—Wait." He drew back an arm, rustled in his coat, and passed up a square of paper and a nub of pencil. "Here, Kate. Draw us, on Tonchu."

"What?" I lowered my voice. "I haven't drawn in years."

Not since my parents had shown my sketches of Kuyen to the psychiatrist.

"Between the two of us, you're still better. Anyway, it's the intent that matters, your focus, not how it looks." He peered over my shoulder, close enough that his hair tickled my ear. He murmured, "Just concentrate on this moment, not how it looks, but how we feel, here, together."

Over by the bridge, the Wogra lifted its head, scanning, scenting the breeze.

Cor hissed, a quiet sound of annoyance. "I lost the binding a moment. Draw quickly, please?"

"No pressure," I muttered under my breath, but I got to work. 'Focus on the moment' was the easy part.

My finished drawing wouldn't win any awards, but it had the right trio: two riders curled together, leaning low over the neck of what looked like an oversized mutt from the pound.

"Perfect. Now we just need... Remember those paper flyers we made, for racing?"

"Um, paper airplanes?" My confidence in his plan cooled, but he was already urging Tonchu into a walk again.

"Yes. You always won. When we get closer, throw it off to the left. The Wogra will follow and—"

"Cor, this is insane," I hissed. The Wogra hadn't seen us yet, but it must have sensed something was near. It turned satellite-dish ears back and forth, lifting its blunt muzzle to scent the air like Tonchu did so often. It kept looking even bigger than perspective could justify the closer we got.

"It's not insane. It will work." Cor tightened his arms around me, resting his chin on my shoulder in a brief hug. "I promise."

"You promise a lot of things," I said under my breath as I folded the drawing.

"And I never lie. Ready?" He brought Tonchu to a halt in the shadow of a shard of stone. The Wogra was maybe thirty feet away, close enough for me to see its shovel-broad paws, its squinty, wide-set eyes scanning the rocky landscape. Its wide, heavy jaw looked powerful enough to crack bone like candy. It hadn't seen us, but it seemed impossible that it hadn't heard us yet, no matter how quietly we had whispered.

I nodded so I didn't have to make any noise.

"Good." Cor breathed the words. "When I drop the ward, throw the drawing that way. Then hang on."

I didn't have time to protest. The Hunter's head snapped around in our direction. It leaped down from its perch among the rocks and charged toward us, unstoppable as an avalanche.

"Throw it!"

The ridiculous little plane sailed through the air and then an image of us appeared ahead of the Wogra. Our doubles, two riders holding tightly to the back of a *morsai* pounding away from the trail through a gap in the boulders, following the flight of the little plane. The Wogra snarled and dug in its massive paws for traction, crashing its way through the rocks after the Seeming.

Tonchu burst into motion, rocking me back against Cor. He held me safe as the *morsai* sprinted toward the bridge. Behind us, the Wogra roared. Either the Seeming or the binding had failed and the thunder of the charging Hunter veered back toward us. On the winding, rocky path, the *morsai* couldn't stretch to her full speed. Cor straightened a little, twisting around to glance back.

"Hold on!" he shouted into my ear.

It registered all at once: the path jagged around a chest-high boulder right at the foot of the bridge, far too tight for Tonchu to make the turn; a bellow from the Wogra, too close behind us; and the realization that I had nothing to hold on to, riding up front in the saddle.

Tonchu leaped, vaulting into the air over the stone, taking the straightest path to the bridge. The Wogra slammed into it a moment later, scrambling and snarling. For a weightless moment in the air, it felt like it would work. Then Tonchu landed on the bridge.

The impact jolted me out of the saddle. I lurched sideways, my feet shaken free of the stirrups. Tonchu's claws scrabbled on the slender, rail-less bridge, her balance ruined by my weight sliding over her side, even as her momentum pushed her forward. She wouldn't have space on the narrow bridge to adjust her footing and she was running too fast to stop.

Behind me, Cor's weight slid in the opposite direction. One arm locked around my waist, but he reached past me with the other to grab the edge of the saddle.

Tonchu scrambled, her feet slipping on the smooth stone as we teetered on her back, but each long stride led her farther from the edge of the bridge and closer to the other side of the canyon.

With a final bound, Tonchu cleared the bridge and she stumbled on the rocky ground. My knee slipped farther over the front of the saddle, but Cor had me, braced in the stirrup, leaning half over the *morsai*'s side like a Wild West desperado. I caught at the edge of the saddle, pulling, and Cor hauled the both of us up and onto her back.

Tonchu ran, a flat-out sprint over the open ground that left the Wogra's fury farther and farther behind.

Once we reached the deep shelter of the forest, the *morsai* slowed, dropping out of her sprint into a lope, then a walk. The bridge lay far behind us.

Cor still had his arms around me, holding me steady. I squeezed his hands, the best gesture of thanks that I could offer from the back of a *morsai*.

"Next time let's take the long way around," I said, still a little breathless.

"That came a little closer than I liked, yes," Cor agreed, pressing his face against my hair. "I would never have let you fall, Katen. I would have slipped us away."

I'd never even thought of it. But Cor had, and I didn't doubt he would have, if he hadn't been able to keep us on Tonchu's back. "I know."

"Good," he breathed, almost too quiet to hear. He straightened, loosening his hold on me. "We need to keep going. I can walk, so Tonchu can have some rest. You should ride, so you don't get too tired. It's night, on your side." He shifted his weight, preparing to slide off of her back.

"Cor, wait," I said. Tonchu's ribs still pumped like bellows. She really should have rest. Still, I found myself asking, "Can you stay? For a little while?"

"We can go slowly while she catches her breath," he agreed. "But then we'll need to pick up the pace. The Wogra couldn't have crafted that bridge. No single person could. It may have found this place and claimed it for itself. Even something as stupid as a Wogra could hold onto it there for a season or so, but someone had to make it."

His suspicion needled at me, sneaking up my spine to settle in the tight muscles at the back of my neck. "You think they're still around here somewhere?"

"Maybe I'm imagining an ambush in every shadow." He sighed and I wished I could see his face. "Perhaps we've just been unlucky, but I would feel better the farther we are from this place."

"We'll do whatever you want," I said. "After all, you just saved me from a monster with a paper airplane."

He gave me a quick hug. "It would never have worked without your drawing. But I do hope I never have to do that again."

CHAPTER FIFTEEN

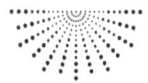

We traded between walking and riding, but the day seemed to last forever. 'Saddle-sore' didn't begin to cover it. I limped through my morning at work and when I got home, I fell into bed, hoping for a few hours of deep sleep before going back to Kuyen.

Noise dragged me back to consciousness. The alarm. I smacked it. No, not the alarm. My cell phone.

No one called my cell phone.

"Hello?" I mumbled, still half-asleep.

"Katie?"

Great. "Yeah, Mom. What's up?"

"Were you sleeping? You sound like you just woke up."

"I was taking a nap." I pushed myself up to sit against the headboard, trying to clear my head of cobwebs.

"In the middle of the day, honey? It's almost five. Won't that make it harder to fall asleep tonight?" The concern in her voice made me feel like a child again. "You know how you get if you can't sleep at night."

Crazy, she meant. I held the phone away so she wouldn't hear me sigh. "It's fine, Mom. What's up? Why did you call?"

"I can't call my baby just to talk?"

"Of course you can." *You just don't.* "But I thought maybe you had something on your mind."

"Well, your father and I were just talking last night, and we thought it would be nice if you came home for a visit."

While I tried to come up with an answer to this, she added, "I tried to call you last night, but your phone just rang and rang." She didn't have to make it a question. Her tone did all the work for her.

I hated lying, but I couldn't tell her the truth. "I took my meds early. You know how it knocks me out. I didn't hear it ring." I hadn't bothered to check for missed calls, either, since I never had any.

The silence stretched long enough I thought I should have come up with something else.

"Is something wrong, honey? Going to bed early yesterday and napping today...that's not like you. Are you getting enough iron?"

"I've just been..." Inspiration finally made an entrance. "Sick."

Mom's voice went dead serious. "Have you talked to Dr. Vargas?"

"No, Mom!" For once, I hadn't even thought of it like that. "It's just a cold. Regular sick."

"You don't sound like you've got a cold."

"It's not a head cold." I hated to lie, in part because I sucked at it. "It's like a stomach thing. The flu. You know, one of those twenty-four hour stomach flu things."

My mom sighed into the phone. "This is why I wanted you to stay with us, Katie. Who do you have to take care of you in San Jose? No one. You should come home."

"Calm down. It's fine." I tried to keep my voice level and ignore the sudden twist in my gut. I was not giving up my life here to go back and be someone's invalid, not even my mother's. "I have a friend helping me out."

"You've been making friends? I'm so proud of you."

Like I was six years old. I was lucky she and Cor couldn't compare notes on how incompetent they thought I was.

Then I remembered Cor hinging his plan for the Wogra on contributions from me. He'd trusted me to help save us.

"What do you think, Katie?"

"What?" I dragged my wandering attention back to the present.

"About coming to visit. We miss you."

This would be the worst possible time. My parents would never gamble on some agreement I'd made with a citizen of Insania. I'd be back in Bayshore before I could blink. "But this is Dad's busiest season. And I'd have to talk with my boss at work."

"Okay." Only moms could put that much disappointment into one word. "Well, you talk to him and let me know, all right? Then I can book your plane ticket."

When she finally hung up, I slumped back down to my pillow and pulled the covers over my head. "Things can't get any worse."

I was wrong.

CHAPTER SIXTEEN

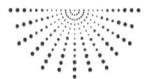

As soon as the sun set, I crossed into sparse forest overgrown with scrub and brambles. I squinted through tatters of a cold dawn mist. Cor must have been around here somewhere.

Then I heard a guttural shout, abruptly silenced. A form crashed toward me through the brush—Cor, fighting astride Tonchu. Around them swarmed attackers, jabbing at him with pale-bladed spears.

The *morsai* twisted and lunged. Something gleamed in Cor's right hand, nearly invisible, just a long, thin shimmer in the air. He swung with it, knocking weapons and opponents aside. From one blink to the next, the horde resolved itself to a half a dozen or so lizard-like creatures, dressed in rags. They looked small compared to the *morsai*, too short for the tops of their heads to reach her saddle.

A high-pitched cry erupted from the brush behind me and weight hurtled into my side. The lizardman and I fell in a heap. He fumbled with a spear in one clawed hand, too close for an easy jab, and latched on to my wrist with the other hand. My backpack caught on a branch and I wrenched away, kicking at the lizardman in desperation. My heel connected solidly with his belly and he went tumbling. He snapped to his feet and scrambled after his dropped spear.

I lurched back away from him, screaming, "Cor!"

When Cor caught sight of me, his eyes widened and he urged Tonchu toward me.

The lizardman found his weapon and more were coming. The creature gathered himself to leap at me. My muscles felt leaden, caught in some nightmare paralysis. I threw myself to the side, but I wouldn't get far enough. He plummeted at me, point first.

Tonchu snatched the attacker out of the air. She snarled deep in her throat, shaking her head from side to side. The lizardman whipped about like a stolen sock in a terrier's jaws. The spear flew out of his grasp and Tonchu flung the body after it. The creature twisted as he fell, as lifeless as a rag doll.

Cor slid from Tonchu's back and turned to meet the oncoming rush of the remaining creatures. He tossed off an order in Thurei to the *morsai* and snapped in English, "Stay behind me."

He had a heartbeat to find his footing, feet planted wide, shoulders steady, and then they were upon us. I caught a glimpse of the blade he held, slightly curved like a samurai sword, visible only by the blood smeared across it, but I lost sight of it as he moved.

He blocked the first opponent's charge, knocking the weapon out of its four-fingered, green hands. Another flick of his wrist and blood blossomed from the lizardman's throat.

The remaining three attackers clearly saw me as an easier target, but they couldn't get past Cor and Tonchu. The *morsai* leaped as neatly as a show jumper over a spear thrust, spun about as she landed, and crunched her teeth down into the back of her foe's neck. It didn't have time to scream.

I'd lost sight of Cor in the meantime, but the sounds of battle died. Seeing no further enemy on the field, Tonchu threw back her head and howled, a sound half-bay, half-roar. The cry made my teeth ache and raised goosebumps on my skin.

Cor turned to me. He looked like he'd lost a paintball fight, but all in red.

Blood.

A lot of blood. Cor's?

My stomach twisted. I spun away from him and vomited my

dinner in the bushes. It wasn't until I'd emptied my stomach that I noticed the lizardman corpse beyond the brush. The curiously straightforward part of my mind noted that, judging by the rips in the scaly skin and the disjointed tumble of its limbs, this one must have been one of Tonchu's.

My stomach heaved again.

I buried my face in my hands, curling into the forest duff, and wished myself fervently home. But slipping back took concentration, and the only image in my mind was the lizardman, its green skin waxy in death, stretched over a triangular, lipless face, wide eyes staring blindly into the forest canopy.

Cor's voice filtered its way up to my attention. I had no clue how long I'd huddled there or what else he might have said. His voice held the same placating tone the nurses used when they calmed a patient in the ward. "Kate. Katen, are you hurt? Katherine, listen. Kate."

As if he needed to use all my names to get my attention.

I opened my eyes to find him crouched beside me, bloody and wide-eyed. I pulled him closer, nearly toppling both of us. I croaked, "You're okay, you're okay."

He wrapped his arms around me and took a shaky breath. "I'm okay. Are you? Were you hurt?"

"No, I'm fine. Sorry I was sick," I added, still fighting the twisting of my stomach. What a stupid thing to say, but my brain seemed to have stalled. "I've never...seen anything die."

Cor hugged me closer. "I'm sorry, Katen. I didn't mean for it to be like this."

I looked back up at him, surprised to hear an apology. "Don't be sorry. You saved us."Something eased in his expression and he pulled me tighter for a moment. Then his eyes widened and he pulled back from me and looked down at himself. He hissed a Thurei curse and added in English, "I'm getting you filthy."

Cor stood and shucked out of his House coat and the blood-stained tunic beneath it, wiping his hands clean on the soiled fabric. Cleaner, anyway.

"I can wash my clothes," I said, but that was the least of my worries. Blood had soaked straight through Cor's shirt, shockingly vivid against his pale skin beneath his collarbone. *No, wait.* "You're bleeding. You need a doctor."

He glanced down and probed the gash gingerly. "It can wait. I have bandages in the packs."

Cor held out his hand to help me up. Blood had dried in the creases in his palms. I closed my eyes for a moment to settle my stomach and then let him help me up.

"They attacked as I was getting ready. I need to finish packing and saddle Tonchu." He tilted his head in a direction off to the left. The gesture seemed awkward until I noticed him surreptitiously rubbing his palms on his trousers.

My legs felt as hollow and unsettled as my stomach, but I stayed close to his side as he headed back toward camp. Cor carried his coat bundled under one arm, his tunic bunched together and pressed high on his chest. To stop the bleeding? As we walked, I reached for his free hand, gore be damned. He glanced at me, surprised, then curled his fingers around mine.

Tonchu fell in behind us. Her nostrils flared wide at every shift in the breeze and her pricked ears twitched at sounds I couldn't even hear. The skin between my shoulder blades drew tight at the thought that we might not be alone here. I tried to push it out of my mind.

The important detail was that *I* wasn't here alone. I had Coran and Tonchu with me.

He had told me he'd been keeping me safe. I'd thought of it in terms of the wards he'd left outside my apartment, or what he'd said about sitting on my roof, like the ward security guard sitting at his post and making his rounds. His quick thinking and hard riding that had gotten us past the Gorvas and the Wogra were different, like a clever hero in a fairytale.

Cor wasn't a watchman. He was a warrior. Faint scars crisscrossed his skin, mapping worse battles than the one with the lizardmen. If I had a Thurei anatomy book, I could probably tag every bone and muscle in his torso, his strength sleek but obvious under his skin in the corded muscles of his arms, the controlled way he carried himself, even injured in the aftermath of a fight. He was so slender, it was easy to forget how strong he was.

What little his camp contained lay scattered across the small clearing. He retrieved Tonchu's saddle from a stand of bushes. One of the saddlebags had been ripped open, spilling dried fruit and broken flatbreads along with a few scraps of cloth or clothing, a small knife, a metal jug. The bandages, in the second pack, were still usable. He hefted the jug.

"Is that water?" I asked. Why hadn't I thought of a first aid kit? Did I have antibiotic ointment somewhere in my bathroom? I shrugged off my backpack, glad I at least had sterile, bottled water. "Here, let me do it."

Cor handed over the cloth and I poured some water on it. His breath hitched when I started dabbing at the wound, so I worked as gently as I could. The injury just below his collarbone, rough around the edges from the serrations on the spearpoint. I wasn't sure how deep it went. Too deep, I could tell that much. At least the bleeding seemed to have stopped.

"You really should go to a healer. This looks bad."

"I will, after we find Issai. If we leave now, there is no guarantee of returning to the same place. We might have to start over entirely." He glanced down at my hands as he spoke. His brows drew down and he caught my wrist. "You got hurt."

I hadn't even noticed. A cut ran across the tendons of my left wrist. Any deeper and it could have done a lot of damage, but this was shallow enough I hadn't noticed it until now. I wiped it clean with a corner of the damp cloth. It stung, but it was the least of my worries. "It's nothing."

He bit at his lip, clearly weighing options. I made an educated guess and said, "If you won't take a break from this to see a healer for your stab wound, don't make a big deal over a scratch."

"Havro will tend this long before it becomes a danger, I assure you. Make sure your wrist is cared for. Please."

"Yes, Nurse Cor. Now, where're the bandages for the hole in your chest?" I bound the wound like he instructed, winding the cloth over his shoulder and across his torso. When I finished tying the ends, he covered my hands lightly with his own, holding them against his chest. It made a little pocket of warmth and safety, though the look on his face had settled into serious lines.

"Thank you, Katen."

I felt my cheeks flush, embarrassed to be thanked for having done so little. Glancing back the way we'd come, I changed the subject. "What were those things?"

"Visenis." Cor shook out his tunic, looking it over. It wasn't as gory as I'd first thought, but dried blood made darker patches on the gray fabric. Cor pulled it over his head anyway, muffling his voice for a moment. "They're lesser Hunters, like the Wogra."

"That Wogra was huge, and you tricked it with your skill. Those things were so small." My voice broke, so I stopped talking. The Wogra had been frightening enough, but it hadn't done us any harm. The Visenis had come inches from killing Cor.

"Seeming is a bit of skillwork I learned. The *zaret*—the blade—is the Thurei skill. My skill." He looked up from wiping off his leather coat to meet my gaze. "I put my life into learning it so that I could protect my House, myself, and you."

"I could tell," I said softly. Growing up, Coran had turned every game into sword fighting if he possibly could. He'd been a swash-buckler, a Musketeer, a man in black eager to face giant rats and impossible cliffs. A hero. But those had been games. Though Cor's bandage was hidden, I could see the slice the spear had left in his shirt. "Couldn't you have slipped away?"

"They would have killed Tonchu and used her bones for spear-blades." He glanced back at her, still standing guard at the edge of the clearing, on full alert and ready to protect us. "I thought I could finish them before you arrived. What if I had slipped away just as you came with your token and found yourself alone?" He answered his question before I could. "That nearly happened, anyway."

"But then you and your *zaret* saved the day," I said. "And here we are."

"Here we are," he agreed, his lips curving into the shadow of a smile.

I gave him my best version of a smile back, under the circumstances. "Now, can we get out of here?"

As eager to leave as I was, Cor saddled Tonchu while I gathered the last of his things.

"I think Issai is close," he said, lacing the saddlebag closed. "Perhaps the Visenis were drawn to the edge of the land she claimed."

"How close, do you think?" Once I could defend myself, Cor wouldn't have to do this anymore. No, I wouldn't have to *think* about this anymore. The thought turned my stomach and I took a deep breath to steady myself.

"Tomorrow, perhaps?" He held Tonchu's stirrup for me to mount. "The wilds are hard to predict, but it'll be soon."

"Good," I said, swinging onto the *morsai*'s back. It couldn't happen soon enough for either of us.

CHAPTER SEVENTEEN

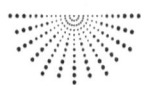

The next day at work, Rose gave me a full rundown of her show opening while I set up some posters for a graduation party.

"What's that?" she asked, in the middle of detailing her first sale. She came over to take my hand and turned my wrist bandage-side up, all her humor gone.

"Nothing. Just a scratch. I put ointment it when I got home last night. It was hardly worth it, really."

"Can I see? My mom's a nurse."

I pulled off the bandage. "It's no big deal."

She looked at my wrist for way too long. "Katherine, what happened?"

I could hardly tell her the truth, so I made something up. "The neighbors have a nasty cat. He got out. I tried to pick him up and get him back home."

"That is not a cat scratch."

I wished I could ask her what she saw, but I couldn't. To me, it was just a shallow cut, deep enough to scab over, but definitely not bad enough for stitches. Probably too deep for a cat, but I couldn't think of anything that would make a better excuse. 'Lizardman claw' wasn't going to work.

Oh. The concern on Rose's face finally clicked.

I hadn't even considered it, and I should have. I'd known enough cutters at Bayshore. I made a face. "It's not what you think."

"Oh?" She made a face right back. She must have learned hers from her nurse mother. "What do I think it is?"

"I didn't do this to myself," I said. *But.* The word hung there in my mind as I slapped the bandage back into place.

"Is this about that guy?"

"Cor? No."

When she pressed her lips together, I realized I should have gone with, 'What do you mean?'

"Okay, look. I know you've been stressed out lately and you're not sleeping and stuff, but if you need to talk, you can talk to me."

"Thank you," I said, and I meant it. She was being nice, even if she was on the wrong track, and I would love to talk to her. To anyone. I just couldn't.

"Things were pretty messed up at home when I was growing up. You never talk much about your life, but I just want you to know I'd understand. I know what it's like."

Not what this is like. Especially because I was having such a hard time deciding what it was like on my own. I hadn't done this to myself, I knew that much.

But. But a homicidal lizardman did it?

If I'd really been attacked, wouldn't it have been worse? Self-injury was common enough in schizophrenics, though I'd never done it. I could hear Dr. Vargas' voice in my mind. *These characters you see, do they tell you to hurt yourself, Katie?*

No. No, that wasn't it at all. But I knew what Rose thought. I knew what my parents and the psychologists would think, if they knew. What anyone sane would think.

I was so close to finishing this. All I had to do was keep it together until we found Issai and she taught me what Cor thought I needed to know. Then I wouldn't have to worry about it anymore.

≈

"Here, put some of this on that cut." I tossed Cor the tube of antibiotic ointment.

He looked up from adjusting the *morsai*'s saddle in time to catch it out of the air. "I told you, the Temarel healer will see to it when we finish here. I'll be fine."

"Do it for my peace of mind, then."

He unlaced the neck of his tunic. The wound below his collarbone looked worse than I remembered, a puffy, angry red. Cor spread on the ointment and grimaced. When he saw me watching, he turned away.

"Cor, that looks awful." How long would it take something like that to get infected? For a moment, I considered asking Rose.

He flicked my concern away and handed the tube back. "I believe Issai is just ahead. We can speak with her first, then decide what to do."

After several more hours of riding, Cor stopped us at the edge of the forest. The trees ended abruptly, like the landscape had been sliced with a knife and scraped away, leaving an empty stretch of packed earth behind. The sun seared, brighter and hotter than I'd expected this far into fall. A single hut sat in the center of the broad, flat sweep of dirt, like a garden shed plopped into the center of a football field, only more post-apocalyptic.

"Is this what we were looking for?" I asked.

"Well, someone's here and I doubt it's a Hunter." He motioned for Tonchu to wait among the trees and started toward the hut.

This place felt awful. The earth had been baked hard and bricklike in the sun, which was jarring after the soft loam of the forest. Here and there, I could see bits of wood imbedded in the hard soil. Roots, I realized, sheared right off at the surface. Rocks, too, sliced cleanly away, level with the ground. It felt like a graveyard or a battlefield, eerie with the memory of destruction.

Beside me, Cor worked the toe of his boot under the edge of a rock, flush with the surface. He pried it out. About the size of a golf ball, it had one normal side, lumpy and rough. The other was perfectly flat, like a geology specimen on display. He turned it over and over, then shoved it into the pocket of his coat. "Come on. If Issai is here, we can get our answers."

Against the featureless stretch of scoured earth, the hut looked tiny and drab. Compared to the massive stone structure of Scholars' Hall, this place looked like a toy.

But we still found a Shevern waiting at the door. She had the same short, broad build and bald head as the Scholars I'd met at the Hall, but her copper skin had a wrinkled, weathered look to it that had been absent in her former colleagues in their hilltop sanctuary.

"Scholar Issai." Cor swept a low bow.

Even without the elegant robes and impressive surroundings of the Scholars, she still had the same haughtiness as her colleagues. She managed to look down her nose at him, despite being nearly two feet shorter. "I'm not a Scholar anymore. I'm sure they told you that before they sent you here. I don't want anything to do with another human."

"Another?" Cor echoed. "You know other human worldwalkers?"

"Not worldwalkers." The Shevern peered at me like an experimental subject. "Humans are unsuited to worldwalking. It damages their minds."

He frowned. "There is nothing wrong with Kjelgaard's mind. She is quite capable of slipping herself here."

"She can control her travels?"

"Of course I can," I said. *I can speak for myself, too, shorty.*

Cor gave me a look, then dialed up his own politeness. "You've met other humans who have trouble with it? Here on Kuyen, or on Earth?"

"Here." She looked past us over the empty landscape. "He stumbled into Kuyen on his own, but he had no control over where he slipped or when. He couldn't control worldwalking any more than he could control his skill. *Jeira* in a human is unstable and dangerous." Her gaze sharpened, focusing back on us. "I argued that we find a way to deal with the problem preemptively, but I was overruled."

Cor ignored this ominous statement. "We're here for your help. Kjelgaard needs to learn her skill and—"

"Help you? Look at this!" She flung a hand out and I flinched away, but she was only motioning to the flat, featureless ground around us. "It's a curse. Why would I help a human to get better at this?"

"This, Scholar?" Cor trailed off and silence settled over us, smothering with the implications in her words. The empty earth spread in every direction, scoured down to the subsoil as if everything above had simply...vaporized. Disappeared.

A flick of Cor's hand broke the moment. "No. Tell me what happened here. You are sworn to tell the truth."

She narrowed her eyes. "I know my responsibility to the truth. I left the Scholars because they chose to taint memory and hide what they know."

"Please." I interrupted, needing an answer. "Tell us what happened."

I might have been better off not reminding her of my existence. She made no attempt to disguise her dislike.

But she told us. "A Sennag looked through the human male's memories and pieced it together for us. He was young. His people had been training him for something—a spiritual vocation, perhaps. You know how unclear Sennag readings can be. Then there was an attack and his people were slaughtered before his eyes. The house burned. He escaped and hid." She slipped into the pedantic style I remembered from the Scholars, losing some of her venom. "We credit the awakening of his skill to a combination of his training, physical trauma, and grief. He hid himself so desperately that he slipped across the gap and found Kuyen. When he got here, he rejected what he found. He disbelieved so strongly that the forest ceased to be."

"It can't be that easy," I said. I had the disbelieving part down. Or at least I had, once.

Issai bared her teeth, a grimace or a threat, I couldn't tell. "Scholar Bemos approached him first, here on this plain. Bemos was unmade. The human was a murderer and a destroyer, whether he intended it

136

or not. His mind became unhinged, crazed. Kuyen is no place for your kind."

"Not Kjegaard," Cor said. This news had shaken something in him, but he was too stubborn to give up. "There is nothing in her like that. She needs your help. We seek only to protect her from Hunters. I grieve for Scholar Bemos and the young human, but help me make sure no one else dies."

"Easy, you called it." Her gaze held me like a fly in amber. She might not have heard Cor's speech at all. "Why? Truth now. Do not pollute your words with lies."

I wished I could turn this conversation back to Cor. "If all it takes is disbelief, I'd have done it already." It sounded bad, sitting out there as a simple statement, so I shoved more words after it. "Please, just teach me. Then I can go back home and I swear I'll never set foot on Kuyen again."

That worked, but not like I'd hoped. She swung back to Cor. "You would trust her with a power like this?"

"I would not hesitate to place my life in her hands," Cor said, but Issai tilted her head like he had left something out. He tried another approach. "The Scholars said you would help us."

She held up her hands, blocking his words. "You shame yourself with these lies, Thurei."

"He's not lying," I snapped. I tried to remember exactly how they'd put it. "They said you would give us answers, if I came here."

"They knew I would never help you. The Scholars' Council wanted to wipe this out of Kuyen's memory." Her gaze cut back to me. "Rare as *jeira* is among your kind, they feared to see humans made into weapons. Earth is an empty world, so they thought ignorance and dishonorable lies would be enough of a defense. I stayed here, to keep the truth from disappearing. They were wrong, for here you are in the hand of a Thurei, ready to be wielded as surely as his *zaret* and far more dangerous."

Dismay flashed across Cor's face. "Kjelgaard will be no one's weapon. I only want her safety. She's a target for Hunters, even on her own world. Her skill would be used in defense of her life."

"Go back to your own land, human." Her tone was flat and utterly final. "You don't belong here. Kuyen will ruin you as surely as you would ruin it."

"You would let her die, then, after all your effort to keep human lore alive?" Though Cor managed to keep his voice level, he held his hands clenched into fists at his sides.

"Yes," she hissed. "I chose exile for the sake of truth, not for the sake of her kind. I pick my world over the life of a stranger."

Cor opened his mouth to make some fresh objection, but the Shevern was done with us.

"I have nothing for you. Go home." She pushed the door of the hut closed, but Cor caught it with his palm.

"Wait—"

But you couldn't hold a worldwalker, if she wanted to go. Issai faded, leaving us alone.

∼

Cor slammed the door of the hut and swore.

"Now what?" I asked.

He took a deep breath, then let it out. "I don't know. I wish the Shevern had not been such a fool. You wouldn't do what she claimed."

I didn't reply. Issai had told the truth. I didn't belong here. I'd fallen into the trap of believing again and Kuyen would destroy the normal life I wanted so badly if I stayed. Everything I'd learned here, at the Scholars' Hall, at House Pareshol... Everyone could see that I would just ruin everything I touched.

Everyone but Cor.

My plan lay in shambles. I'd pinned the end of this episode on that Shevern and now it had all unraveled. "How can I finish our agreement if no one will teach me?"

"She said they had removed mention of humans from the lore, but that could only be where the Scholars can reach. Surely, something must remain in private collections, someone—"

"You said you've looked already." I shook my head. "I'm not going on a wild goose chase. That wasn't the agreement. You heard her. I don't belong here. This whole thing is ridiculous."

"You gave your word." He played it like a trump card, but the stakes were too high for me to lose.

"And? What's the next step? You promised, too. This wasn't supposed to be a trap. You said you'd leave me alone if I did this. I don't belong here, Cor. I know it and you know it and she was right. I'm just going to ruin everything." My life. His life. This had been a mistake from the beginning. "Is that what you want?"

"She's wrong, Kate." He clenched his hands, like he could keep me here if he only held on tightly enough. "There's nothing wrong with you being here. All those years when we were young—"

"Stop." Something Issai had said prickled in my mind. "All the danger has been here. All the Hunters, all the violence, it was all here on Kuyen. I was never in danger on Earth."

"You never saw Hunters on your side because I kept them away! You see how real the danger is. Do you want to face a Wogra with no way to protect yourself? Alone?"

His words unraveled all of it, the whole tapestry I'd built to convince myself that any of this was possible. Beating a monster like the Wogra with a paper airplane? It was all smoke and mirrors, sound and fury, my illness trying to make me afraid. To make me give in. I rubbed the bandage I still wore over my wrist. Maybe Rose had been right to worry about the cut. "I should have known it wasn't real. It was too easy."

"Easy? I learned everything anyone would teach me, wards and Seemings and melee with the *zaret*...and now you won't believe me because I made it too safe? No."

I'd lived for years among very ill people, with bad news and breakdowns and crises as common as potholes in a country road, but I had never seen anyone look as stricken as Cor did right then. His fingers flicked again and again, like a tic. "Katherine Kjelgaard, I beg you to release me from our bargain. Let it be like it was before and you'll never need to see me again, anyway. Please. You would be dead if not for me."

"I'd be normal if not for you." Or he would end up dead. *No, stop it. None of this is real.* I couldn't hold both possibilities in my head anymore. He would never leave, if I didn't make him go. I forced the words out. "I did what you asked. We found Issai. You swore you would go away. Are you going to break your word?"

"We're done, then," he said, his voice gone toneless. "You can't learn if no one will teach you. You kept your word. I'll keep mine."

"It's better this way." I couldn't keep myself from saying it, despite everything. "You get your life back."

"Not like this."

I had to go, now, before I caved. No part of Kuyen was as hard to deny as he was. None so tempting to believe. I took a deep breath, gathering my concentration to slip home.

"Wait," Cor said. "Promise you will keep the token I gave you, in case you ever need me. Please."

At Bayshore, they'd made me throw away all the silly little trinkets I'd claimed my friends had given me. A line had to be drawn, reality on one side and nothing else on the other. I'd broken that rule and look where it had gotten me.

But I still nodded to him before I wrenched myself back across the gap, home.

I should have felt elated, back in my dark living room. My life could get back to normal. I wouldn't have to call the doctors. I had Cor's word that he would stay away. The hallucinations would end and I could put this episode behind me.

I stumbled through the dark to my bed and fell into it. I should have felt happy.

What a miserable victory. All I could think of was the lost look on Cor's face as Kuyen had faded away.

CHAPTER EIGHTEEN

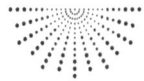

O n my way to work the next morning, I focused on the relief that this thing with Kuyen was over. One way or the other, I wouldn't have to worry about it anymore. I concentrated on setting up the till and turning on the computers and equipment until Rose got there to distract me.

"I'm so ready for this semester to be over!" she announced as she breezed through the door.

Not 'ready,' but 'so ready.' Maybe I could learn from her enthusiasm, now that I didn't have so much to worry about.

"You only have a couple more weeks, right?"

"Yep, just under. Twelve more days. Two hundred eighty-eight more hours." She lifted a hand to tick off fingers. "In that time, I have to cram for a statistics final, finish my contemporary literature paper, do my figure drawing self-portrait, put together my lithography portfolio, go over slides for my Renaissance art history exam, and do a write-up on my show."

Most of the time I envied the opportunity she had for college. Right now, she might as well have been talking gibberish. I fumbled for a reasonable response. "Sounds like a lot."

"Yeah, first world problems, right? That's why I'm playing pool tonight instead. You in?" She said it politely, though I'd never taken her up on an evening invitation. I'd been too afraid to before.

Well, not anymore. Not after what I'd paid to have the opportunity. "Sure. I need to get out of my apartment."

Rose raised her brows. "Who are you and what did you do to my friend?"

I laughed. "Come on. I'm—" Then I saw the look on her face, the one that said it was possible to be 'the crazy girl' even when she didn't know my diagnosis. "I'm not going as your pet project."

"Not at all." Her expression had more kindness in it than judgment. Maybe Rose was just being a friend, like she claimed. I could use one. I'd run out.

"Okay." I hesitated, then added, "Just so you know, everything's much better now and there's nothing to worry about."

"I'll take that at face value as long as you'll still come with us."

"Us who? You and Troy?"

"A whole group of us from school. It'll be good for you, getting out into the wider world. They're all artsy types, so you'll fit right in."

"But I'm not any kind of artist."

"You have an artistic soul. It's the intent that matters."

Intent is what matters, not how it looks. I could almost hear Cor's voice in my ear, feel his arms around me. I shoved the memory away.

Today seemed like a great time to meet new people. "Yeah, I'd like that."

Rose showed up right around sunset. Not that I had to worry about that anymore, but my heart stumbled at her knock.

She looked gorgeous, like always, in black skinny jeans and a sleeveless, shimmery pink halter top with a chunky silver necklace and hoop earrings. I'd dressed up some, at least compared to my usual outfit. I wore my nicest pair of jeans and a blousy kind of shirt, lavender with a V-neck and long sleeves. A little warm for the weather, but I wasn't taking chances. Rose hadn't said anything more about the cut on my arm and I didn't want it brought up again.

"You look lovely, darling, but accessories are a girl's best friend." She swept past me into the apartment and looked around. "Where do you keep your pretties?"

"Um, jewelry?" For all that she was speaking English, I felt the need for some translation. "I don't have any, really."

"Oh, this'll work!" She fetched something off my bookshelf. The hair comb from Cor. "I haven't seen a real tortoiseshell comb in ages. Where'd you get it?"

No harm in the truth, this time. "It was a present."

"It's beautiful. You should wear it more often. Here, do your hair up in a twist."

I followed her directions, rationalizing that if Rose could see it and approved, I wasn't too likely to make a fool of myself. The comb looked nothing like tortoiseshell to me, but it didn't matter. Not anymore.

She fiddled with my hair and the comb for a moment, then stepped back and gave me a onceover. "There. That's perfect."

As Rose drove us over to the university campus, I kept the conversation on her classes and she didn't seem to notice. I didn't have anything of my own to add.

The blocky cement student union building held a bowling alley and billiards room on the ground floor. On a Sunday night two weeks before finals, students filled the space, rowdy with procrastination. Rose led me past the packed snack bar to the handful of pool tables that dominated one end. Bowling lanes stretched down the other side of the area, the background rumble broken by the clatter of pins and the occasional cheer.

Rose's group of friends gathered around a couple of pool tables near the wall. She introduced them as Clara and Harvey, theater majors; Logan, Chloe, and Eric, all from fine arts; Troy, of course; and Ryan, who gave me a wry smile and said, "I'm not enrolled. I work at Dragon House, the dumpling place downtown."

"While he chases his muse," Rose added, reaching out to muss his already ruffled dark hair. He ducked away, laughing. "I worked on one of his shows last year for my gallery installations class." She nudged me with her elbow. "Katherine's never played pool before. You're pretty good, though, right? Want to show her the ropes?"

"I never turn down the company of a beautiful lady," he said, turning up the wattage on his smile. He had the kind of blue eyes that should be making me think about the ocean or something equally dramatic, but all I could think was, *They make him look so human.*

"As soon as Chloe finishes dusting the boys over there, you guys are set." Rose pointed to the farthest table, where the tall blonde watched a striped ball drop neatly into a corner pocket, then bent to line up another shot. Harvey and Logan stood a little off to the side, bemused expressions on their faces. Harvey had long hair drawn back in a ponytail that would have made a Thurei proud, for all that it was plain, dark brown.

I had to stop thinking about Cor.

Ryan looked at me as Rose headed off to Troy's table. "Ever notice she's a bit of a matchmaker?"

I rolled my eyes. "I'm getting that vibe."

"Let's go find you a cue before she thinks up something more obvious."

Stick selected, we picked a couple of stools by the wall to watch the end of the game while he explained the rules to me. Chloe worked her way methodically through the remainder of the striped balls, ending her turn by missing a shot at the green one. Logan stepped in with relief to take his turn.

Having completed his tutorial, Ryan hunted for another topic. "So, Rose didn't introduce you by your major. Are you taking classes somewhere else, or just undecided?"

"Um, no. I guess I'm kind of...trying to decide what I want to do from here, you know?" I had options. Maybe more options now than I'd had a month ago. It just didn't feel that way.

"I completely understand, trust me." Ryan chuckled. "Did your parents mind that you skipped college?"

But he didn't understand and never would. I pushed the thought away, trying to concentrate on the moment. Ryan might not understand, but he was being sympathetic. He didn't need the full truth, just an answer. "No, not so much. My dad didn't go to college. He owns his own business. Mom did, she majored in English, but now she does the billing and scheduling for the nursery business. So I guess they never viewed it as a requirement."

They had, in fact, never viewed it as an option for me, since they didn't think I'd be sane enough to handle it. The so-called schooling provided at Bayshore was hardly college prep anyway.

"You're lucky," he said, and I was sure he believed it. "Every time I go visit my parents, I still have to hear about how much I could have accomplished if I had only applied myself."

"But you are accomplishing things. Rose said you've done your own gallery shows. That's impressive."

"Thanks. Working at the restaurant still pays the bills, though." He grinned, a little sideways curve of his lips. "Want to see some of my work?"

"Sure," I said, pretending this felt natural, like I had normal conversations with normal people all the time. Like I was normal and didn't have anything to hide.

Ryan pulled his phone out of his pocket, tapped through a few menus, and leaned in so we could both see the little screen. "They're like the photography version of sketches. I go out and take quick shots around the city looking for things to explore later, so these are pretty rough."

They were beautiful. A city park at sunset. Rush hour taillights reflecting off a rain-slicked street. A construction site with streamers of orange plastic netting blowing in the wind. Face after face of the city, each scene familiar but made striking by the light, the angle, the composition.

"What do you think?" Ryan spoke so close, I could feel his breath on my ear.

I concentrated on what I saw before me. "These are great. It's amazing how you can find wonder in all these places."

"Photos can capture things no one's ever seen or known before.

People think only a drawing or painting can do that. But fact can be just as surprising as fiction."

Downright fake can blow your socks off, too. "I believe you."

He bumped his shoulder against mine. "Your turn. Tell me something no one else knows. About yourself, I mean."

"Well..." *I spent six years in a mental hospital for believing I could transport myself to a fantasy realm.* Right. Something else. It seemed like everything about me led back to that, though. Like that fact was the only part that mattered.

The thought woke a snarl of loneliness. I pushed the ache away. I was here with a group of friends, talking to a handsome, talented guy who seemed to be enjoying the conversation. Who cared if they knew nothing about me? I should have been glad. I needed to get used to it. "I can make an entire origami zoo with my eyes closed."

"Like cranes?"

"Like lions and tigers and bears, oh my. Cranes are for amateurs. Got any paper on you?"

He patted his pockets like he might have an errant notebook stuck in his jeans by mistake, but of course not. Just then Chloe sunk the final ball.

Harvey waved us toward the table, not looking the least bit put out by his loss. "Your turn, guys."

Rose and Troy peeled away from the other table when they caught sight of Ryan racking the balls. She brandished her cue. "Girls against boys?"

Ryan lifted a brow. "You mean you're not going to insist on couples?"

"Have I been heavy handed?"

Her boyfriend caught her around the waist and planted a kiss on her lips. "Not you. Never you, Rosie!"

Undeterred, she wriggled away and turned to me. "Is that what we've got? Couples?"

I held up my hands, feeling a blush across my cheeks. "Look, I just wanted an evening out of my apartment."

"And if I get pushy, you'll never leave the house again! Got it." She teased with her usual enthusiasm, but concern showed in her eyes.

Troy wrapped his arms around her with the ease of long affection. "You two ignore her. I'm not sure why I put up with her myself. Come on, babe, you need something sugary and caffeinated. I don't think you're hyper enough."

They headed off to the snack bar.

"Good," Ryan said. "You don't even know how to shoot yet."

He told me where to stand and demonstrated the right way to hold the cue, but my first shot managed to bounce off three of the bumpers without hitting a single ball.

Ryan set the white ball back in its place and stepped close. "Here, like this." He curled the fingers of his left hand around mine and leaned against me to put his right over mine on the cue. He shifted my hips with his, tilting us together against the table, explaining something about angle and ricochet.

"What was that?" I asked, unable to concentrate. More nerves than attraction, and the too-close memory of someone else's body pressed against mine.

He chuckled softly, a rumble of his chest against my back. He stepped back and I could breathe again. "Just hit it. Hard enough to bounce things around."

I did and it worked and I didn't make a fool of myself, or at least no more than I might have already. When Rose and Troy returned, we played girls against boys, though it seemed the guys hampered their own effort by being so quick to help us make perfect shots, especially when such help involved minute adjustments of elbows or hands or hips. I tried to enjoy the attention and think of nothing but my present company.

Ryan was nice and funny and it shouldn't matter that we were practically complete strangers. Maybe that made it better. All I had to do was take care with what I told him and ignore the hollow feeling hiding behind my ribs.

As it grew late and the games wrapped up, Rose nudged me and said, "I'm headed over to Troy's after this. Do you mind if Ryan drops you off?"

I gave her my best scheme-quelling glare. "You're not trying to set me up with him, are you? Seriously?"

"Of course not." She looked up at me with a saintly look of innocence. "That's up to you and him."

Impossible imp.

Ryan and I said our goodbyes soon after, though Logan begged us to stay longer and give Chloe more opponents to beat.

Chloe just laughed and shook her head at him before turning to me. "Come back sometime. For whatever you like, it doesn't have to be pool."

"Sounds good," I said and I meant it.

The walk out to Ryan's car threaded another minefield of answering personal questions without saying too much and Ryan wasn't even being nosy. Just friendly.

When I gave him my address, he pulled directions up on his phone. Before he could think up anything else to ask, I pointed to his car stereo. "Got any good music?"

"Sure thing," he said. He had clearly put some money into the stereo system and seemed happy enough to show it off. We listened to something fast and loud and German on the way home and it was perfect because then we could ride without talking.

He spun the volume down when we reached my apartment building. "Want me to walk you up? It's pretty late."

I hardly heard him, my attention snagged on a figure standing just beyond the pool of streetlight at the property's eastern edge. I couldn't see much more than a vague shape.

Cor? A Hunter, waiting for me?

Something touched my shoulder and I jumped, biting back a yelp of surprise.

"Katherine, are you okay?"

"Yeah," I said, willing my heartbeat to slow down. I glanced back out the car window. Of course, it was the bus stop. Just a man waiting at a bus stop. "Yeah, I'm fine."

"I can walk you to your door," he offered again, looking past me at the night beyond the car. I must not have hidden my reaction as well as I'd thought.

"No. Um, thanks, but no." The last thing I needed was someone to see me acting crazy. I opened the door with trembling fingers, forcing myself out of the car. I would not give in to this. I was done with hallucinations.

"Katherine," Ryan said before I could close the car door behind me. I stopped, ducked back down to see him. "I had a nice time."

"Yeah, me too," I said, wanting to be polite, but really wanting to be back home, where I didn't have to worry about hiding the fact that I might see something. I swung the car door shut.

"Hey." His voice stopped me again, halfway up the walk. "Can I call you 'Kate'?"

"No one calls me 'Kate' anymore," I said, and I went up to my apartment, leaving the night behind. This time, when I found the ward—bit of ribbon, strip of cloth, trash, I didn't care—in my pocket along with my keys, I threw it away.

CHAPTER NINETEEN

I thought about the last few days as little as possible and threw myself into finding a new routine. I had the freedom now to do whatever I wanted. Finally. I concentrated on that.

I learned to cook stir-fries. I went to Rose's show, escorted by the artist herself. She took another break from finals prep for some 'retail therapy' and gave me a budget fashionista makeover at her favorite thrift store. I made arrangements with my mom to visit in a few weeks.

It worked, mostly, to keep my mind off of other things.

When Rose asked me to take another evening shift for her, I told her it would be no problem. My apartment was starting to feel cramped and, of course, I didn't have to worry about being out at night anymore.

I believed it until Frank and I closed up the shop for the night. While I pulled on my heavy denim jacket, Frank waited for me, propping the store's back door open with the toe of one bright blue-and-gold sneaker. He was checking his phone, probably the score of the Warriors game. He'd been telling me about his favorite team for most of the last hour.

The shop had posters and advertisements covering the storefront windows and I hadn't thought much about the night outside. I shouldn't have been thinking about the night outside, that was the whole point. But the jittery nerves I'd had after the pool game crept back on me, anyway.

"You doing okay?" Frank asked, his black brows drawn down in concern.

"Yeah, of course." I tried to project the confidence I should have been feeling as I flicked off the shop's lights and waved Frank out the door ahead of me. I didn't want anyone seeing me act paranoid over nothing. "You'd better get home before the game's over."

He grinned back and headed for his car. "See ya later, Katherine."

I headed for my bicycle as he pulled out of the small employee parking lot. When I'd locked the bike up behind the shop this afternoon, I hadn't thought about how dark it would be by the time I got off of work. The bike lock hung in the pitch-black shadows where the light above the back door didn't reach. As I jabbed at it with my key, growing impatience made me more fumble-fingered than ever.

The parking lot stretched empty but for me and the shadows. I was alone here. No Cor—

It wasn't supposed to matter anymore, but that didn't stop my chest from working itself tighter with every breath. A dog barked, making me jump, even though it was probably half a block away.

Why am I not using my phone flashlight? I groaned at myself and reached into my jeans pocket. Empty. My jacket pockets, too. I rummaged through my purse, all but turning it inside out, but my phone wasn't there, either. I must have left it inside. *Dammit.*

I'd have to enter the reason for resetting the store's security alarm on my timecard: *dumb mistake*. At least I could use the back door light now, standing right below it and shuffling through my keys to find the work set.

Something scraped as I slid the key into the door lock. Not the key. Even as I turned around, I told myself, *It's nothing.*

One shadow detached itself from the dark mass of the neighboring building. Tall and bulky, its movement was alien but familiar. Claws scratched across the asphalt in time with its deliberate strides.

I couldn't make my body move.

"Where is your House guard, little human?" The Hirach's low voice slipped into a mocking chuckle. "There's no Truce here to stop me."

I still held the key in my nerveless fingers, seated firmly in the lock. The Hunter snapped into motion the instant I did, the two movements so close together, I couldn't say which of us acted and which reacted. I twisted the key and then yanked the door open. I felt a tug on my jacket, but I flung myself through the doorway, pulling free.

The Hirach roared as I dragged the door closed behind me. It slammed, rebounded, refused to close. He roared again. The Hunter yanked his smashed hand out of the gap between door and jamb. Before he could get his claws back in, I jerked the door shut. I heard the lock engage and I darted deeper into the small store, crashing into a filing cabinet in the dark. The pounding and snarls from the other side of the door made it impossible to think straight. Light switch? *No. If the Hirach can see inside, it can get inside.* I scrabbled in the darkness, dragging my hands over countertops suddenly unfamiliar. Something beeped a warning, but I couldn't pay attention to it right now. My phone had to be here somewhere. *Where?*

Silence.

Then the security grille over the storefront rattled in its track. I bit back a scream and scrambled under the counter, but the steel held against the Hunter's assault.

So far.

The store's alarm went off, blaring loud enough to make me cover my ears. The grille rattled again. Of course, there were no alarm systems on Kuyen, so why would he stop? The police would come. That would chase him off, wouldn't it?

I had nothing else to do but wait and hope, curled under the counter and helpless.

After an eternity, silence.

Silence.

Then sirens. More pounding. "Police. Open the door."

I crawled out from under the counter, my back hurting and wet, my body cramped and shaking from the aftermath of adrenaline. I opened the door to a pair of policemen with drawn guns.

The older one opened his mouth to question me but stopped when he saw the blood. It surprised us both. He sent the younger officer back to the patrol car to get first aid supplies and call for an ambulance. He helped me to sit down. "What happened?"

"A Hunter. Outside...I..." My voice shook and everything blurred. I heard the policeman speak, but I couldn't be sure if I answered or not.

The arrival of the ambulance stopped his questions.

Hands. Movement. Pain.

Darkness.

CHAPTER TWENTY

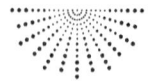

My first memory was of a suburban forest, the tree section of my family's landscaping nursery. The leaves turned innocent breezes into mysterious whispers. Trundling beetles and the occasional flick of a lizard hid among the plastic pots and wooden crates. It was easily the wildest place in my entire young life.

I didn't recall feeling surprised the evening that secret grove revealed a gray-skinned girl with oddly bent legs and an orange-haired boy with yellow eyes just like a cat's. I couldn't understand a word they said, but words matter much less to the very young.

The little boy's outstretched hand said 'come with us' as clearly as any speech.

Someone was holding my hand. Bright hair. A little boy running and laughing under the birches. Coran.

I opened my eyes. Rose sat in a chair drawn up to my bedside, holding my hand in hers. Her dark eyes were worried. "How are you feeling?"

"Confused," I whispered, trying to put together a whole story out of scattered pieces. The hospital was wrong. The wrong room, the wrong smells. The many beeping, flashing machines did not belong. My back ached, a dark red throb of pain.

"I should say so, after that attack. The nurse said you were in shock when they got you in here."

I put together that this was a medical hospital, not the other kind. "It was real."

She laughed a little, nervously. "Eighty-four stitches of real. From what I gather, someone tried to jump you after Frank left. He cut you across your back before you could lock yourself back in. Smart thinking, there. The outside of the door's all scratched up. That guy was psycho, whoever it was. Did you get a good look at him?"

Claws. The glint of teeth. Growls and pounding at the door. The cloaked form looming out of the darkness, the shape inhuman and monstrous.

Rose squeezed my hand. "Are you okay? We don't have to talk about it."

Was I okay? She hadn't meant anything by that question, but it echoed through me regardless. The Hunter was real. The attack was real. I shuddered, waking a snarl of pain across my back. My forehead itched. When I reached up, I found an IV in my hand and a swath of bandages up near my hairline, the hint of an ache beneath.

Considering I might not be crazy, I was okay. Sane, even.

"Yeah." I took a deep breath and felt the painful pull of the stitches. "Other than the stitches. And bandages on my head. Aside from those, I'm fine."

It was weak humor, but she was kind enough to laugh.

"Well, Mr. Parker called to ask if I could work for you this morning. When he said you were in the hospital, I came right away. The doctor said you can go home this afternoon."

"Good," I said automatically, while I thought about bus routes and hospital bills.

She must have seen some of the worry on my face. "Do you have someone to take you home?"

I shook my head. "My parents are in Oregon, and I don't have anyone around here."

She narrowed her dark eyes. "Of course you do. I'm right here and I'm your friend. I'd be happy to take you home." She looked away, toying with the end of her braid. "Besides, if it weren't for me, you wouldn't be in the hospital at all. You were covering my shift."

"Don't say that." What if the Hunter had caught me at my apartment, away from the steel door and the security grille? I'd have been dead now. "There's no way to say what would or wouldn't have happened. What if you'd been there and gotten killed? I'd rather have stitches than a funeral."

She gave me a wan smile. "Thanks. I still feel bad, though."

I wasn't sure what to say to make her feel better. "I really appreciate you being here."

"That's what friends are for."

That wasn't the only thing friends were good for, Rose proved as the day unfolded. The doctor came to outline for me the extent of my injuries—stitches, minor concussion, shock, but the blood loss hadn't been too bad—and give me an estimate of when the stitches could be removed, when I could get back to work, and instructions I needed to follow while I healed. Rose took notes. She tucked the bottle of prescription painkillers into my bag, which the nurse returned to me. Rose fetched me a new shirt from the gift store.

I stared long and hard at my back in the bathroom mirror. The gash ran from one shoulder to about mid-rib level on the other side, covered with bandages. Visible around the edges, two shorter welts ran in parallel stripes on either side, where the thick denim of my jacket had taken the brunt of the damage and literally saved my skin.

No knife-wielding mugger could have done this, slashed three times across my back as I'd dashed through the door. *Believe it, Kate*, I told myself. *The Hunter is real and he will kill you.*

I needed Cor.

I didn't have any right to ask for his help after all that had happened. I'd be lucky if he didn't laugh in my face and tell me I'd gotten what I deserved. But I didn't have any other choice.

The policemen came to take my statement before I left. I stuck with the story they could believe: a mugger who caught me at the end of my shift, a knife in the dark. Mr. Parker, the After Image owner, arrived somewhere in the middle and assured me that the business would cover the medical expenses, since I had been at work and my assailant was likely after the money in the till.

"You should have let him take the money, Katherine," he told me. "It's not worth your life."

I agreed and thanked him and wished fervently, privately, that this problem had such a simple solution.

Rose drove me home, slow and careful, while I sat on the edge of the seat and tried not to bump against the back rest. I hated the stairs up to my apartment, but I made it, glad that she was there to carry my bag and complain companionably about the lack of elevator.

I motioned for her to dump my stuff on the card table after I got the door open. Exhaustion rolled through me and it felt like the painkillers were wearing off, but I didn't want to seem ungrateful for all of Rose's help. I dragged out a serviceable, "Can I get you anything?"

"My God, no!" She waved the suggestion away. "You need to get in bed and mend. You heard the doctor: lots of rest. In fact, can I get you anything?" She looked around the tiny living room. "Like some chairs?"

I was deep enough in her debt already. "I'll go to bed, how's that?"

"You have my number, so you better call me if you need anything." She pulled the pain pills out of my bag and set them down on top of the doctor's list of instructions.

"Thank you, Rose."

"Take care." She let herself out and I locked the door behind her.

It wouldn't take the Hunter any time at all to break through this flimsy wooden door, or the glass window that opened on the fire escape. I shivered. Hallucinations didn't slash up jackets. The police hadn't been certain how one man with a knife could have managed three cuts across the back of my jacket, but they agreed that that was what had happened. Any other explanation was beyond their ability to believe.

A Hunter, though, had more than enough claws to do the job. I'd been lucky my jacket had taken some of the damage.

The Hunter was real. Kuyen was real. So was Cor.

It was surprising that I still had to remind myself of that with so many stitches in my back.

When I plugged my phone on the charger, it lit up with messages from my parents. *Great.* I should have thought of this at the hospital. I had emergency contact information in my wallet. I sat on the edge of my folding chair while the phone dialed.

My mom picked up on the first ring. "Katie? Thank God. Are you okay?"

"Yeah, Mom. I'm okay." Tears surprised me, spilling down my cheeks.

"What happened? They said you got attacked." There was a rustling sound and then she added, "Your dad's here, too. You're on speaker phone."

"Hi, Katie," my dad said, his deep voice worried.

"Hi, Dad." I related the version of events that the police had given me and played down the extent of the cut. This wasn't a problem I could escape by running home. That would just bring danger to them. It took some doing, but I convinced my parents that I didn't need Mom to fly out here immediately or start making plans to quit my job and move back to Oregon.

"It was just a freak bit of bad luck," I lied. At least I could be honest about the next part. "I'm going to be very careful, I promise. I'm pretty tired, though, so I think I should get some rest."

They finally let me off the phone and I sighed.

I had hours yet before sundown, hours before I could do anything that could actually help. Hours before the Hunter could do anything, either. I suppressed another shiver and grabbed the bottle of painkillers on my way to bed.

My back hurt even worse when I woke up, which I hadn't thought possible. I dressed gingerly, in a lavender button-up shirt that had been part of my wardrobe makeover. Compared with pulling on a T-shirt, it was easier to maneuver over my stitches. I took the bandage off my forehead, finding a scabbed-over cut just above my hairline. The skin around it felt tender and swollen. This must have been the slight concussion, from crashing into the counter in the dark. No wonder my head pounded. I barely remembered.

I went out to the kitchen and made myself some peanut butter toast so I could take my next dose of painkillers with food. Gingerly, I sagged into the folding chair, careful not to bump my injury against the chair back. I had to figure out some way to convince Cor to help me. I'd spent years denying his existence—even to his face, which I had to admit would frustrate anybody. This last time, he had come to help and I had agreed to play along, only to take advantage of our agreement and use it to send him packing at the end.

I might have been able to tell myself that he had been better off, since it freed him up to live his own life, but that didn't excuse the cruel way I'd done it.

Maybe, if I were very, very, very sorry, he would forgive me. Cor was generous and kind and loyal, far, far better than I deserved. Maybe he would take pity on the helpless, as he had before.

I sighed and rubbed tears out of my eyes. I'd be lucky if he agreed to see me at all. I deserved to do more than a little groveling for my lack of faith. Lots and lots of groveling. I spread out a sheet of paper, toyed with my pen. "Forgive me, Cor, please..."

No. I had no right to call him that now. I started over. "Forgive me, Coraven. I was an idiot..."

I crumpled the paper and flung it across the room. The sun would set in a few minutes and I would never come up with the right way to word this, even if I had all night. All night, alone in my apartment. He'd warded it, he said, but I had no idea how long those wards would last.

What if he wouldn't come?

He had made me promise to keep the bird token, in case I needed him. I fetched it from the drawer of my bedside table. Even if he was mad at me, I'd be safer with him than on my own. Surely, he wouldn't turn me away, if I showed up on his doorstep.

Not like I'd done to him.

CHAPTER TWENTY-ONE

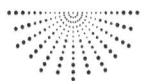

When night finally came, I slipped across the gap the moment the sun went down. I found myself in a sitting room, its style familiar from my time at House Pareshol. Pale dawn light washed across the room, picking out the flame of Cor's hair.

He slouched in an armchair near the door. No, he slept, his head leaning into the upholstery. He wore a tailored blue shirt and fitted black trousers that looked like evening clothes he'd nodded off in. A short black jacket lay draped over the end table beside him, along with a leatherbound book splayed face down on a stack of papers, and a goblet stood by an empty carafe.

Exhaustion smudged dark circles under his eyes, but sleep had at least smoothed the usual tension from his face. I hesitated to wake him and see his expression turn angry or offended or, worst of all, dismissive.

However it went, I'd earned it and he still deserved my apology.

I went over to stand in front of him and cleared my throat. "Um, Coraven—"

He stirred, then rubbed a hand over his face and cracked open his eyes. He gave me the sweetest smile I'd ever seen on his face.

Then he bolted upright in the chair, his expression an uneasy mix of wonder and panic. "Katen!"

Startled, I stumbled backward. On reflex, I blurted out, "Sorry. I didn't mean to scare you."

His gaze darted around the room, like there might be a Hunter hiding there. He winced when he saw the cast-offs on the table, then ran his long fingers through his hair before meeting my eyes again.

Guilt twisted tight in my chest. "I...I can go. Wait, no, I can't. Cor. Um, I mean Coraven..."

I should have prepared better.

Cor stood slowly, looking at me like he expected to wake up for real in another moment or two. "You're here."

"Please, let me start over." Nervousness chilled my fingers and I twisted my hands together. If Cor turned me down, I would truly have nowhere else to go. I tried my best for the right air of Thurei formality so he wouldn't think I was taking this lightly. "Coraven Temarel."

Like a charm, his full name drew him up, straight and solemn. "Yes?"

"I beg you to forgive me for my lack of belief."

"Ah, Katen." He let out a breath and relaxed again. "Of course."

"I was afraid you wouldn't. Not after how I treated you. I've been awful." By the end of the sentence, I was crying. Stupid tears, but I couldn't seem to stop.

Then Cor was there, gathering me into his arms. "It's okay, Katen."

His hand brushed across my back and I gasped at the jolt of pain. He pulled away so fast, I staggered. When I looked up, his expression was carefully neutral. Turavi couldn't have gotten a better mask out of him.

"It's just the stitches," I explained, wiping tears off my cheeks.

"Stitches? I thought that was sewing."

"It is. That Hunter, the one from Scholars' Hall...maybe not the same one, but he did say I didn't have my guard with me..." *And whose fault was that?* I barreled on. "I was leaving work when he showed up and he clawed me before I could get back in the building and lock him out. The doctor sewed it up, but it still hurts like hell."

Cor's eyes had gotten wider with each word. "The Hirach found you? And you escaped him."

"I got lucky," I said. "If I hadn't had my hand on the door already, I wouldn't have made it in time. He was so fast."

He flicked his fingers emphatically. "You were smart. That was quick thinking, not luck. Then you...they sewed you." He gave the English term odd emphasis, like it still made no sense. "Like a piece of cloth. Why did they not heal it? What do your healers do, anyway? Let me take you to Havro."

I weighed the unpleasantness of my last encounter with a healer against the black line of pain etched across my back. No contest. "Sold."

"This is no merchant healer. Havro uses his skill for any Temarel, and you are—my guest. The House cares for its own."

But I wasn't 'its own,' just Cor's guest. Even he had to scramble to come up with a way to justify it just now. "Are you sure it's okay? I don't want to get you in trouble with your *denet*."

"The *denet* is out of the House at present, and Havro will be honored, I assure you."

"Did you get that spear wound taken care of?" I reached for the spot under his collarbone.

"I did." He caught my hand, careful as if it might break. "Tell me, Kate. How do things go from here for us?"

There would be no disbelieving from now on. "If you're willing to help me, I'll do whatever it takes to learn how to defend myself. If we can't find a way to do that, then I need to come up with another plan. You shouldn't have to be my bodyguard."

"Tell me you won't send me away again."

I laced my fingers together so I wouldn't embarrass myself by reaching for him again. "I was trying not to be crazy before. It wasn't about wanting *you* to go."

He waited.

"I won't send you away."

"Thank you," he said. He glanced down at his wrinkled clothes and ran a hand through his hair. "Let me change? Then I'll take you to our healer."

Freshly dressed and looking far more awake, Cor led me to an airy, white-walled atrium full of greenery like the one I'd seen at House Pareshol. Cor was right, the tawny-furred Lewril healer did seem genuinely honored to meet me. He bowed deeply when Cor introduced me.

Cor relayed what I'd told him about my injury, stumbling over the Kuyene word for sewing. Havro shrugged it off with a ripple of his short fingers. "That's a common field dressing on worlds with no healing talents. Come, Kjelgaard, you will need to remove your shirt."

"I can wait outside if you want," Cor offered.

"No, it's okay." Heat crept up my cheeks, but I wouldn't ask him to leave. Not anymore.

He took a sudden interest in the healer's collection of plants on the opposite wall and strolled over in that direction. I unbuttoned my blouse quickly and lay down on the cot Havro indicated. I could tell the moment Cor turned back around because he caught his breath.

With a hint of rebuke in his voice, Havro told him, "The one who treated her did fine work. That will make my job easier. Just relax."

I think he meant the last part for me. I tried, but I couldn't do it. He placed a palm on either side of the injury and the velvety fur at the edges of his hand tickled my skin. Then an alien consciousness was present in both my body and my mind.

Sanity was irrelevant—I feared this, even if I knew enough not to fight it. I found a corner of my mind that the healing didn't require and I hid.

Sleep pulled away from me like the tide. In my entire life, I don't think I'd ever felt this good. I lay with my eyes closed for long moments that flowed as slow and golden as honey. My blood sang in my veins with every heartbeat. My skin tingled like it was newly made. Every breath tasted sweet as it slid down my throat and into my lungs.

I must be dreaming. I didn't mind. Getting to feel like this now would be worth the disappointment of waking to real life later. I opened my eyes to a white space as surreal as the inside of a cloud.

And Cor, looking down at me, a smile softening his mouth.

"Coran." I smiled, delighted that he could share this dream, too. There had been too much pain and sorrow in his face lately. He deserved some happiness.

"You're not dreaming," he said. "It's the healing."

Had I said some of that out loud? I blinked, trying to clear my wonderfully muzzy head. *Healing. Healer. Okay. Got it.* "Was I talking in my sleep?"

"A little."

"What did I say?"

"Nothing to embarrass you. Can you stand?" He held out a hand to help me up.

When I reached for it, my back didn't hurt. Either I'd said that out loud, too, or he read my broad grin. "Havro says you're all healed, though there will be a scar. Your body had begun mending itself. No healer can undo the body's own work. He gives his compliments to your doctor."

Probably the first time I'd ever heard Cor say something nice about human doctors. Of course, he was quoting someone.

I shrugged, glad to be able to do such a simple thing again without pain. Something occurred to me. "Is that why you have so many scars?"

"Ah. In part. Sometimes it wasn't safe to leave right away and I had to wait for the dawn. Others weren't serious enough to trouble Havro."

Though I had gotten to my feet, Cor had not let go of me. I was fascinated by the feel of his hand in mine. Weighty and warm, smooth and rough under my fingertips. I almost missed what he said next.

"He found a corruption that the Hirach had set into the wound.

He was able to unwork it because he got to it so soon." The words came out clipped and tense. He must have been upset.

I wasn't. I felt too good to be upset. Just curious. "What does that mean?"

"It means—" He cleared his throat, starting over. "It means that you would have sickened and died if you had not come back, although the wound on its own wasn't life-threatening."

His eyes were molten gold and shadowed by fear. I didn't want him to be afraid anymore. No more hurt, or sorrow. I didn't feel those things—why should he? So I took the one step toward him that brought our bodies together, wrapped my arms around him, and tucked my cheek up along his collarbone. He froze for a breath, then slid his arms around me. He pulled me tightly against him, as if he thought I might fade away. His heartbeat thundered against my ear, harder and faster than my own, and his breath tickled through my hair. We fit like two puzzle pieces, matched together.

I'd hugged Cor before, but not like this. This was what I'd wanted while we'd huddled under the blanket in the rain and I tried to ignore the fact that I should ignore him, that I should be ready to walk away and forget about him.

Silly, to think that I'd ever felt good before now.

"Thank you, Coran," I whispered against his neck.

He took a deep breath and let it out. "How are you feeling?"

"Perfect." Warm. Safe. Just where I should have been. "I've never felt this good before."

"It's the healing. It makes you feel differently. Less...concerned." His arms loosened around me. "It's affecting you, I think. I don't want you to regret anything once it wears off."

I let go and stepped back. It woke a prickle of loneliness, but my newfound calm soothed it away. "I don't regret you."

"Tell me that tomorrow," he said, but he smiled. "Now, are you hungry?"

My stomach answered for me with an epic gurgle. "I ate before I left the apartment!"

"Yes, but then you were healed. Your body did the work. Havro only guided it. You'll need to eat, then sleep. Trust me. I know the steps in that dance."

"You dance?"

"When I have to." He brushed the comment off with a shrug and led me out into the hallway.

CHAPTER TWENTY-TWO

"Coraven," someone called from behind us as we left the healer's. Two someones, young men about Cor's age, dressed in casual House clothes. One had a braid the vivid green of an over-fertilized lawn, the other a short ponytail the blushing yellow of an apricot.

"Havro brought the most interesting story to the kitchens just now," the pony-tailed one said.

"Birasef and Zimero," Cor told me, gesturing at the green-haired one, then the one who'd just spoken. To them, he added, "I make known to you Katherine Kjelgaard, guest of the House."

"We've met, but that was years ago." Birasef gave me an appraising look. There had been a gaggle of Thurei kids around when I'd been little, but I didn't remember them well. He didn't look like he expected me to. "Guest of the House, huh? It's one thing to saddle the *morsai*, Kjelgaard, but you muzzle it, too?"

"What's that supposed to mean?" I asked, honestly puzzled. Cor and I weren't going to ride anywhere.

By Cor's expression, he knew exactly what the man had meant. "Mind where you set your feet, Birasef. She *is* a guest and deserves courtesy."

The glare went unheeded. "Put up, Coraven. You know you never duel." Birasef cut his glance back to me. "Did I say something wrong? I would hate to put Coraven in the awkward position of being unable to draw blade before his guest."

Zimero's snicker made that double entendre clear. Cor shifted his feet, just enough to square up his posture, and the hallway suddenly seemed too full of testosterone.

Cor murmured something in Thurei that got Zimero's attention, but the green-haired guy brushed his words off with a theatrical ripple of his fingers.

"Of course, of course." Birasef sounded nonchalant, but his posture remained too stiff. "We'd hate to interrupt your hospitality."

Seeing the Pareshols insult Cor had been bad enough. This was Cor's own House. His kin. I wasn't quite sure of all the currents swirling in this conversation, but my new confidence urged me to jump right in.

I smiled at the pair of them. "I hear Coraven is pretty good with his *zaret*. You aren't really challenging him, are you?"

None of them had expected that. Zimero tried to swallow a laugh and ended up coughing on it. Cor looked pleased.

Birasef, not so much. He backpedaled. "But Coraven's blade is dedicated to a higher purpose, eh, cousin? Dueling is an unnecessary risk."

I looked to Cor. "Is it?"

He rippled his fingers in a shrug. "The *zarets* are a part of us. If they are damaged, no healer or smith can mend them."

"What a shame," Birasef said, his voice brimming with regret, "to have such an exquisite blade at hand and be unable to use it."

Cor's eyes narrowed, but he didn't rise to the bait.

Well, I could. I didn't need a translation to figure that taunt out. "Your blade gets a lot of use, does it?"

Birasef grinned. "You must have heard of me."

"Actually, I haven't. I was just wondering how many Hunters you've gone up against."

That wiped the smile off his face. Rather more politely, he said, "I have never fought a Hunter, Kjelgaard."

"Really?" I hadn't expected him to have faced as many as Cor, but I did think it would have been more than zero. I looked at Zimero. "What about you?"

"Many Thureis never see a Hunter outside the boundaries of Truce or House," Cor put in, with the attitude of someone providing a helpful little side note. "Don't think less of them, just because they're unblooded."

Score one innuendo for our side.

To my surprise, Birasef bobbed an appreciative little bow at the dig. I'd been mocked enough on the schoolyard, but none of those kids had ever shown a sense of humor about themselves. "Much as I would love to discuss the merits of various types of practice, you need to feed your...guest."

Zimero spoke up. "Ah, for this, I would be happy to run back to the kitchen."

He looked like he would actually run so that he didn't miss anything.

"Thank you, I'd appreciate it." I beamed at him, more than a little curious about the outcome myself. He took off, as promised.

Birasef gazed after him like he'd be happy to get out of there, too.

"You offered a demonstration for my guest," Cor said.

"No, I believe this all started with..." Birasef trailed off and looked to me instead, his expression entreating. "You weren't really offended, were you?"

"That you think I'm...what, his *nochel*? I would expect Turavi Pareshol to make insults like that, but not here in your House."

Birasef glanced between us, his expression gone serious. "I would never say such a thing, Kjelgaard."

So I'd misread that one. For all that I thought I followed their little taunts, I'd missed the meaning somewhere. Was it really so terrible to imagine a human and a Thurei together?

"I think I misunderstood," he continued, a half-apology. He offered half a smile to go with it and spread his hands wide. "Consider me chastised. Comparing me to the exalted *denet*-kin Pareshol cuts deep enough that we can spare Coraven's blade."

"Ah, no." Cor didn't let him off that easily. "I think this will be a good reminder for you. There are always *tironas*, if you don't want to risk *zarets.* "

It was Birasef's turn to look insulted. "We are not children, to duel with sticks."

"You made a child's insult," Cor pointed out.

Birasef appealed to me instead. "Did I really offend you?"

I may not have read his meaning right, but I'd been teased enough to recognize the signs. "I think you meant to, even if I didn't understand what you said."

Cor beat him to the explanation. "He said you insulted me by coming here as my guest."

"That's not—" Birasef glanced at Cor and decided not to say any more.

"I would never insult Cor. Coraven, I mean." *Whoops.* They'd been sticking to the more formal address. I added, "At least, not on purpose."

"Not a duel then," Cor said. "A demonstration, to see whose experience carries more weight."

Birasef waggled his fingers in a shrug. "Walked right into this, did I? Fine. Sticks." He turned on his heel and headed back down the hall.

As soon as he was out of earshot, I rounded on Cor. "What was that all about? Is it really an insult to you that I'm here?"

"Of course not. I'm honored to have you as my guest." He shrugged, human-style, and gestured for me to walk with him. "This is the latest word in a long conversation with my cousins."

"So this is a pissing contest?"

He blinked for a moment over the English phrase, but he was male. He figured it out. It surprised a laugh out of him. "If you like. Your healing must not have worn off yet."

"Why? I don't feel—" I didn't regret hugging him. Maybe I should have, considering how shocked Birasef had been at the *nochel* thing. Cor had wrapped his arms around me, but maybe he had just held me because I'd wanted to be held. That was Cor, always careful of my feelings. I needed to stop putting him in that position. But I had to add, "I still don't regret you."

"I don't regret you, either." He stopped at one of the doors and held it open for me. "And I will make sure my cousins know it."

"Are you really going to beat this guy up?" I stepped past Cor into a huge courtyard. Around the edge of the square ran a line of columns that supported a lattice sunshade. Perhaps thirty Thureis were scattered across the space, divided into pairs or small groups. Most of them held long, wooden rods, sparring. The clatter of wood on wood filled the air, punctuated by the occasional words of an instructor. I didn't see the green-haired cousin.

"Do you think I can?" He grinned.

"I thought you were pretty good."

"I am, I assure you, and I appreciate your faith."

It had been years since I'd seen Coran smug. I liked it. But starting some sort of honor duel—*demonstration*—between Cor and his cousin didn't seem like such a good idea anymore, so maybe the effects of the healing were wearing off.

"But you're not really going to beat him up, right?"

Before I got my answer, Birasef strolled over with two of the long, wooden rods. A couple more of his friends, plus the one from the hallway, followed him. Some of the other students and instructors in the courtyard fell silent and stopped their practice as they saw the group head for us.

Birasef bowed when he reached us, a little less jaunty this time, and offered Cor one of the sticks.

Loud enough for his words to carry, Cor said, "A guest of the House is eager to see if your skill matches your words. Will you satisfy her curiosity?"

"Anything for a guest of the House," Birasef said, all courtesy now, twisting the *tirona* in his hands.

His friends made their bows deep enough even I could see the mockery, but I wasn't sure if it was aimed at me or Cor. Or Birasef, for that matter. Zimero handed me a large, cheese-filled roll, still warm from the oven. His smile, at least, seemed genuine.

One with blue hair traced a wide circle on the packed dirt around us. We moved away, leaving Cor and Birasef alone in the center. The three young men gathered around me.

Cor eyed them and said, "I believe Birasef would encourage you to leave her alone."

"But she's a guest of the House," objected the blue-haired one.

As Cor scowled, Zimero leaned down to me and added, "That makes you our guest as much as Coraven's."

The friends murmured amongst themselves as Cor and Birasef started circling each other. They spoke Thurei, so I didn't catch much beyond a few numbers. The youngest one, with pale yellow hair, switched to Kuyene to ask me, "Do you think he is more angry or more showing off?"

"What was that?" I asked, and I saw Cor's gaze flick over to us from across the circle. Birasef capitalized on his distraction to lunge at him, but Cor parried easily with a crack of wood on wood.

"We're making bets on how quick Coraven gets that stick off him," the boy explained. "I think it depends on whether he's angry at Bir or just wants to show off. Which is it, do you think?"

Birasef, in the ring, was trying not to smile at this audible lack of confidence. A couple of people in the audience snickered. Cor ignored it.

"I think you're trying to distract him," I said, trying a severe look on the boy.

"Bir needs all the help he can get." Zimero shrugged with his fingers. "He's ages away from master, if he even tries for it."

"I can hear you," Birasef called.

"We know," they chorused back. More laughter.

I let myself relax. This wasn't the bloodthirsty scene I'd imagined it would be after my experience at House Pareshol. If it had begun as a joke at my expense, they were sharing it more equally around now.

Birasef moved steadily forward, like he meant to circle around all day, but Cor reached out with the stick and then they were both in motion.

I'd seen Cor fight before, but the battle with the Visenis had been desperate and chaotic and terrifying. He'd been very good, then. More than good, he'd saved my life. Against Birasef, he was beautiful, lithe and sure, not a single movement wasted.

His opponent was faster, flashy. He also seemed outmatched, despite his dazzling speed. Cor just never seemed to be there to catch. When Birasef struck, Cor shifted aside a hairsbreadth, or he angled his weapon so the attack slid off without any real resistance, fouling his opponent's balance.

"Bir moves too much," the blue-haired one said, moving to stand closer to me. "He's wasting his momentum. Cor could have the edge off him any time he likes."

Zimero nudged him. "As if you would do better in there, Val."

"Ah, I never said that." Val looked down at me. "You heard me, I never said that. I don't need Coraven making a demonstration out of me."

After a string of unproductive tries, Bir settled back, waiting, his stick held low and ready. Cor lunged forward, aiming for his right foot. His opponent skipped back a step, but Cor didn't press the attack. He just shifted his posture, bringing his *tirona* up and a few inches to the left. Birasef changed his own stance in response, eyebrows drawn.

Cor's *tirona* flicked out again, glancing off Bir's ready weapon rather than making serious contact. Again, they shifted. Cor threatened, Bir moved a little in response, and this time, a titter of laughter ran around the watching Thureis. They moved again and a girl on the other side of the circle said, "Four."

Birasef feinted aside and lunged at Cor, who deflected smoothly. He knocked Bir's guard wide but didn't take the advantage the opening gave him. Instead, he moved in from a higher angle, prompting his opponent to step back and away.

A chorus of younger students chimed, "Five."

Around me, Bir's friends started to chuckle.

"What are they counting for?" I asked, watching as Cor started up with that move-and-stop routine again.

"He's putting Bir through the dance," Zimero said.

The younger one added, "These are the practice positions for children starting out in the circle. And Coraven is correcting his form while he's at it."

The crowd around us counted up to eight when a voice beyond the circle boomed out, "I have never gathered half so large an audience for my lessons."

An older man stood at the edge of the group with his well-muscled arms crossed. "But then, I never thought of using a live puppet."

A murmur of amusement ran through the audience. Birasef and Cor stepped apart and bowed, very low.

"The House armsmaster," Zimero murmured to me.

At least it's not the denet.

The armsmaster's scarlet hair matched his mood perfectly. He glared at Cor. "I don't recall assigning you advanced students. I thought you were too busy. Are you telling me you have the time now?"

"I hoped it would be a single lesson only," Cor began.

Birasef stepped forward. "I asked for it. Believe me, I did."

The man snorted. "I have no trouble imagining that." He swept his tawny gaze to Bir's friends, clustered around me. They all stood a little straighter under his attention. His gaze snagged a moment on me, but his words were for them. "I didn't expect any of you here today. If you have enough idle time to spend loafing around the training courtyard, I could speak with the House Master on your account."

They all quickly declined the armsmaster's offer and took their leave. The audience dispersed back to their own lessons.

That left Cor and me under the armsmaster's stern look. He gathered us up with a gesture and led us out of the courtyard.

CHAPTER TWENTY-THREE

The armsmaster brought us to a utilitarian version of Cor's sitting room. Racks of *tironas* lined one wall, shelves and cabinets on the others, and the furniture was plain, serviceable wood. I dropped into one of the chairs. We hadn't been out in the courtyard long, but it felt like I'd been standing for hours.

Cor swept another low bow. "My guest, Katherine Kjelgaard. Kate, this is Seretun, my instructor as I was growing up."

The middle-aged man snorted. His strong features had lost their sternness, though the air of authority he wore seemed as much a part of him as his red hair. "I could still teach you a thing or two, cub. I will, if you ever make me sound that old in front of a lovely lady again."

"Pleased to meet you," I managed, too relieved to blush. "Thank you for not being mad."

Seretun chuckled. "Considering the circumstances, I believe Coran may be forgiven." He leveled his gaze at Cor. "As Biren will be, too."

Cor looked to me, a question in his eyes. "If Kate wishes."

"I forgive him, of course," I said.

"Your generosity speaks well of you." He took another measuring glance at his student. "Try to nudge Coran in that direction, if you can."

"I don't know anyone more generous than Cor," I said.

Cor bobbed an ironic little bow to me for that and settled in the chair next to me.

Seretun took one opposite and raised his brows at Cor. "Then tell me, peerless emblem of generosity, what's your plan from here?"

Cor dove into the conversation like they'd merely paused in the middle. "If the Scholars destroyed information about humans, as Issai claimed, then that explains my failure at the Lore Hall. I might check the private collections among House allies."

They discussed some options, names and Houses I didn't know, sources of information that might be worth investigating. Tired as I was, I stayed quiet and let their voices flow around me. What I did catch from it was that Cor had been on this mission long before he'd approached me, and his teacher seemed to know all about it.

Things would have been so different if I'd believed all along. That thought led me to another, hopefully more productive one. When I caught a break in the conversation, I asked, "What about Shom, would she know anything?"

"The Lan girl?" Seretun asked.

Cor moved a hand in agreement. "She may have come across the odd bit of human lore by chance. Did you ever write to her?"

I opened my mouth to say *no*, but it turned into a yawn, so I just shook my head.

"Where are your manners, Coran?" Seretun used his armsmaster glare. "She's going to fall asleep in her chair before you can get her back to her House."

"Cor's not my...my *babysitter*," I protested, tumbling out of Kuyene into English, too tired to find the right word in time.

Cor, who knew the word perfectly well, muttered—also in English—that it was clearly past my bedtime.

Seretun tilted his head. "And that means?"

"It's not Cor's job to look after me." I tried to concentrate on the armsmaster and not let my gaze stray to Cor. "The fact that he's helped me so much is a blessing and I'm grateful to have such a loyal friend, but he's not my nursemaid." *And shouldn't be my guard.*

"I imagine not." Seretun chuckled. "Well said, Katherine. I would hate to see all my good training go unappreciated." He stood and offered me a hand up. "I look forward to more visits."

"Thank you," I said, nodding. "Me, too."

I didn't remember he wouldn't recognize the gesture until Cor and I had already slipped back home.

"Sorry I almost got you involved in a duel," I said, feeling for the light switch in my dark living room.

"A fight with Birasef would hardly count as a duel." Cor snaked an arm past me and flicked the light on. He steadied me with a supportive hand on my elbow. "I should have slipped you back here to rest right after the healing. It affected you more strongly than I realized."

I shook my head. "You're not my babysitter. Didn't you hear what I just told your teacher?"

"Ah, but did *you*?" He kept most of the smile off his lips, but I saw it in his eyes. "Help from a friend is a blessing."

"I'm glad you thought it was funny," I said, mockingly stern.

"So if you have a friend who knows the steps to this dance, it falls to him to lead you." He demonstrated by steering me toward my bedroom. "I'd forgotten what it's like to have a serious healing for the first time, but I can do my best to make up for it now."

"All this talk about dancing." I hid another yawn as he turned on the bedside lamp. "Do you dance like you fight?"

"I don't try to embarrass my partners, if that's what you mean."

"No, you were...great." I'd started to say 'beautiful.' Maybe he was right and the healing had temporarily stolen my good sense. I sat on my bed and leaned down to tug at my shoelaces. "One of your cousins called it dancing."

Cor knelt, batted my hands away, and started picking at the knots.

"Training with the *zaret* is like a dance, I guess. Done to a pattern, with each step taken the right way in the right order." He tugged off one shoe and set to work on the other. "I'm counted pretty good at dancing."

"Which kind?" I grinned at him, thinking of his sparring match.

He grinned back, near enough that I heard the laugh hiding beneath his breath. "Both, actually."

"I thought you didn't have a girlfriend."

"Dancing with a girl doesn't make her a *nochel*, and I have never done more than that." He freed the second shoe and tilted his face up to meet my gaze. His eyes caught the lamplight and I wondered if hypnotism might be a Thurei skill. "For instance, I have never kissed."

"Me, neither," I whispered.

"Never?"

If I hadn't yawned then, I might have made a much bigger fool of myself then I had in the healer's. When I looked up again, Cor was halfway to the door.

"Where are you going?"

"To keep watch," he said, his hand on the knob. "The air might do me good."

"Cor, stay safe."

Not that he needed the reminder that there were monsters out there.

"I promise," he said, and the door clicked closed.

CHAPTER TWENTY-FOUR

I took a long, sober look in the mirror at the new, pale scar stretching across my back the next morning. The price of my disbelief, and I'd been lucky to get away so lightly. At least I would be safe until sundown.

My phone rang while I was pouring water into the coffeemaker. I fished it out of my pocket. "Hello?"

"Hey, how are you feeling?" Rose asked.

"Good. Uh, considering."

"Do you feel up to some visitors?"

"Sure."

She must have heard the hesitation in my voice. "It's just me and Troy and Ryan. We won't stay long and we're bringing get-well-soon presents."

"Oh, wow. Sure. I mean, thanks."

"Okay, we're at the curb. We'll be up in a sec."

Somehow, I should have expected that. When I opened the door, Rose entered chair first. On the stairs behind her, Ryan and Troy balanced a circle of wood that I could only imagine was a tabletop.

"Most people bring flowers. Or a card." Even I knew that. You could get cut flowers in the ward, so long as the vase wasn't breakable.

Rose nudged me aside with the chair legs. "How long have you lived here?"

"Um, four months." And sixteen days. Some hours. I'd never felt freer than when I'd signed the rental agreement.

"Then it's about time you had some real furniture." She plunked the chair down. It had simple lines, with straight legs and a high, curving back. The dark finish was scuffed in places, but it looked sturdy. "There. Get well soon."

"Thank you." *If you only knew.* Rose hadn't known me for years. We'd barely known each other any time at all. Tears prickled at the corners of my eyes. "This is wonderful."

"That's the only answer when she gets like this," said her boyfriend, as he and Ryan negotiated the doorway. "You may have noticed she's kinda bossy."

"Hey, if you've got the skills." Rose shrugged. "It's only yard sale stuff, so don't get too excited. I'd have taken you down to pick up a set yourself, but I thought you probably wouldn't be up to it." She paused and looked me over more closely. "You're looking pretty good, though."

"Thanks. I've got good pain pills, so I slept well," I lied, reluctantly, and retreated to the kitchen. "Anyone want coffee?"

To general agreement, I fetched down four mismatched mugs and poured.

"Hey, did you do this? It's pretty good."

I turned to find Ryan holding a sheet of paper over by the card table. I went over to find the sheet covered with doodles. So Cor must not have spent the entire time out in the cold. He'd finished the jigsaw puzzle, too.

"No, a friend of mine stopped by last night," I said, trying to run the scenario through my mind before I let it out of my mouth. "He must have done it."

I recognized the sign of his House and a few words in his tidy Kuyene handwriting that looked like subjects to pursue in those private collections he'd talked about with the armsmaster. He'd written a few other things in the looping, tangled Thurei script that I'd never learned. The names of those allies to check with?

"Is this in, what, Arabic?" Ryan's brows drew down. He tapped the clusters of Thurei. "These look tribal. Is he a tattoo artist or something?"

I shook my head. "No. He must have just been bored."

"Here, with you?" Ryan dropped the paper back on the card table. His smile had an edge to it. "So, talented but not very smart."

He said it like I should take it as a compliment.

I didn't. "He's brilliant. I was sleeping at the time. That's hardly his fault."

The look on his face soured.

"Ryan, you're supposed to be moving that," Rose said behind us. "We've got the table legs. You want it in the same place, Katherine?"

"Yeah, that's fine." I retrieved Cor's paper from the card table and Ryan lugged the table over to the wall. Troy produced a screwdriver from somewhere and set to work assembling the new table.

"I'll get the chairs." Ryan disappeared out the door.

Rose brought over my coffee. "That's what guys are for, doing manual labor while we supervise."

"I heard that," Troy said, laughing.

She nodded her head at the paper in my hand. "He's talented and multilingual, this mystery friend of yours?"

I shrugged. I could acknowledge I wasn't crazy, but that didn't make Cor any easier to explain to someone on this side. "You could say that."

"That was nice of him, to stay with you. I didn't even think how freaked out you must have been after that. Want me to stay over tonight?"

"Thanks, but I think I've got my evenings covered for a while."

I forgot how far Rose could stretch a single scrap of drama. "That means you and Mr. Ghost-from-the-Past are getting along again, huh?"

Behind me, I heard Ryan set down a chair and close the door. His footfalls clattered back down the stairs.

"He's just being a good friend," I said. "Not that it's any of Ryan's business."

Rose scooted over one of the new chairs. "Ryan's a nice enough guy, but it's not like you promised him anything."

Troy tilted the table up onto its legs and waved her over. "Come on, busybody. Help me move this."

Once the table and chairs were arranged to Rose's satisfaction, they took their leave. Ryan was polite but not particularly friendly.

Rose was right. I hadn't promised him anything.

"I thought I slipped over to the wrong place."

I turned from the stove to find Cor looking at the new table. At least he wasn't talking about the cooking. I returned to the cookbook I'd gotten from the library last week. "It was a gift."

"A fine gift. How did you get it up all those stairs?" He pulled a chair over to the edge of the kitchen, since the space was too small to hold more than one person at a time. Especially if there was cooking going on.

"It took three people, but Ryan and Troy did most of the heavy lifting." I tasted the tomato sauce, added a little more salt. "Rose was shocked when I told her I'd had a boy stay over."

It shocked Cor, too. "You told her about me?"

"A little bit. Not enough to sound insane."

"Of course not." He sat silent for a moment, frowning, and I thought he was working out exactly what and how much I might have said. I was wrong. "Why should she be surprised if you have a guest stay the night? You may have a *nochel*, if you want. If this Rose is your friend, she should be glad for you and not judge."

"Ha. Are you kidding? A boyfriend is the last thing on my mind. And Rose would be delighted, by the way. She tried to set me up with Ryan."

"Ryan the table carrier."

I looked at him. He looked back at me, the neutral-polite that Thureis specialized in.

"That smells delicious, by the way," he offered.

"Thanks. It's just spaghetti. I'm making it out of a book." I leaned against the counter, glad to be off the boyfriend topic, and waited for the sauce to thicken as promised.

His orange brows drew together and he repeated the sentence. "You're making it out of a book?"

The image of a plateful of pages drizzled with tomato sauce popped into my head and I laughed. "No. I'm using a cookbook. It has instructions on how to make food. That's all. I never learned to cook before."

"Ah." He paused, maybe contemplating the wisdom of withholding knives and open flame from mental patients. "I never learned to cook, either. May I see this book?"

I handed it over. While he flipped through it, I stirred occasionally, as the book instructed. Half to himself, he said, "Perhaps I could find something like this on my side. I have no idea what most of these ingredients are."

The water in the second pot came to a boil and I added the noodles. He flipped the book shut, then crossed his arms on the back of the chair, setting his chin on his wrist. I had the urge to brush his vivid orange hair off his forehead, though the effects of the healing had worn off by morning. I concentrated on dinner.

"I heard from Shom." Not in a good way, by his tone of voice.

"What'd she say?"

He took the kind of deep breath that meant he was busy editing his words. "She might help us, if you talk with her."

"That promising, huh?" I thought of Shom as I'd last seen her, furious at my insistence they leave me alone. I couldn't blame her. I'd betrayed her friendship.

"We can make the round of House libraries, if you wish, but we may have luck with Shom. She is a—in English, a maker? A crafter?"

I'd been to the county fair a couple of times growing up, but I didn't think he meant that sort of crafting. "What is it that she makes?"

"The common kind of skillwork requires the right materials and form as well as the focus of your *jeira*." He paused until I nodded. "Shom works to find out what those materials and forms are."

"So she's a scientist?" I asked, trying to picture it. "Or a magician."

"Scientist, if you must call her something."

She had always hated it when I used the word 'magic' in connection with Kuyen. *It's hard work, not wand waving*, she'd say, serious about it even then.

"Thanks for the tip. You really think she'll help us?"

He held up a small metal trinket. "She sent a token, so she must not be too angry."

"Okay." I would give it a try, even if I didn't think much of my chances. I pulled two plates from the cabinet. "Are you hungry?"

He scooted the chair back to the table and I joined him, glad of Rose's gift. He watched me twirl the long noodles around my fork before trying it himself. After swallowing his first bite of spaghetti, he said, "This is excellent. I've never had anything like it."

"Thanks. It's just a cookbook recipe." Still, it was nice. I'd never cooked for anyone before.

CHAPTER TWENTY-FIVE

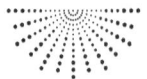

Shom's token brought us to a plain alcove, set in a larger room that looked—and I'd never tell Shom this—exactly like a wizard's, packed with books and bundles and tools and *stuff*.

"It was much easier bringing you across this time," Cor said. "Yesterday, too."

"The medications are probably out of my system by now."

He lifted his eyebrows at that, but Shom walked in before he could answer.

"The fool and the faithless," she said, just as pleased as I expected.

Nothing else about her was what I'd expected at all. If not for her voice, I wouldn't have recognized her. From what Cor had told me, I'd expected a grown-up, geekier version of the slim, curious child I'd known. Instead, Shom the Adult looked like she could tear phonebooks in half. She was shorter than me but had a burly, broad build and her glossy, black hair was drawn back in a serviceable ponytail. The gray skin of her hands and forearms bore marks that looked like burn scars.

She leaned against the open archway of the alcove, arms crossed. "You came back. Why?"

"I told you why," Cor said, keeping his voice soft.

"You know, I can still read after all these years." She barely glanced at him. "I wasn't asking you. I was asking Kate."

Shom had no patience for dissembling, so I didn't try. "A Hirach attacked me. There's nothing like a mess of stitches to make a person open their eyes, right?"

She wasn't having humor, either. "Why did you let those people tell you we didn't exist?"

With Cor, apologies held a power all on their own. With Shom, only the facts mattered, but the facts had become shifty, changeable things.

"Everyone here can worldwalk. There's magic here. Yes, okay, not *magic*. Skill, *jeira*, whatever you want to call it. On my side, there's nothing like that. Kuyene has a word for crazy." It was an insult, not a diagnosis. "On Earth, that's what they call people who see things others don't. You remember how my parents acted when I told them you were right beside me."

"You could see us. So what if they didn't?" Shom had never been uncertain of her own opinions.

"But everyone reacted the same way." I spread my hands wide. "I was twelve and everyone said I was seeing and hearing things that didn't exist, or things that weren't what they should be. I'm sorry I believed them, Shom. I know I was wrong, but when dawn came, you and Cor left and I was stuck in my world with them."

She mulled that over for a moment, then said, "Tell me why this Hunter attacked you. A single Hirach is not beyond Cor's abilities. I'm still not clear on why he couldn't handle it."

"We had an agreement," I said softly, wishing I could leave it at that. "I thought I was still hallucinating and I just wanted to be sane again. His end of the bargain was to stay away. He wasn't there when the Hunter showed up."

"Is that so?" She raised a brow and looked at Cor. "She kicked you out again?"

I found Shom a hell of a lot more intimidating now than she'd been as a girl, but Cor met her gaze without hesitation. "I was never in. You'd understand, if you'd stayed."

He'd played the diplomat between us often enough as kids, but it didn't work now. "I thought for certain he convinced you." Shom narrowed her dark eyes at me. "But you made him leave when he got in your way and now you're in trouble, so you called him back for his trusty service again? I'm not so easily led about as Cor."

"I'm not trying to lead him around!" I took a deep breath and forced my volume back down. "Or you. If I'd known what was going on, I'd have told him to stop." I'd been the worst kind of burden and never known it. Thinking of the things he'd said at House Pareshol, I shook my head. "I want to be able to keep myself safe so no one else has to. I'm not here to take advantage of anyone."

She looked over at Cor, whose face had gone impassive, then back to me. "Okay, Kate. If I can help you, I will, but I won't put myself in the Hunter's jaws for you when you wouldn't do it for us. In return, you sort this out as quickly as you can and cut him loose."

"I plan to," I said. "I don't want him stuck with me any more than you do."

"Enough," Cor said, his voice hard. "Shom, if you're willing to help, then help. Stop playing games."

"I'm sorry, Shom," I said. He shouldn't have had to be the one making a case here, forever coming to my defense. "I would do this on my own if I could, but I can't. I don't want to be a burden to either of you."

She grunted and turned to Cor. "You were coy over what Issai told you. What is this skill you need me to teach her?"

"She said the human boy could unmake things with his denial. He came by it through a mixture of training, physical trauma, and grieving." From his pocket, he pulled the rock half he'd taken from Issai's wasteland and passed it over into Shom's broad, gray palm. "He had never worldwalked before. The crossings killed him, before he learned control."

Shom shot me a glare. "I'm surprised you didn't get rid of us sooner, then."

"I never wanted you and Cor *gone*. I just wanted to be normal." I sighed, tired of everything being a fight. "Maybe normal's overrated."

Shom tilted her head in acknowledgement but moved us back to the task at hand. "Have you checked the Lore Hall yet?"

"Years ago," Cor said. "But the Scholars removed anything useful."

"Hm. What did you look for?"

"Humans. Earth." Cor's fingers rippled in a self-conscious shrug. "I didn't find much."

"Amateur." Shom shaded the word with a hint of teasing, so at least she didn't hate Cor. "All right. We'll start there."

Worldwalking was the only practical way for us to get to the Hall, so I slipped us to my apartment long enough for Shom to take us back over to our destination.

The Lore Hall looked more like a postcard cathedral than any public building I'd ever seen. Pale gray stone had been carved into fluted columns and arches, covered in twining, abstract organic shapes that reminded me of vines or tree branches. It was huge. I stared. "This is the library?"

Cor glanced down at me and grinned. "Of course."

Of course. Why not?

I grinned back. "That's a lot of books."

"Perhaps some of them have answers for us," Shom said, leading us up the steps to the massive, open doors.

The inside was in keeping with the outside. Bookcases stretched a full two stories high, beneath an arching ceiling. I couldn't guess how many floors might have been above. The shelves held books, no surprise there, but also metal-banded boxes, chunks of stone, carvings, even a bleached skull, and other things I didn't recognize. Here and there, members of Kuyen's various races sat or strolled between the shelves.

The main hallway led into a circular hub. A crescent of low shelving filled with thick, leatherbound volumes lined the walls.

"The catalog," Cor explained as Shom headed for it.

We watched as she pulled out a couple of volumes and stacked them on top of the shelf. She opened one and started flipping through pages. She paused to glare up at us. "If you want to help, you can start searching for entries under 'inherent skill theory.' Checking on '*jeira* development principles' would help, too."

Cor pulled a volume over, turning it to face us. "Would you take this one? I will fetch the next."

I looked at the colorful, angular Kuyene script stamped on the cover. "I can't read this."

"Not the formal script?" He ran a slender finger over the imprinted letters.

"No, just the handwriting. From notes and things."

"Well, of course. When would you have had the chance to learn?" It was a rhetorical question. He flipped the book open and started scanning the list of entries. Shom, at the other end of the shelf, had a slip of paper out, making notes.

I leaned against the shelf, feeling like a third wheel. An illiterate third wheel. The three of us hadn't been together in years and things had been so different then. Shom was helping now, but I didn't confuse that with forgiveness.

"Here," Shom said, holding a slip of paper out for Cor. "Why don't you find the ones on this list for me and grab whatever else you've come up with? Be useful."

"When am I less than useful?" Cor mused, easy as if we were still grade schoolers goofing around in the Kuyene afternoon. He raised a brow at one of the titles on the list. "*Hunter Survey*? I have a copy of this in my rooms, Shom."

She snorted, not even looking up from the catalog volume. "Kate can look at the pictures."

Ha ha. Very funny.

"Come with me, Kate?" he offered.

Shom answered for me. "No, she can stay here."

He slowed on his way to the door. I could understand not wanting to leave me alone with *Denet* Pareshol, but Shom?

"The quicker you go, the quicker you'll be back," she said, sounding just like a mom.

It worked. He left.

"What was that about?" I asked.

"Would you rather wait to show me your scar when he gets back? I got the distinct impression that you two weren't that way."

"He saw it at the healer's already." At the moment, we were the only ones in the catalog room. I turned around and lifted my shirt high enough for her to see the scar across my back.

"It's not that bad. I got worse in training with the *tol*'s troops, before I settled on skillcraft."

"I got lucky," I said, tugging my shirt back down. "That Hunter would have killed me if he'd been a couple of minutes earlier."

"What are your people thinking, to keep themselves so defenseless?" Shom drummed her fingers on the pages in front of her. "What happened, exactly? Firetop's note was short."

I told her.

"The healer said there was a corruption in the wound?" She looked concerned for the first time.

"I think that's what he called it." My memories from right after the healing fuzzed at the edges. At the center of them, I mostly remembered holding on to Cor. My cheeks heated just thinking about it.

"Well, you know how to pick an enemy," Shom said, hopefully not noticing my blush. "If the Hirach could set a corruption into the wound that fast, then we're not talking about some low-pack growler."

"What does that mean?" I asked.

"He didn't even tell you that much?" She slapped a hand down on the polished tabletop. "What good does he think it's going to do, refusing to tell you anything?"

"He's not refusing to tell me," I began, but Shom glanced past me and I turned to find Cor in the doorway, his arms piled with books. He looked like he'd just found a hungry tiger behind door number three.

"How is it," she asked him, enunciating every word with precision, "that you have not explained to Kate more about Hunters? Don't you think she deserves to know?"

"Ah. Hunters. Of course." He cleared his throat, set the books down next to Shom, and came back to me. "I haven't told you more about Hunters because you already know enough to worry you and we've had little time for lessons."

"It's okay, Cor. Shom, leave him alone."

"Come on, you two." She grabbed the list she'd been working on and waved us toward the aisle. "Let's find someplace to sit. Carry those."

Shom led us to a smaller room and Cor set his stack of books at one end of the table. Commandeering that end, she waved us to the other. She lifted one of the smaller books and held it out to Cor. "You have plenty of time to explain it all to her now, while I'm going through these ones. Unless you have something else you want to talk about?"

"Hunters it is." Cor took the book and sat next to me. He flipped it open, then paged through until he came to a detailed illustration of a Hirach. "Greater Hunters. The one we saw at the Scholars' Hall, Tharkesh—he would be the Finder for their tribe."

"You came across him at the Scholars' Hall?" Shom asked, from behind the barricade she'd built of opened books.

"As we were leaving," Cor said. "He was on his way in. Why?"

"Odd that his folk would send a Finder to the Hall, that's all. If they needed a question answered, they could have sent someone with a lower rank. A Finder," Shom added, directing the information toward me, "can cause a level of trouble that would test even Cor's skills."

I looked at him, chilled by her casual warning. He gave me a little shake of his head. "A Finder can call his own pack on a hunt, that's true. But you likely injured him slamming his hand in the door. He'll have to wait until he heals to continue the Hunt."

"Unless he gets it healed," I said, imagining mobs of the monsters breaking down my flimsy apartment door.

"Healers won't treat a Hunter." Cor set the book aside so he could face me squarely. "I swear to you that I will keep you safe until you're able to defend yourself."

"But Shom just said—"

"Shom doubts my abilities."

"No." Shom cut in without looking up from her book. "Your abilities are well known. I doubt your sense."

I expected her dig to wind him up again, but he just grinned. "You're not the only one."

"Maybe he'll lose interest and leave me alone," I said, not wanting to sit here and listen to her rag on him.

"I think she means the Hirach," Shom pointed out, and Cor rolled his eyes.

He shifted his chair, turning a little away from her, and tugged the book closer. "Hiraches take trophies. You'd be valuable to this Hunter, if he thinks you're dangerous."

"And if he doesn't? What if we made him think I'm harmless? That shouldn't be hard."

Cor flicked the possibility aside. "He's already on the Hunt. He'd kill you regardless and count you as easy prey."

"Don't forget, Cor's been brought to his attention, too," Shom added. "He'd would make a worthy trophy for any Hunter."

I looked at him, but a quick flick of his fingers undercut her concern.

Maybe he was that confident, but it was starting to seem a lot more like he was just trying to reassure me. Shom wasn't the type to overstate a danger. "Can they follow you back to your House?"

"No Hunter is mad enough to attack a full House of Thureis," he assured me, and that sounded logical, at least.

"So you'll be safe, once I'm trained and you can stay home."

He looked back at the Hirach illustration. "Yes."

One problem solved. Whatever reputation Cor had accumulated for himself while acting as my protector, it wouldn't endanger him once I got out of the way.

That only left all the other problems. I sighed. "I just have to make sure I don't go insane in the meantime."

"I thought we were past that," Shom said, eying me over her stack of books. "You said the doctors were wrong. That's the only reason I'm here."

Well, that's good to know. Out loud, I said, "The Scholars told us that humans and Kuyen don't mix well."

"They're right, to a point," Shom said. "Slip your mother here and I doubt she could handle it. Kuyen is something she can't bend her mind around. But you're not blind."

Cor frowned. "Why would the Scholars say so, if it's not the truth? They're Sheverns."

Shom rested her elbows on the table. "Tell me what they said, exactly."

So we told her about the visit to the Scholars' Hall, as verbatim as the two of us could manage. Then, under the microscope of Shom's follow-up questions, we went through the conversation with Issai, as well.

"If Issai's right, the Scholars deliberately erased the truth," Shom pointed out when we were done. "That removes it from the reach of all Kuyenes."

"More than that," Cor said. "They lied about what Issai discovered. That's the worst crime, for Sheverns. Their memories are their skill. Information is the only thing that matters to them."

"Then why tell us at all?" I asked. "If it was important enough to lie about it, why did they end up sending us to Issai, if she'd gone into exile for refusing to hide the truth? They could just have told us she died or something."

Shom cocked an eyebrow at Cor. "Threw your weight around, did you, Houseboy?"

He spread his arms out and leaned back in the chair, emphasizing his slender build. A *denet's* heir, if he'd remained one, would have had a different type of weight than that, though. I tried not to think about it.

"It was more like stalling than arguing," I said. At the time, I'd chalked it up to hallucinations. Those didn't have to make sense. But now... "Then we met the Hirach outside."

Cor met my gaze, his amber eyes gone as hard as chips of yellow glass. "They asked what overland route we would take, too. I told them exactly how we planned to get there, and we tripped over Hunters every step of the way."

"Don't gut yourself on this one," Shom said. "The Scholars have based their reputation on being trustworthy. Maybe they buried the truth about humans if they thought that information was too dangerous to spread. But you're implying they sent Hunters after you. They're Sheverns, Cor. They're fact keepers, not blood spillers, even by proxy."

"Perhaps I'm trying too hard lately to find meaning in things where there isn't any." Cor rested his chin in his palm, eyes focused beyond us. "I do think Issai told us the truth. Worldwalking and the exercise of his skill killed the boy she told us about."

"He saw his family murdered in front of him," Shom said, as blunt as ever. "And ended up on a world he'd never seen. He didn't know what he was doing. I don't think it had anything to do with him being human, beyond that. Even the worldbound on other worlds at least know there are other places out there."

What Shom said tracked fairly well with what I'd been thinking. I'd grown up believing Kuyen was real and the pressure of everyone around me denying it had still been enough to make me agree with them. I'd refused to believe what was in front of me. What would it have been like for that boy to be dropped into such a strange place in such a horrifying time?

"I think you're right," I told her. "He never had a chance to believe what he was seeing."

"You do, though," Shom said, before turning her attention back to her research. "So don't waste it."

I glanced over to find Cor watching me. I whispered, "I won't."

He flicked me a smile.

While Shom went through her stack of books, leaving once to gather some more, Cor covered the basics of Hunters and some of the more common ones. Lesser Hunters, like the Wogra, were opportunistic predators and often solitary. Greater Hunters like the Hirach were more intelligent, strategic planners and selective in their choice of prey. Though the Truce and other pressures from the other peoples of Kuyen had reduced the practice, the more vicious among the Hunters all preferred sentient prey, for status, or power, or the challenge of it.

"Why have the Truce anyway?" I asked him. "Why don't the rest of the Kuyenes wipe Hunters out?"

"They are thinking beings, Kate. We defend ourselves, but slaughtering an entire people would make us no better than they are."

"Right," I said, since he looked so scandalized, though it still sounded like a good idea to me.

"Okay, students," Shom said, saving me from a response. She set the book she'd been looking through aside. "I think we've got enough to start. I've written ahead, so we can use the trials arena."

CHAPTER TWENTY-SIX

C or volunteered to slip us over to my side so Shom could take us back to the arena.

The murmur of waves reached my ears and my shoes shifted on soft sand. I opened my eyes to a view of the ocean, silvered by moonlight. Beyond the beach, a cliff rose thirty feet high. A tenacious pine clung to the edge, defying gravity and the wind that pulled at its branches.

I could almost be convinced my own world had turned into something fantastic, if not for the faint smell of gasoline beneath the salt scent of the sea, or the soda can half-buried in the sand near the high tide line. The rumble of traffic carried on the breeze.

"Where is this?" I asked him. I didn't believe he'd slipped us here at random.

"Not far from Bayshore."

"Oh." I could imagine him walking there in the beginning, after the arguments we'd had. Or later, when I'd refused to acknowledge him at all. While he had stood on the beach beneath the stars, I would have been asleep on my hard hospital bed, drugged for insomnia, with no view out the barred window but city walls. "It's beautiful here."

"Sightsee on your own time," Shom said, pulling us back to Kuyen.

The trials arena was a large, empty building, with a floor of loose sand. Thick, metal bars crisscrossed the walls, set into the plaster in a pattern that reminded me of prisons. Crafted with dampening effects, they were perfect for containing the destructive force of experimental skillwork gone wrong, Shom explained.

"In a way, everyone begins the same," she said. "Underneath the trappings, it's all *jeira*. We should be able to make this work." She pointed toward the middle of the space. "Kate, you head over there. Cor, you need to wait outside."

"I prefer to stay," he said, in the same tone someone might use to say they preferred the onion rings to the fries.

The kind of tone that took acquiescence as a given.

Shom wasn't having it. "It's not safe. She won't be able to control herself while she learns."

"Katen won't hurt me."

He planned to use my don't-send-him-away promise to the fullest extent of the law, I could tell.

"That's some optimism you have there." Shom glanced over to me, but when I made no objection, she just pressed her fingers to her temple for a moment. "Fine. You want to stay, you put your back against that wall over there. Got it?"

"Isn't this just as dangerous for you?" I asked her, tucking my cold hands in my pockets as Cor walked toward the edge of the arena. Somehow, I'd imagined we could do this in a way that didn't endanger anyone. Maybe that was naive.

"No one's found a major skill that will affect a Lan te Kos, not on any world. We can use minor skillwork, but Thurei swords will not cut us. Gorvas can't put their fear in us. Don't be the exception, and we should both be fine. But Cor will be safer if he leaves."

I shook my head. "That's up to him. He wanted to stay."

"If only the two of you could get your stubbornnesses pointed in the same direction. But that's your problem." Shom led me to the center of the arena and then sat down in the sand, cross-legged. "Lie down."

I settled myself in the sand.

"Shift around until you're comfortable."

I wriggled my shoulders and hips until the loose earth molded to my shape and tried not to think of it working its way into my hair.

"Roll your head until you feel the exact angle it joins your spine. Now your shoulders, until the shape of the muscles is perfect, your shoulder blades flat beneath you. Now your hips... Now your spine..." Shom tweaked my posture, until I lay perfectly aligned in the cushioning sand. All the tiny distractions of my body—things I hadn't consciously noticed until they'd been gone—faded away.

Shom's voice, soft and insistent, became the flow of my thoughts. "Find the place in you that feels the edges of this world, the place where you focus when you worldwalk."

I searched and found it.

"Don't pull, as you do to slip across the gap. Push. Gather the power there so it doesn't spread out around you any longer."

I tried, imagining curling myself up tight to hide away. Long moments ticked by while I struggled to do as she said. Finally, I sighed. "I couldn't do it when Cor tried to teach me, either. He said to sharpen my focus and make it...thinner, somehow."

"He was teaching you the way he was taught, like a Thurei. The basic principles are the same, but the details make a difference." Shom tilted her head to the side, rubbing her chin. "How about this instead? That space inside you is a room. Imagine yourself standing there. That's your space. That's you, your center, where your *jeira* lives and where you work your skill. You're the only one with a key and you can come and go whenever you want. When you want to, you can gather your *jeira* there to conceal it from Hunter senses. Try that."

The plain white walls around me and the lock on the door didn't take any imagination at all. I knew all about these kinds of rooms. For a moment, my heart kicked up a beat, but I took a deep breath and concentrated on the rest of what Shom had said.

This room belonged to me. I held the key to it. I could stay or leave when I wanted.

"Good job, Kate," Shom said, real approval in her voice. "At first, it will take effort to stay there, but you need to practice until it's second nature. Until you can do it in your sleep. You'll need to, if you won't have Cor there. Now, sit up and open your eyes. I'll be right back."

Shom came back to sit beside me, holding a clay sphere about the size of a softball in her hand. She placed it in mine.

"Feel the weight of it. The texture. Color. Close your eyes again."

I let my lids drop. The ball felt heavy in my hand, gritty and dry. In my mind's eye, I could see the reddish-tan curve of it in the paler curve of my palm, all in perfect detail.

"Kate, there is nothing in your hand. The ball I gave you does not exist, has no weight, no shape, no texture. It is illusion, it is imagination, it is air."

The weight in my hand did not shift, nor did the image in my mind. The sphere's solidity belied her words. I imagined Issai's clearing, Cor's half a rock.

I peeked, but that just confirmed what my hand was telling me. I had a big clay ball in my palm.

"We could try trauma if you want," said Shom, dry enough to spark.

"No, thanks." I closed my eyes again. Tried to imagine my hand empty.

No luck. I thought of the story Issai had told, a terrified boy fleeing from murderers, finding himself suddenly in the middle of a wilderness. I tried to think of it as he might have, a waking denial of what he'd seen. I visualized the ball in my hand fading away, as if it slipped from one world to another, only I let it slip into nothingness. I opened my eyes to see the last of the clay melting in my hand, flowing through my fingers, disappearing before the dust hit the dirt floor.

I let out a whoop of triumph. "I did it!"

"Not yet you didn't. A clod of dirt is a far cry from a Hunter leaping at you. Wait here." Shom headed for the wall across from the door. On it hung several racks. From one she selected a long, wooden rod like the *tironas*.

"Shom, what are you doing?" I couldn't see Cor's expression from here, but his alarm came across plain enough.

"Kate didn't come here to learn picnic games. She came to survive a fight. Or do you want the Hunters to eat her up next time? We have a healer here, for non-Lan. Grant me the ability to avoid breaking things if I try."

Cor said something too low for me to hear.

She laughed. "As easy as the Hunters will."

I eyed her as she came back, swinging the *tirona* idly, Barry Bonds on his way to the batter's box. Standing seemed like a good idea.

"This stick is not real for you, Kate. Concentrate on that space inside you." Then she swung it at me. The blow glanced off my forearm as I flailed away, turning three of my fingers numb. My feet tripped up in the soft sand and I fell hard.

"Again. Focus, Kate."

"No." I rubbed the throbbing ache in my arm. "How can I stay focused when you're trying to hit me?"

"You can think and move at the same time. And I can hit you down there just as easily as I can when you're standing, and you'll have a lot less chance to dodge. Just a friendly piece of advice, but I'd get up if I were you."

She didn't look like she was kidding. I got up.

"This stick," she repeated, "is not real."

Just like worldwalking. Concentrate. I ducked beyond her reach and the stick hummed past my shoulder. It wasn't real. *Not real, not real—*

Pain, as the end of the staff caught me in the ribs. I dropped to the sand. My body curled itself into a little ball without any prompting from my head. I may have groaned.

"Again."

"Shom!" Cor called. Merciful Cor.

"Catch your breath," Shom told me as she walked away.

I could hear them from where I lay. I didn't bother to roll over to look. Didn't know if I could.

"What are you doing?" Cor kept his voice low.

Shom, not particularly. "She's here to learn. Sometimes learning hurts. Believe me, I can appreciate the irony."

"Don't hurt her just because she hurt you."

"I don't forgive the way you do."

"If you'd stayed, you would've seen what it was like for her. Then you wouldn't judge so harshly."

Shom chuckled. "Who says I'm judging harshly? You should see how *I* was trained."

When she strolled back over, she offered, "Want to try the clay ball again?"

Like hell. I climbed to my feet, fumbling for that mental space. *My skill. This is me.* "Again."

She smiled and swung at me.

Not real not real not real not real.

My shoulder.

Not real not real.

My thigh.

Not real not real not real.

My stomach, which left me gagging and struggling for breath on the sand.

Not real not real.

A smack across my butt, meant to humiliate instead of hurt.

Not real not real not real.

My hip.

I rolled over to get to my feet again. I stopped when Shom pointed the end of the very hard, very solid stick an inch from my nose.

"Kate. For you, this stick is not real. Come. I know you've practiced."

She didn't mean this session, here.

"My bruises will be real in the morning," I muttered.

"Yes. And your scar."

I held up my hand and she granted me a pause while I closed my eyes and searched again for the place she'd taught me. I spun it into an image of the ward, Dr. Vargas peering over his notes at me. *These things you claim to see aren't real, Katherine. You must realize they are not consistent with reality.*

I opened my eyes. Shom swung, overhanded, her weight behind it. I ducked, knew it wasn't enough. She'd still hit me. I braced for the blow, eyes squeezed closed.

"It's not real!" My words rang out against the wooden walls, the echo of a memory of the ward, drugged and desperate, unable to believe anymore.

No pain. When I opened my eyes, the last of the stick drained away through Shom's fingers. She wore a smile as hard as the *tirona*. "Good, Kate."

I straightened from my crouch, trying to slow my heartbeat down.

Shom turned toward the door, instructing over her shoulder, "You'll need to practice. I haven't the time to work with you more, but you've got the basic feel for it. Cor can guide you beyond that. Careful you don't dissolve him."

When she reached him, she held out a hand to stop him on his way toward me. "Don't overlook the cost of this, Coraven. She's dangerous. You'd better be sure of what you're doing."

"I am." He bowed, holding it long enough to show deep gratitude.

"Fool. Watch yourself." Then she was gone.

"Do you want a healer?" Cor asked when he reached me.

"No, they're just bruises." I remained grateful for Havro's work, but I didn't want a healer inside my skull and skin again if I could help it. This session with Shom had been unsettling enough.

"You must be tired. We can continue tomorrow."

My gaze flicked involuntarily to the rack of sticks.

"I wouldn't hit you, Kate."

"Not since we've grown up," I replied.

"Ah. Well." He offered me a slim smile. "I mean, I wouldn't train you Shom's way."

I sighed, stretched my stiffening muscles. "Okay, you've got a deal."

CHAPTER TWENTY-SEVEN

W e slipped back to my apartment in the wee hours of the night. I settled into one of the new chairs carefully, out of respect for all my new aches.

Cor sat across from me. "How bad is it?"

Dark, spreading blossoms of pain across my skin everywhere Shom had caught me with the stick. "Not too bad."

Cor pressed his lips together, but he didn't mention the healer again.

I shrugged with the shoulder that had escaped the beating. "How is it that you don't hate me like Shom does?"

"She doesn't hate you," he said. "Shom's never been a forgiver—"

I flicked my fingers at him and he stopped evading.

"I could never hate you. I admit, it hasn't always been easy to understand why you would believe people who were almost strangers over us and the evidence of your own eyes." His voice held a ghost of the frustration that had flared between us so many times over the last couple weeks. I couldn't blame him. "But I know you didn't want to send us away. They made you. It was different for Shom. The Lan te Kos...do not bow. They have their own leaders, of course, but they have nothing like Houses and *denets*. A son of the House must learn to bow." He added softly, "I know what it's like, to face another's insistence and have no power to deny it."

He didn't say it in anger, or as a complaint. He made the statement a simple fact, an answer so I would understand.

I studied him, wondering how much of an act he put on to show a calm face. "You don't always bow to your *denet*."

"And you are here now," he said. "So you don't always bow, either."

Like my return was a triumph of will rather than a panicked defeat. I changed the subject. "What would you be doing now, if not for me?"

"If we never met? Much of what Damen does now, as *denet*-heir. She joins our father at high council meetings. She sits with him when he hears matters of the House." He twisted his lips into a wry smile. "You saw how pleasant Thurei politics can be."

"So you don't miss that. What else?" I tried to imagine Cor seated in some sort of ostentatious, formal hall, surrounded by Thureis in fancy dress and serious expressions. Mounds of paperwork around, no doubt.

He'd probably be good at it, even if he didn't like it.

"I already train some of the youngers with the *tironas* as part of my House-debt," he said, continuing to paint a picture of his alternate life. "Perhaps I would have more students. Of course, I have nineteen years now, so I'd be married to Turavi. I've heard being a husband can be something of an effort in and of itself. I believe it, if Turen is the wife."

I didn't like hearing the intimate form of that woman's name in Cor's voice, but I tried to keep that opinion off my face. Instead, I said, "I doubt things would be as dull as all that. Some part of it has to be better than pulling guard duty all day."

He traced the woodgrain on the tabletop with a long finger. "I have never seen the sea on my side. I could go, of course, but somehow I doubt it would be the same."

"No fast food wrappers or soda cans," I said. *No girl stuck in a psychiatric ward, refusing to see you.*

Cor laced his restless fingers together and looked at me. "Believe it or not, there are some things more amazing in your world than could ever be in mine."

"Like what?"

"I have found some humans to be quite remarkable." He said it airily, like a joke.

"Oh, yeah?" I laughed, playing along. "How many humans do you know?"

"Not many," he admitted. When I raised a brow, he added, "Just one."

"Coran—" I had to clear my throat and start over. He'd never lost faith in me like my parents had, or given up on me like Shom. "Thank you for everything you've done for me. It's good to know that I always had someone who believed in me." I felt guilty as I said it because I hadn't done the same for him. I'd done what I could. "Things will be better once we're done with this, right? Your *denet* won't be so mad at you?"

He twisted his lips into a bitter smile. "Have no fear on my account. I can bow as low as a *denet* could wish."

"I never meant to get you in trouble."

"You didn't. I told you, Kate, it was my doing, not yours. My vow cannot be unmade. But I have grown too big to spank." Making a joke of it, again.

You're not too big to be disinherited, little comic, I thought darkly. Instead, I found myself saying, "I'm glad you don't have to marry that Pareshol woman, at least." And, on the heels of that surprise, I added, "And I'm glad you aren't still angry with me, like Shom."

I must have been too tired to properly edit my tongue.

"We never held grudges, you and I," he said.

I nodded, trying to stifle a yawn.

His bright brows drew together. "You used a lot of your energy. Your skill will always tire you some, but especially in the beginning. You should sleep."

"But—" I meant to live up to some sort of standard as a hostess, but Cor cut me off with a wave of his hand.

"It's afternoon on my side and will be first light here soon. I'm not tired at all."

I slept better, knowing he was out there.

The next day, when Cor brought me back to his House, I opened my eyes after the crossing to find us in a room lined with shelves full of folded cloth. Some trunks stood against the wall.

"I thought you might appreciate more appropriate clothing," he said, counting up and across the shelves for a particular cubby. He pulled out a stack of folded clothes. "Here. It's training clothes, so yours will stay in better shape."

"Wait, I thought you weren't going to be hitting me with things."

"Have faith, Katen." Cor pointed me to a changing room. I bit back my curiosity.

The bundle proved to be a shirt and a pair of pants made from a sturdy, pale fabric, like I'd seen the students wearing in the courtyard. The outfit had a straight, simple cut, suitable for Thureis, who didn't tend toward curves. Cor had found a set more or less big enough for me. By the breadth of the shoulders, it was probably a men's size, but the laced closures were moderately forgiving. I had to roll the sleeves and pant legs up several times. But they would work.

Cor took a couple of lumpy sacks out of one of the trunks and we went out into the courtyard. He picked a spot beneath the lattice, a little distance away from the other students, and set the sacks on the ground. He gazed up at the framework above us a moment, then leaped into the air and caught the edge of the wooden screen with one hand. As agile as a gymnast, he swung and twisted, flipping himself up and onto the roof. In a heartbeat, he was kneeling at the edge, holding out his hand. "The bags, please."

I heaved the bags up one by one, grateful he was able to catch my clumsy throws. Other students near us cast furtive glances our way.

Some of them were adults, but some boys and girls were young enough to be in elementary school. At best.

"Do all Thureis do this?"

"Train? Of course." He carried the bags away from the edge, chose a spot by some criteria known only to himself, and knelt again. "It's our duty to be ready and able to defend the House."

"I thought you said most Thureis never face a Hunter."

"Ready in principle, then." From the bag, he began pulling out pouches roughly the size, shape, and color of plums, each wrapped in a long cord. He lowered one through the lattice, tying it off with the string. "Tradition has a long memory and at one time, House Temarel stood as a small place alone in the wilds."

"Plus it keeps you in shape for dueling," I added, remembering what Birasef had said. "Which you don't do."

He chuckled, glancing down at me through the gaps between the wooden slats. "Why should I? My honor stands in a safe place."

It must, if he was that good of a fighter. A master, his cousin had said. "Why didn't you just beat Birasef then and be done with it?"

He paused in his odd task long enough to shrug, a ripple of purple-tinted fingers. "He wanted a lesson, so I gave him one."

"It wasn't to show off, then." I said it straight. I knew him well enough to know the answer.

"I never show off."

Yep.

"There," he said, tying off the last string. He had made a small galaxy of the spheres, a filled circle about ten feet across, the pouches irregularly spaced, varying in height from about even with my shoulders to a few inches off the ground. He dusted the violet powder from his hands, walked to the edge, and jumped lightly down to the packed earth floor. He came to my side and showed me his palms. Purple pigment clung stubbornly to the creases. "Your job is simple. Get to the center of the circle without getting any of this on you."

"Okay." Sounded easy enough. I took a step toward the circle he'd made.

"Not so fast," he said, with an easy laugh. He walked through it first, set the weighted strings to swinging. I couldn't imagine a way through the swinging pouches without getting covered in the purple powder. "This teaches your mind and body to work together, until physical movement and the concentration on your skill both become reflex."

I must have looked skeptical, because he added, "Half my clothes were purple when I was learning."

"Half your clothes would still be purple unless you cut them all down."

"You think so?" Cor's brows lifted and his eyes sparkled with challenge. He shifted his attention to the maze made by the swinging pendulums, considering them for a breath or two. Then he stepped into a momentary gap. He bent, twisted, evaded one, another, a third, as they swung past. A half-step sideways brought him into another brief space. Here, he was trapped, but his *zaret* flashed in his hand, severing the string of a pouch he couldn't avoid. The blade disappeared in the next instant and he moved again, dodging and swaying, pausing and advancing, his movement supple and as light as a feather caught in a breeze.

A final hop brought him face to face with me, grinning in a refreshingly full-of-himself sort of way. He wasn't even breathing hard.

This was my Coran—easy, confident, and proud of his abilities. I grinned back, enjoying his display as much as he'd enjoyed performing it. Still, I couldn't let him get away with too much. It might go to his head. "You never show off, huh?"

He laughed. "Should I have left you thinking I asked the impossible? It's your turn."

"Okay, okay." I studied the movement of the pouches, looking for a path like Cor had found, but it all seemed like chaos to me. I closed my eyes, reminded myself that they weren't real. They didn't exist, if I didn't want them to. I could walk right through an empty circle, and...

The courtyard went quiet. I opened my eyes. The pouches and strings were all gone. So was a sizable circle of the lattice.

"Well, it worked." Cor's voice seemed loud in the silence. "Perhaps we should start with something else."

"I'm sorry." I forced the words out of a dry throat. The damage to the roof was bad enough, but I was terrified at the fact that I'd done so much by accident. What if someone had walked past?

"The whole point of training is to make mistakes," he said, calm as a comment about the weather, but I remembered how rattled he'd been by the barren clearing in the wildlands. I could end up doing that to his House by mistake. My stomach twisted at the thought.

Cor turned and I followed a shift in the direction of his gaze to find the scarlet-haired armsmaster making his way toward us through the ranks of stunned Thureis. In quick English, he said, "Remember, you don't have to apologize."

Great.

Cor greeted Seretun with a low bow. "Katherine has come for training. As my student."

"Is that so, Katherine? Do you stand as Cor's student while you stay here?" The armsmaster had the stern, appraising look of teachers everywhere.

I tried not to feel like I was ten years old again. Was being Cor's student better than being a guest? I didn't know what the difference was, but Cor had suggested it. I trusted him. "Yes, I do."

That seemed to satisfy him. He waved a hand at the circle of sky showing through the damaged lattice. "So this is the human skill?"

"It is. I..." I swallowed the 'am sorry' and recovered with, "I'm new to it."

He studied the sunscreen a moment longer. "Quite an ability to wield. It's good humans are so rare here. Katherine, I hope to never find you my enemy. Still, I would not expect to find anyone less impressive in the company of my finest pupil."

The armsmaster shifted his attention back to Cor and I hoped my relief didn't show. "But a wise teacher knows his student's limits. Other grounds might be more suitable for now."

"As you say." Cor bowed again, in gratitude.

"I look forward to your progress, Katherine." Seretun nodded to me. "I'll be glad to have you back in the courtyard as soon as you're ready."

The armsmaster turned back to our impromptu audience, barking something in his native tongue. The courtyard jumped back to life. Cor translated for me. "'Those caught standing still fall to the next move.' Come, let's practice somewhere else."

CHAPTER TWENTY-EIGHT

Cor's "somewhere else" involved threading back through what felt like half the House, then out the other side. I stepped through the final door into a small, lush space like a gazebo, one of a linked set, shaded by a pole roof overgrown with vines—leafless now this deep into Kuyen's autumn. Potted plants crowded the corners and a row of palm-like vegetation divided this room from the next ones. To the left, I glimpsed a blue-tiled pool and fountain. Cor headed to the right, down a couple of stone steps, brushing aside the tendrils of an evergreen creeper.

He paused, looking back at me as I dawdled. "This whole side of the House is divided into...rooms of plants? Garden spaces? It's beautiful in summer." He waved a hand at a bare-branched tree pruned along wires to screen off the next room. "This one bears red flowers like flames. They flicker and you can even blow them out, but they don't burn. You'll like them."

My heart stuttered over the next beat. I *could* visit this place in summer. Because it was real and would turn through the seasons like any other place. And because, even once we finished this and Cor would be free to pursue the life he wanted, we would still be friends. He would still be part of my future. I had to have faith in that.

I smiled back at him. "I'm sure I'll love them."

We wound our way through the interlocking spaces, tending generally downward, away from the House. There must have been at least a dozen rooms, growing wilder the farther we went, until we walked through exuberant planted beds bound by nothing more structured than gravel paths.

"Where are we going?" I asked, not that I minded the detour, per se.

"We'll try something different. I still think the *esepras*, the moving targets, have much to teach you. For Thureis, they come between the *tironas* and sparring *zarets* against another opponent. Your skill is very different from mine, though. Your instructor must widen his imagination. Do you remember the meadow?"

"Where we played tag? Of course. That's here?"

Shom and Cor had brought me to all sorts of fascinating places, showing up at night after my parents had gone to sleep. World-walking made sneaking out of the house ridiculously easy, but it also meant I had memories of a range of places without any clue how they all strung together in real space.

"It is safe here, for children," Cor explained. "It's all Temarel land. The climbing tree is here as well, but I would rather that stay intact. Here we are."

We came to a trellised arch in a tall hedge. Beyond it spread a broad meadow filled with tall grasses and other plants. There were few flowers this late in the year, and the grass wasn't so high as I remembered, only about up to my waist. Tall enough for children to run and duck to the ground, hidden from sight.

Somewhere beyond, though, Temarel lands stopped and the wilds began. "What about Hunters? Couldn't they sneak in?"

"We have patrols," he said. "They're an important part of the House duties. I've done my fair share of them."

I could imagine, with as much fighting practice as he'd had. Maybe that's where he'd learned to ride so well.

Cor stopped just past the hedge and turned to face me. "Will you walk with me?"

I didn't mind the idea in theory, but I still ached from my bout with Shom yesterday and we both had reasons to hurry and get my skill ironed out. "Sure, if you'll explain to me how that's part of my training."

"It would be more pleasant if we had a path. Can you do that?"

"What if I can't control it, like inside?" How large a sphere had I destroyed? Ten feet? Twelve? "I don't want anything to happen to you."

He watched me closely. "Will you hurt me, Kate?"

"Not on purpose. I didn't wreck the lattice on purpose, either."

"Here." Cor took my hand, holding it between his calloused palms. "I'm real, aren't I?"

It seemed impossible that someone like him was real. He was the cocky boy I'd tried to forget. He was the deadly fighter who'd fought off monsters to keep me safe. And somehow, he was also the man who stood before me, still afraid I would refuse to acknowledge him.

"You're real," I whispered.

"Just as a reminder." Cor laced his fingers with mine. "I'm not afraid of your skill."

"I could vaporize you by accident." I tightened my grip on him when he shifted his weight to begin walking. He waited. "I know you like a dare, but this is serious."

"I take it seriously. Come, Katen. Walk with me."

He could make his own decisions. More than that, if I was going to learn, I should trust him to pick the lessons. He believed in me. Maybe I could believe in myself. I let out a slow breath and concentrated on the grass in front of us. *Just the grass. Just here.* I imagined a path clearing before us, as if I had an invisible lawn mower.

The meadow obliged. Cor squeezed my hand and grinned down at me. We walked, the path clearing a few feet ahead of us. Cor steered us in an arc to the left.

After a minute or two of silence, he said, "Taking a dare was the best thing I ever did."

The path-clearing stopped, my concentration broken. "What do you mean?"

Cor looked meaningfully at the grass ahead of us. "You have lost your grip. How did Shom say it? The space she told you to make. You're outside it. It gets easier with practice, but for now, you have to concentrate."

"You distracted me," I grumbled, but I focused back on the space inside me that Shom had described.

"I promise I'm less distracting than Hunters," Cor replied gently, but he stayed silent until I could clear a path through the grass for us again. When he resumed his train of thought, I managed to keep my concentration steady, though the width of the path wobbled. "How else do you think we ended up in your father's garden that night?"

"Who dared you? Shom?" The path before us narrowed as I shifted my attention to speaking. Heavy autumn seed heads brushed, tickling, against our hips. The path stopped completely. I groaned.

Coran laughed and tugged lightly on my hand. "Patience, Kate. Soon enough, you will be able to walk and have candy."

That broke my focus again for a moment, but then I figured it out and started the path up again. "You mean walk and chew gum at the same time?"

"Yes, that." He grinned. "It was Shom's older brother who dared us. He didn't expect me to stray that far from my *denet*'s gaze. No Thurei would have made a dare like that."

"So you've been a rebel from the beginning."

He just laughed.

His confidence was contagious. I could feel it in the light clasp of his hand in mine, his easy stride as we walked a path I'd cleared with the focused power of my disbelief. We meandered in curves and switchbacks, some route of Cor's devising, and he told me about the dreadful trade luncheon, where a young *denet*-heir was expected to be quiet and polite even if he was bored out of his mind, and then the wonder of finding my family's nursery lot, a tame wildland all tidied up in rows on the other side of the gap. And hiding in the middle like it was her very own House, a little girl who shouldn't have been able to see him—but could.

The sun crept low in the sky by the time my path flagged beyond my ability to restart it. I stared at the grass before us, silently pleading with it to melt away, but nothing happened.

Cor's fingers tightened on mine and he coaxed me to turn back the way we'd come. "Look at how much you've done already."

The arch in the hedge was a distant shadow. The trail I'd cleared wound and zagged through the tall grass. Near the gate, it looked like a line painted by a clumsy child. Farther along, the path grew steadier as my control improved. The pattern of it tugged at some buried memory and I squinted. "You wrote something. In Thurei."

"*You* wrote your name." He pointed to parts of the knot-work path. "Well, *Ka-the-ri*. The final consonant was meant to curve a little beyond us."

I blinked at him. It was hard to concentrate on anything, after the unfamiliar strain of using my skill, so I couldn't figure out why it warmed me to know he'd walked us in the path of my name. Maybe anyone would have done the same, given the unusual opportunity, as he had doodled his own name sitting at the table in my apartment.

A thought made me giggle. "I just graffitied my name in your *denet*'s field."

He grinned back. "I see it as my duty to keep things interesting for my *denet*. Only children come here, really. My cousins will enjoy your path. If any of them read it, they'll hardly be surprised. Let me take you home. You need the rest. Tomorrow's lesson will not be a stroll through the meadow."

CHAPTER TWENTY-NINE

The next morning, I decided I needed more practice and I needed to get some breakfast. Or dinner. I would really need to do something about this schedule when my medical leave ran out. Luckily, the diner near my apartment had the same menu all day.

Before I left, I gathered a notebook, a couple of loose sheets of paper, and a blank square of stationery Cor had left on the table. I stuffed it all in my backpack and headed downstairs to get my bike.

While I waited for my sandwich, I jotted down some notes about what steps Shom had led me through to center my concentration, what it felt like to shift myself over the gap between worlds, and use my skill.

Then I experimented. I made one small pile of pea-sized paper balls from a strip of printer paper and a second pile from part of the thicker stationery. The waitress glared like a school teacher as she set down my plate, likely annoyed at the mess she thought I'd leave. I smiled my sweetest and she went away.

I mixed the bits of paper together until I couldn't tell which were from my side, which from Cor's. I spread them out on the table's surface and closed my eyes, finding the place Shom had shown me. I pictured the scraps on the table. *None of you belong. Go away.*

Only half of the scraps remained. I unrolled one to confirm that they were the cheap copier paper from my apartment. So my skill would work here, even in the daytime, but I could only affect things from another world. If I faced a mugger, not a Hunter, I'd be out of luck.

For trial two, I tore the rest of the stationery into little squares. On six of them I penned an 'X' and arranged them all in a grid. I'd practiced my control in the meadow, but I needed to do better. I didn't want to vaporize any of those stick-wielding Thurei kids.

Good thing, too. On my first try, I disintegrated the entire upper corner of the grid for the sake of one marked square. Like yesterday's practice hadn't even happened. I thought of Issai's dustbowl and shivered. *I have the atomic bomb of defense skills.*

I tried again as I ate my sandwich. And again. Gradually, the circle of destruction grew smaller until the only square that disappeared was the one I'd intended.

After I paid the bill and turned for the door, I heard a couple of waitresses whispering about me. I didn't know how my experiments had appeared to them, but it was clear they thought I was nuts.

I headed for my bike, suddenly queasy. As much as I'd been through lately, as certain as I was about the evidence of my own senses and experience, I still lived in a world where Threis and Lan te Kos and Hunters didn't exist and the only people with secret powers were characters in comic books.

As long as the sun was up, all that was true.

I had decided to believe, and it had been easy with stitches in my back or Cor's hand in mine.

In the future, I would be careful to practice at home.

I'd meant to run some errands, but Cor was right about how tired my skill made me. It seemed to use an absurd amount of energy, although maybe it was harder to do on my side or during the day. I didn't have enough experience yet to judge. Either way, when I got home I crawled straight into bed.

I dreamt I was back in the hospital.

A knock on the door woke me. I didn't even open my eyes. The nurse would come in for bed checks whether I spoke up or not. Sure enough, the door swung open. Footfalls came toward my bed. Paused.

"Katen?"

The sound of Cor's voice unmoored me. Not the hospital. I snapped my eyes open to see a dark form in a dark room. Icy fear raced up my spine. I gasped, flinched, and Cor spoke up again. "Kate, it's me."

"I was dreaming of the hospital." My voice shook. I took a deep breath and let it out. "What if I forgot and believed you weren't real?"

A pause. "Then I will work on being unforgettable."

"It's not a joke! I'm afraid. What if I did something—"

"You wouldn't. You would never. You will be safe and well and the Hunters will never be able to touch you again. Things will be well." Clear-sighted in the dark, he covered my hand with his own.

I took another deep breath. "I hope you're right."

"I am. I promise."

He'd claimed to be unafraid of my skill. I was terrified.

Back at House Temarel, the training clothes fit perfectly. Cor shrugged it off, claiming that the House tailor would be mortified if they didn't. Someone had patched the hole in the lattice, but we used a corner well away from the rest of the students.

After the first couple of hours, I looked like an eggplant, my clothes dyed purple from the powder in the swinging *esepras*.

"It'll get easier," Cor assured me, hauling himself up to reset the pattern.

I managed not to destroy any more of the building, but control didn't have much to do with it. I waffled back and forth between nuking all the targets at once or not getting my skill to work at all.

When it became apparent I wasn't going to unmake the scenery, Cor drafted a student from a nearby instructor. The boy looked to be about eleven and stared up at Cor with undiluted hero worship.

"Fosemur, I need someone to sit on the roof and tie on *esepras* for my student. Will you help us?"

He bowed his agreement, grinning like Cor had offered him a job as a ninja space cowboy.

"Oh, no," I said, killing his smile. I winced and switched to English. "He could get hurt or worse around me."

"You've improved quite a bit. Fos is old enough to decide for himself."

"That young?" I asked, surprised.

Cor switched back to the common tongue. "There is danger, cousin. You saw—"

"Let me do it, then," someone offered from behind me.

I turned to find Birasef, all decked out in training clothes. Cor narrowed his eyes like he was waiting for an unpleasant punchline.

"I don't have any control yet," I said. "I might hurt you by accident."

"Precisely why you would rather see me up there than little Fosen. Or Coraven for that matter." Birasef shooed the boy back to his instructor and turned a sunny smile on me. "And this way, your teacher can spend more time on the ground with you."

"You helped enough, thank you," Cor said, pushing him back toward the exit.

Birasef eeled around him and dropped into a ridiculously low bow in front of me. "I'm in your debt for my insulting behavior the other day. Allow me to repay you with general helpfulness."

"You, helpful?" Cor nudged him off-balance.

Thurei boys. I rolled my eyes at both of them. "Wouldn't it just be easier to apologize?"

"That would imply I have something to be sorry for." Birasef refused to put the smile away.

I tried to hold on to my stern expression. "Either you insulted me or you didn't."

"Ah." Birasef splayed a long-fingered hand over his chest. "I certainly did, but the circumstances were different. That changes things."

He hadn't had his dignity handed to him in front of half the House, he meant. "Then yes. When you put it like that, I think you'd be perfect up there."

Cor sighed. "Well, get up there, then."

I expected trouble from him, but Birasef stayed quiet while we worked. At first, my fear of hurting him by accident—in spite of his attitude—kept me from using my skill at all. Cor noticed. His instructions grew more demanding, daring me to get past it.

He wasn't the only one who had a weakness for dares.

Between the mental focus, trying not to trip over my own feet, and the endless stream of directions from Cor, I often forgot there was anyone up on the roof at all. By the time Cor called a halt for a late lunch, I'd made real progress.

Birasef dropped down beside us, clapping a cloud of purple dust off his hands. "I'll get us something to eat."

"No need for that," Cor said, but Birasef had already jogged away.

He only went far enough to snag a student who'd just finished her own lessons. He gave her a quick order and sent her off. Probably to the kitchens in his stead.

"That's how you get lunch?" I asked Birasef when he caught back up with us.

He rippled his fingers in a shrug. "I did my share of fetch and carry when I was her age."

"No need to eat with us," Cor said. "I imagine your mark is holding a table for you as we speak."

"And leave you and Katherine in your rooms for the afternoon?" Birasef quick-stepped to the door ahead of us and held it as we walked through, as if he did mean to double down on his claim of helpfulness. "You just put those rumors to rest."

Cor glared. "None of this is yours to worry about, Birasef."

"Actually, it's fine," I said. Rumors from House Pareshol? I would bet Turavi was behind those. If Birasef's presence would at least not make things any worse, I'd take it. Even if Cor wanted to pretend it didn't matter. I changed the subject before he could argue. "What's a mark?"

"You met them the other day," Birasef said.

"A 'mark' is an age group," Cor explained. He mimed a gesture like my dad measuring my height against the door frame. "It comes from being all the same size."

"I thought it came from always picking the same thing to mark us out as unique." Birasef grimaced. "We had a set of House coats made in that awful shade of teal when our mark was younger."

Cor chuckled. "It served you right when your parents all made you wear them until you grew out of them."

He must not have been too annoyed about having an unwanted lunch guest.

"You didn't have one, Cor?" I asked, trying to picture his candy corn hair paired with a teal coat.

"Of course not," Birasef answered for him. "Cor always went his own way. He cut his hair."

Now that he mentioned it, I couldn't recall seeing any other Thureis with short hair. I hadn't realized it was unusual. Coran had always worn his orange hair in a long braid when we'd been little.

"That must have been a surprise," I said, wondering why he hadn't grown it out again.

"Not as much as you might imagine," Birasef said.

"Ah, here we are." Cor interrupted, hurrying us a couple of doors farther along the hall. He swung open the door and let us into his sitting room. "There's a washroom, Kate, if you'd like to clean up."

By the time I'd washed off the last traces of stubborn powder and changed back into my own clothes, lunch had arrived. A tureen of thick stew and a loaf of bread flecked with herbs waited on the table.

"I can take you back after lunch," Cor said, handing me a bowl and a slice of the bread.

"You should stay, Kjelgaard," Birasef said. "With as many Hunters as you met in the wildlands, you'd be better off here. No Hunter would move against the House."

Cor seemed to take this as a slight on his skill. "She would be perfectly safe in her own home."

"She would be. I don't doubt it for a moment." Birasef looked at me. "But what about Cor?"

No question, the House would trump my apartment for safety. Cor wouldn't have to keep watch and there'd be no possibility of a fight. "It's okay. I can just stay here."

Cor flicked his fingers. "Ignore Birasef. It's safe enough on your side."

"Is it as safe as staying here?" I asked him.

Cor glared at his cousin a moment before admitting, "No."

"Then I can stay here until sundown," I said. "I mean, if that's okay."

"Of course it is," Birasef assured me, grinning like he'd won.

Cor muttered something I'd never gotten a proper translation for growing up.

Birasef laughed. "Better than what they call me in the courtyard now, after the little lesson you gave me."

It was an obvious setup, but I was curious, so I asked, "What do they call you now?"

"Puppet. It shortens nicely." He waited, green brows lifted.

"*Shesof*, in Thurei," Cor explained for me. "*Shesan*, if you made a close-name of it."

That one I got, a child's word for a personal bit of anatomy. I bit my lip to keep from laughing. Thurei honor could be a tricky thing.

Birasef flicked his fingers, not at all offended. "I thought you knew Thurei."

I shook my head, then remembered to copy his gesture instead. "Just a little. That's why we're talking in the common tongue."

"I thought it was a courtesy," he said. "Since I don't know any human."

"English," I said. "There are a lot of human languages."

Birasef waggled his hand in a ridiculously overdone shrug. "Whatever."

Cor pushed his bowl away. "Lunch is over, Birasef. Thank you for your company."

"I would be happy to give you language lessons, Kjelgaard." His cousin smiled like Cor hadn't spoken. He clung stubbornly to the friendlier mode of address, too. "Let Cor handle the courtyard training. I doubt either of you would trust me with that. But there are some things that can only be said properly in Thurei."

There was a thump. Birasef jumped and looked at Cor, his golden eyes wide.

So did I. "You did not just kick him under the table."

Cor shrugged, human-style. "He needed it."

I sighed and rubbed my eyes. Hours of concentration and skill-work, a full belly, and I couldn't remember how many days it had been since I'd had a proper night's sleep. While it was entertaining to see Cor spar again with his charmingly exasperating cousin, I was one good yawn away from nodding off at the table.

"I can teach Katherine, if she needs to know Thurei," Cor said firmly. He pushed his chair back from the table and offered me his hand. "Let me find you a guest room."

"No, that's okay. I'll sleep when I get home." I'd had enough of Thurei guest rooms. Cor's sitting room had a bench seat with cushions. It didn't look particularly comfortable, but it would work. "Maybe I'll just lie down and close my eyes for a few minutes."

"On that?" Birasef raised his emerald brows. He hadn't moved from his chair. "Use Cor's bed."

"No," Cor said, too fast to be simple disagreement.

"Not that again," I said, glaring at Birasef. He might have been annoying Cor, but he'd been growing on me. "I thought you were nice."

He widened his eyes. "How am I not nice?"

Cor shot him a look. "Mean and stupid are two different things."

"Well, don't be stupid, either," I said, out of patience with the whole thing. They'd been sniping at each other when we'd walked out of the healer's, but I thought they'd gotten friendlier since then. If Cor wanted to excuse him, I would let it go. I pushed a couple of stiff throw pillows against the carved, wooden arm of the couch and stretched out.

Birasef raised his voice a little and dialed up his innocent tone along with it. "Would it be stupid of me to suggest you get her a decent pillow and a blanket? Or is that going to land me in the circle with you again?"

"No, it's okay," I said. "Really."

But Cor had already disappeared through the door to what I assumed was his bedroom. He came back with a bundle of bedding.

"You would be more comfortable in a guest room," he said quietly, settling the blanket around me.

"I don't mind it here." I burrowed my face into the pillow. It smelled like him. "I can't leave you and Birasef alone. What would happen to your reputation?"

As soon as I had my eyes closed, Cor started a conversation with Birasef over at the table. In Thurei. Though they kept their voices low, I could tell they argued. Maybe I could ask him about it later.

Whatever it was, a knock at the door silenced them both. Cor got up to answer it and his greeting sounded surprised. "*Denet.*"

My eyes flew open. Birasef still sat at the table, though his relaxed posture had been shocked as straight as a soldier for inspection. Cor straightened from a deep bow in front of the open door and then gave ground as a man strode in and glanced around the room. He had a cobalt-colored braid and dressed as formally as anyone I'd seen since House Pareshol, in a richly embroidered jacket over a cream-colored tunic, perfectly tailored midnight-blue trousers, and soft, black leather shoes that looked made for walking around on carpets all day.

The shape of his brow, the line of his mouth, the angle of his jaw, even his general build, all spoke clearly to the blood he shared with Cor. But while Cor's slender frame held the grace and power of a warrior, the *denet*'s thinness and the sharp-edged planes of his face gave him an air of asceticism.

He said something to Cor in Thurei. The most I got from it was that Cor's dad called him "Coraven" even in the privacy of his own rooms.

I sat up, running my hands over my hair, trying to straighten my clothes. Not that it would do much good, since the *denet* had already seen me when he'd walked in. The phrase 'get caught napping' had never sounded so daunting.

Cor answered his father, his tone formal, his words clipped.

The *denet* switched to the common tongue for his answer. "If I wanted to see you, I would send for you after sunset, as usual. I'm here to meet the guest of the House I've been hearing so much about."

He walked past Cor over toward me, his expression forbidding.

I stood hastily, balling up the blanket—Cor's blanket—and stuffing it on one end of the couch. My cheeks burned. Was sleeping in someone's blanket worse than being offered a guest room?

Cor stretched his long legs to catch up. He offered the standard greeting I'd become familiar with, the words spilling together in his haste. "*Denet* Temarel, I make known to you Katherine Kjelgaard. Kate is here as my student."

"You've come here as Coraven's student?" Temarel asked.

"Yes, and thank you for your hospitality," I said, trying to imbue my voice with the proper amount of respect. I might not have thought highly of the man after everything I'd heard, but Cor still had to live here. "Cor—Coraven's been teaching me to use my skill to defend myself. I'm lucky to have his help."

The *denet* turned to Cor. "I've heard Seretun claiming the same thing. You've been too busy to take students of your own House, but now you're turning your oath into an excuse to make a spectacle of the training courtyard. You've neglected your own duties for years. Don't entreat your kin to do the same."

"Excuse me, *Denet*," Birsasef said, popping up from his chair to sweep his own respectful bow. "Cor has offered all appropriate courtesy due a guest and all guidance fit for a student. I can attest to that myself." He stretched his smile wider. "And as to the spectacle, I believe the lesson he gave me was well-earned and efficiently taught."

"It was my fault," I interjected. Not an apology, but nearly. If the *denet* was going to be angry with someone, it needed to be the right person.

"I'm well aware," the *denet* said, his tone sharp.

"My temper outdrew my sense, I admit—" Cor began.

The *denet* cut him off with a flick of his fingers and pinned Birasef with a glare. "Your concern for Coraven's reputation does you credit, but if there's a flaw in his honor, it doesn't rest in the hands of his kin. Now, if you have other business to attend to, I recommend it."

"Gladly, *Denet*. If I may be of any further service to the House, I stand ready." Birasef's second bow was deeper, and he hurried out without a backward glance.

As soon as the door closed, the *denet* rounded on me. "What is your purpose here, outworlder? Why come to my House now? Does it amuse you to give Coraven a shadow of the life he could have led, after keeping him away from it for so long?"

"N-No," I stuttered. His words cut, and I had to suppress the urge to wrap my arms around myself in defense. "I never wanted any of that to happen."

I couldn't mention that I'd never known Cor had been protecting me. Cor took such care talking to people about us, I had no desire to spill any of his secrets in front of this man. I didn't have to guess how he would wield that knowledge. Maybe he hadn't specialized in the *zaret* like Cor had, but he wasn't without weapons.

Surely, he knew that Cor had protected me from Hunters, though. This was his own House, and even the Pareshols—hell, even the Scholars—had known that.

I forced my shoulders square. "I'm here to get the training I need to defend myself. I will forever be glad to Cor—Coraven for all his efforts on my behalf, but I want him to be free to live his own life."

"What Kate intends to—" Cor began.

"She was quite clear." The *denet* pressed on. "Katherine Kjelgaard, you have no place as a guest in my House. You have forfeited your *dacha* rights here and receive no welcome. On Coraven's behalf, I will permit you to finish your training here, provided you act with propriety and refrain from disturbing the House. In exchange, you will release him from any further obligation to you and return his dedication to the House."

Did I just get kicked out? I pressed my hands to my thighs to stop them from shaking. But at its heart, this was the same course Cor and I had already agreed on. Once I was trained, he wouldn't have any obligation to keep me safe. He would be free to live his life the way he wanted. To have the life he should have had, if not for me.

I had hoped I could visit him here afterward, but if this made things easier between Cor and his father, then I'd take it.

"Of course," I said, at the same time Cor said, in English, "Don't."

Startled, I looked over at him. He held himself so stiffly, I worried he'd snap. "You promised not to send me away again."

"Coraven," his *denet* snapped. In his mouth, Cor's name was a rebuke.

This wasn't the time to pause for casual asides, but I muttered a quick, "I'm not doing that."

Cor jumped on it. "*Denet*, with all gratitude for your offer, we must decline the hospitality of the House. Kate will retain my vow and train elsewhere."

"She's given her answer already," the *denet* snapped. "You're not in the position to deny her. Hasn't that been the theme since you swore your vow? She wants no part of being your *dacha*. Your vow is meaningless."

"Wait," I said, cold creeping up my spine. Cor had said he'd sworn a vow that had broken his engagement. He'd lost his position in his House and the future he might have lived. But he hadn't told me what the vow had been. I couldn't ask what *dacha* meant. Not here. I stalled. "I'll need time to consider it. This is an important decision."

Why hadn't he told me? *What* hadn't he told me?

The *denet* cut his gaze to Cor. Though he lacked the warrior's bearing of his son, the *denet* wielded his words as sharp and precise as any attack of Cor's. "You said you would decline the hospitality of your House if Kjelgaard retained your vow. For once, we're in accord. Kjelgaard will reject you, or your House will. Kjelgaard, you have ten days to consider your answer."

Cor looked gutted for an instant, but utter fury scoured it away. He bowed, mechanical as clockwork, and when he rose there was no expression on his face at all. "As you say, *Denet* Temarel."

"Very well," I managed because the *denet*'s piercing stare required some answer from me.

I'd been right at Issai's: I would ruin everything here. As soon as Cor's father left the room, I dropped back down onto the couch, my legs too weak to hold me. "What did I just do?"

Cor pushed aside the blanket and sat beside me. "You stepped into a battle that you didn't start, with no protection. I'd thought he'd be gone longer on House business, but it seems Damen is handling this one. Forgive me, Katen. I should have brought you home."

He'd tried to, but Birasef had talked him out of it. No, he'd talked *me* out of it, as a way to keep Cor safe.

"Forgive you?" I echoed, shaking my head. "Just tell me what's going on. You *wanted* to stop being my bodyguard. That's why you came back in the first place. That's why you left that note on my doorstep. Why did you just tell me not to release you from that?"

"It's complicated," Cor began, but he didn't continue. Instead, he said, "I'll speak with him tonight. He's been threatening to expel me for years. I told you, I can bow when I need to."

I shook my head. I couldn't afford to let him shield me from this, if that was what he thought he was doing. "You said *dacha* was a vow. What does *dacha* mean?"

"It *is* a vow." Cor leaned forward to put his elbows on his knees. He laced his long fingers together and stared at them. "I swore to set you first, above everything else. If you were in danger, my duty before every other duty was to keep you safe. Even the *denet* didn't have the authority to stop me." He gave me a bright-eyed glance, but his gaze slid away again. "I couldn't leave you to die, Katen, not if I had the power to do something about it."

"And you can't have a wife because Turavi won't stand for you spending your days guarding another woman?"

Cor shifted to face me fully, letting me see him. Making me see him. "I can't have a *helon* because *helons* are arrangements made for children and alliances, but each person must still answer to their House. They usually end the union after a time and return to their kin, as my mother did. But a *dacha* is heartkin, more than a *helon*, more than blood or House, dearer to me than my own skin, Katen."

"You..." Every event of the last few weeks flipped on its side. But I could see the truth of his words in his face. I could see everything in his face, now that I looked. "You said it was an insult for people to think we were even *nochels*."

"It's an insult to be called your bed-friend when you're my *dacha*." He took my hand lightly, as if he expected me to pull away at any moment.

I folded my hands over his, unable to ignore the callouses years of training had given him. A *denet*'s hands wouldn't be marked like this.

"I can't let you be thrown out of your House." Not after everything else. I'd done enough damage.

"You promised you wouldn't send me away again." His eyes held mine, golden and intense and so different from anything I knew.

"Why didn't you tell me?"

"I meant to, when you were ready to hear," he said. His fingers were cold. "A month ago, we sat in that restaurant and you...you closed your eyes so you didn't have to see me. I thought if I told you, it would be the end of everything."

"It's not the end." I made my voice firm, though I didn't know where to take things from here. Coran was right. Two weeks ago, I'd thought he was a hallucination, a tempting fabrication of my own mind. A couple months ago, I'd thought of him as little as possible and considered it a success if I didn't think of him at all.

One thing I was sure of, though. "It's time to tell me all of it. No more holding things back."

"Past time," he agreed softly. "I told you I would go to Bayshore some days, if I was free."

After I'd refused to have anything to do with him. I didn't say that. "I remember. You found a Hunter on the grounds."

Cor nodded. "I'd trained, of course. You've seen. I always liked training in the circle. It made a good change of pace from my studies. But it was a very lucky thing that the first Hunter I faced was a lesser one, and more curious than determined." A thin smile flickered across his lips, there and gone.

"After that, I spent all the time on the grounds there that I could. I was sure that if one Hunter found you, others might follow. I was right. Not many, but enough to make the danger clear. Soon I was spending even the time I couldn't spare, skipping lessons, buying or badgering my cousins into covering House duties. You can imagine how that sat with my *denet* when it came to his attention."

I nodded. I could picture it in detail, based on what I'd seen so far. It had also been a long time since I'd heard Cor call his father 'my *denet*.' Did he remain that way in Cor's memory, in the years when things had been different between them?

"For a while, he let me honor the duty I might owe a friend, but when he decided I had overpaid my share, he forbade me. He said your own people ought to care for you." Cor's tone turned bitter. "And I already knew how that turned out."

"But a *dacha* comes before the House," I said.

"Yes. I agreed to do my duty to the House after sunset, but only if I could be there when you needed me during the day."

How old could he have been then? Thirteen? Fourteen? Before Bayshore, if I'd been asked whom I'd thought my soulmate was, I'd have picked Coran without a second thought. But what had I known about love at twelve?

I guessed at the rest of the story. "But it got too hard to balance both halves and you came back so that I could get trained and you'd be free to go."

"That was part of it," Cor acknowledged, then he took a deep breath. "I thought you would be the one to come back, once you didn't have people blinding your eyes to the things they weren't able to see. But you didn't. And then it seemed...you wouldn't. I thought it would take time to get you trained, and in that time, you would find me worthy of...of your affection. Or if you never did, at least you would be safe on your own."

By the time he came back, could he even recognize in me the girl he'd made his promise to—the one who wholeheartedly believed in the wonder and magic of another world?

"What's the vow you made?" I asked.

"Ah." Cor blinked at my abrupt change of topic. "It's made in Thurei and calls on traditions of the Houses. It sounds thin in English."

So that was what Birasef had meant by offering language lessons. He knew. Everyone knew. It had been in every conversation since I'd come back.

The only one in the dark had been me.

"How about Kuyene, then?"

He inclined his head, not a nod, but a slight bow, then straightened. Formal, as anyone might have been, changing their life with a promise. "In the sight of my *denet* and my House, I pledge myself to Katherine Kjelgaard. I follow her through darkness and through light. Everything I have and will ever have is hers, all that I am and will ever become. She holds my love, my honor, and my loyalty above all else."

He added, not quite offhand, "There's a part about choosing a House, but of course that didn't apply."

It was meant to be done in pairs, that was clear. There should be two *dachas*, promising to each other, and then remaining with one House or the other. The vow should be matched, but how could I be worthy of this, after the way I'd treated him?

"Katen, please understand. My vow...it doesn't require anything of you. I know I never asked your permission." His voice wasn't quite steady, but he continued. "If there's no promise you wish to make, you don't need to make one. Only do as you said and don't send me away."

"Coran..." I held on to his hand, my fingers wrapped around his because I couldn't bear to let go. How could I say anything without wrecking everything?

"There, you have all of it now." He rubbed his thumb over my knuckles, a little of the tension in his frame evaporating now that he wasn't carrying this secret. "No need for regrets when you give the *denet* your answer."

I nodded, my throat too tight to get a word out even if I knew what to say.

"Let me take you back home." He urged me to my feet, our fingers still twined together. "You'll sleep better and I want to get outside of these walls."

Not much remained of Kuyen's day, but we slipped back across the gap to a chilly Earth night. Cor excused himself up to the roof to keep watch, or, I suspected, to think. I was supposed to sleep, or, I intended, to think.

But my mind refused to move past the obvious.

I couldn't get Coran kicked out of his House.

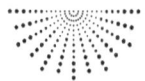

CHAPTER THIRTY

F osemur sat on the roof for us the next day, tying on more *esepra* when Cor called for them.

"Where's Birasef?" I asked.

"Seeing to his duties, like a responsible son of the House." Cor smiled, like it might be an everyday, self-deprecating joke.

"Well, that's a shame," I said, playing it up with a wistful look into the distance.

"Hm." Cor looked a little suspicious but followed along anyway. "Why is that?"

"At least he has a sense of humor," I teased. "He doesn't seem as stuffy as some of the other Thureis I know."

"Thanks so much for that," he said, keeping his tone serious. But he did relax enough for his smile to reach his eyes. "I can spot stalling when I see it, Katherine. Fos has your targets ready. Let's get to work."

But he kept the smile.

I *had* wanted to see him smile, but I hadn't been stalling. With the *denet's* ultimatum, we didn't have much time. I had no doubt that Cor would still offer to finish my training elsewhere, but it had become clear that his loyalty carried a stiff price. He'd paid too much already.

We pushed on past lunchtime, though Cor sent Fos off to fetch a snack to tide us over. By late afternoon, though, I'd reached my limit and Cor called the session over.

When we—and Fos, on Cor's invitation—reached his rooms for an early dinner, I spotted the difference right away.

"You're kidding me," I said. The lovely but marginally comfortable wooden bench seat had been replaced by a luxurious upholstered couch. It would probably swallow me if I lay down on it. At least the blanket and the pillow on it were the same ones from yesterday.

"I doubt it has a sense of humor," said Cor, looking over my shoulder.

"You went and got a couch for me to sleep on?" Ridiculous as the idea sounded, I had to admit the couch looked inviting.

"Why not?" Cor turned to his little cousin. "Fos, how many couches do you think the House has?"

"Hundreds," Fos said from where he sat at the table, spooning a helping of sliced fruit onto his plate.

"Less than hundreds, but plenty." Cor gave me his getting-his-way look. "There are guest rooms if you want one. But if you prefer to stay here, why shouldn't you be comfortable?"

"Well, I'd rather stay here," I said, too conscious of the fact that the head of the House wanted me out as quickly as possible. I wasn't Temarel's guest.

"I would rather you did, too." He gestured toward the table, laid out with sliced bread, fruits, meat, and cheeses for a late lunch. Fos already had a loaded plate, though he hadn't dug in yet. "First, would you care to eat?"

There must have been some teeth behind my joke that we'd needed Birasef as a chaperone, because after lunch, Cor had Fos fetch some books from his latest lessons. We wouldn't be spending time alone.

At least it meant we wouldn't be having private conversations.

"We could just go back to the courtyard again," Fos said, spreading his study materials out on the table.

"But Kate needs rest," Cor said, slanting a glance at me and smiling when he caught me smothering a yawn. "She's done her lessons. But how can I face your teachers if I keep you from finishing yours?"

Fos' young face turned serious. "I won't embarrass you, cousin."

"Thank you, Fosen." Cor seemed to find the boy as charming as I did, by the look he gave me over Fos' head. In English, he added, "If you're tired, you should sleep. He's working on history."

It made sense. Even though I wouldn't be working in the morning, I still slept better at night than during the day, at least in theory. In truth, I'd tossed and turned most of the night last night. But more importantly, I was running out of days with Cor and I didn't want to waste the hours sleeping.

Instead, I sat at the table with Cor and his cousin, trying to follow a Kuyene history lesson taught in Thurei. Cor did his best to hustle a language lesson in there for me, but he took his tutoring duties seriously. I couldn't imagine the boy's regular teacher would have any reason to complain.

As Kuyen's sun traveled its last few minutes to the horizon, I slipped back to my apartment alone and then stayed up to watch Earth's sun rise. Safe for another day.

Nine days left.

Then we did it again the next day. In between, I drilled with my skill in my apartment. Bit by bit, I improved.

When I was down to one day before the *denet*'s deadline, I could make it to the center of the circle of swinging targets, only dissolving those I couldn't dodge.

The armsmaster walked up as Fos tied on another set of targets.

"I'm planning to marvel," Seretun said, the hint of a smile spoiling his otherwise stern expression. He stood beside Cor in our corner of the training courtyard, on the other side of the swaying constellation of *esepra*.

From above, Fos called, "Bring honor to your teacher."

I understood the phrase in Thurei. Cor used it often enough in his tutoring sessions.

I took a deep breath and stepped straight at the target in front of me. It swung past just ahead of me, leaving me in a space that would be safe for a moment. I stepped sideways, dodging another, but miscalculated the speed of the third. It arced toward me, but I concentrated and it disintegrated into a whiff of purple smoke before it made contact. From there, I lunged forward, ducking under a high target, twisted to the left. I unraveled the string of another *esepra* blocking my path and kept going.

I would never be as agile as Cor, so by the time I reached the opposite side of the circle, there were fewer targets hanging than he would have left, but I'd worked hard and I had the basics of my skill down, at least. No purple powder marred my clothes.

"Congratulations, Katherine." Seretun offered me a shallow bow that mirrored his words.

Beside him, Cor beamed.

Seretun's gaze slid over to his own pupil. "Did Coraven tell you how long it took him to accomplish the same thing?"

Cor just laughed. In the training courtyard, he had an easy mastery that the other students and instructors respected. He'd been a patient and effective teacher to me, but others frequently came to him in quiet moments to ask advice while Fos was setting up or I was working independently. More than once, I'd overheard arrangements for lessons in the evening, though I noted he hadn't made any past tomorrow.

I wondered if *denets'* sons could become armsmasters.

"Well, I admit," Seretun continued, "it wasn't that long. He's always been a quick learner."

"Not always," Cor said before offering me his own congratulatory bow. "Now, among Thureis, this is the point where you would begin sparring *zarets* with a partner. But that's not an option here." The comment sobered all three of us some. Cor continued. "There's only one true target of your skill. If you're willing, perhaps this is time to take the fight to our enemies." Then, his voice quiet, "And soon you'll need to speak to the *denet*."

"Tomorrow," I said, trying to ignore the way my heart stumbled.

Cor called up to our young helper, releasing Fos to his regular instructors.

"You could teach me next," the boy said, no hint of begging in his serious, straight posture. Hero worship or not, he had his pride, I'd noticed. "Now that Katherine's done."

"You have an excellent tutor," Cor said gently. "You must bring honor to her."

"Thank you for my lessons." Fos bowed low, to Cor and to me, and headed on his way.

I squared my shoulders and followed Cor and Seretun back to Cor's rooms to discuss how to kill a Hunter.

The meal Cor called for us reminded me of calzones, wrapped in flaky crust and fragrant with spices. The wine complemented it, a crisp, tart variety a couple of shades lighter than Cor's eyes. My stomach tied itself in knots and I couldn't eat more than a bite or two.

"We should assume the Hunter is waiting for us," Cor said. "Your apartment has wards, and no Hunter would dare move against the House. So you have been beyond his reach since the attack. He'll be looking. All we need to do is draw him to a place beyond Truce where he can strike without fear of reprisal."

"Sounds easy enough," I managed, my mouth gone dry. I reached for my wineglass. It wasn't only talk of the Hunter. All the training, and even the lessons with Fos, had distracted me, allowed me to keep Cor at a distance emotionally, even in close quarters.

Now, with his gaze intent on me, every heartbeat made itself known.

Seretun set his plate aside. "Kate, you said you injured him?"

"I—I think so," I said, remembering the solid bash of the door on the Hunter's clawed hand.

"There's no way of knowing if he's recovered by now from his injury," the armsmaster said. "There might be a wait for him to find you. Keep your ears up for other Hunters who might find you first."

"I think he'll be faster this time," Cor said. "He's found Katen once and now he has somewhere he'll start looking."

"Luring Hunters somewhere close to my work sounds like a bad idea," I said, pushing away memories of claws and darkness. "Won't that make it more likely that others might follow? And we'd be in the middle of the city."

"It's a risk," Seretun agreed. "Hunters have many ways to track their targets."

"We'll find a place." Cor caught my gaze with his. "I promise, we will find a place and everything will work out."

He wasn't just talking about the Hirach. I nodded and laced my fingers together in front of me to keep from reaching for him.

I didn't know if taking his hand would even be acceptable, in front of the armsmaster. Such a simple thing and I had no idea how it would play out among Cor's people. If I reached for him, I didn't know what kind of future I'd be leading him toward.

As if summoned, a knock sounded on the door.

I jumped and Cor and I stared at each other a moment longer, eyes wide, before Cor got up to answer it.

I have one more day, I thought, furious at having even a moment stolen.

But it wasn't the *denet*.

"Shom, come in, come in." Cor held the door wide as she walked inside, relief and welcome clear on his face.

She gave me a nod of approval when she saw me sitting at the table. "Good to see you here, Kate." She gave Seretun a small bow of greeting as well.

"I didn't mean to interrupt," she said, looking at Cor.

"Not at all," he said, leading her to the table and offering the empty seat. "We were discussing where the road leads from here." He gestured to me, inviting me to sketch out the map.

"We're going to try to lure the Hunter out," I said, focusing on that single but potentially deadly step. "Cor's been a good teacher. I think I'm ready."

Seretun lifted an eyebrow. "You've been a quick student. You have a talent for controlling your focus. I'm impressed."

"Thank you," I murmured and didn't add that my practice had

come from years of pushing Kuyen out of my mind. I needed to let that go, now that I knew what was real.

"I knew you were capable," Shom said, with her typical effusive praise. "But I'm here with bad news, I'm afraid. Cor, it seems you weren't wrong about the Scholars."

"They were involved?" Seretun asked, the words reluctant.

"It's not clear yet how much," Shom admitted. "But one of the lorekeepers remembers a Hirach coming in with questions about a sickness that had struck among his kith, looking for treatment or a cure. Tharkesh os Chigaf, Finder of the Akevad. That's the name you mentioned, wasn't it?"

"Tharkesh, yes." Cor tapped his fingers on the tabletop. "Then the lorekeepers sent him to the Hall? That's not unusual."

"It's not. But a friend of mine is paying off her debt to the Hall by working as an aide. She was able to look back through the ledger and she found the entry for Tharkesh. Twenty-two days before you said you went."

"So he asked his question and after twenty-two days, he came back," Cor said, his voice pensive. "That's after I started writing to them with questions."

Shom added, "And his debt was to be paid in service, not in goods. Few Hunters can provide a service the Scholars would want."

"Sheverns asked for assassination?" Seretun grunted, appearing unconvinced. "This friend of yours paid her debt in service. It doesn't seem unusual."

"Among Hunters, it is," Shom said. "They rarely visit the Hall, but when they do, they pay for their answers in things that can be collected in the wildlands, or from more dangerous worlds. Places where Hunters can travel more freely."

Shom's conclusion made sense. The Sheverns had all but asked Cor to abandon me to Earth, danger or no, rather than pursue any more information of my skill. They'd exiled Issai just for knowing the truth. But hearing it in such bare terms chilled me.

"They didn't ask us for any payment," I pointed out. "Cor offered."

Cor's fingers flicked in confirmation. "In fact, they said our debt would be discharged by making the overland trip to Issai."

Something else occurred to me. "Why do they keep a ledger, anyway? Aren't Sheverns supposed to have amazing memories?"

"They do," Shom explained. "But they don't all know the same things, and Scholars' time is worth more than a clerk's. They trade their knowledge in part to cover the mundane tasks that are required to run a place like the Hall. Maintaining a list of petitioner debt across generations isn't worth it."

Seretun leaned forward. "Did Tharkesh show up in the ledger on the second visit?"

"No," Shom said. "Kate and Cor weren't entered at all."

I nodded. "Why would they leave the first visit in? They lied and hid other information. Why not this?"

"Lying is the worst of all crimes for them," Cor said. "I doubt they have much practice, so it might not have occurred to them. But what about the others we met on the journey? They were all lesser Hunters. I'm not sure they would visit the Hall."

"My friend didn't have long to look through the ledger," Shom said, by which I guessed the aide had snuck in where she wasn't supposed to be. "I'm sorry I don't have something more concrete."

"My thanks for what you've brought," Cor said.

"It's enough to take to our *denet*," Seretun said, his expression grave. "This should involve the House."

"Katen's not part of the House." Cor's gesture there was decisive.

"That's a technicality. Besides, this Hunter has made note of you as well." Seretun wore a look of fatherly concern that I doubted the *denet* ever showed. He sent a quick glance at me. "Even if you're not a specific quarry of this Hirach, Coran, you're still tied to this. If Shom is correct and the Scholars are involved, this pits the primary Shevern lineage against a son of the House."

Cor stood and offered his teacher a bow of thanks but deepened it, shading his gratitude with something more profound. He held a hand out to me. "We need to speak with the *denet* in any case. Shom, will you wait for us? I need to ask about your *tol*."

I took Cor's hand, holding on tightly. Maybe I shouldn't have, but I couldn't say what I needed to say without it.

But Seretun spoke first, his brows drawn in a frown. "Her *tol*? I doubt you'll need mercenaries for this. You'll have all the blades you need here."

"I don't need her services." Cor squeezed my hand. "But I might offer her mine."

The armsmaster widened his eyes, just as dismayed as I was at the prospect. But what else would he do, if I took him away from everything he had?

"Coran, I can't let you get kicked out of your House." I had to force the words out. Cor's shoulders sagged and I hastened to add, "I'm not rejecting anything. There has to be another way. I'll talk to your *denet*. I'll beg." I was too conscious of our audience. "But you can't lose your House because of me."

Cor shuttered his expression, hiding a flash of hurt and surprise behind the mask I'd seen him use so many times. "It's your choice to make." He turned away from me to his guests. "My thanks to you both for your help."

It was sincere, but obviously a dismissal. Shom lingered an extra moment, glancing between the two of us before settling on Cor. "Let me know how it goes."

When he'd escorted them to the door and closed it behind them, Cor stood, staring at it, though he must have heard me walk up behind him.

"Coran." I rested a hand on his back, but he remained tense and unmoving. Just then, it didn't matter that I didn't have a way to fix everything, to balance it all. I had to try to fix this at least. I slid my arms around him, pressing my cheek in the hollow between his shoulder blades. "Please, I'm not going to send you away. I just don't want you to lose everything because of me."

He turned in the circle of my arms and pulled me close. "Katen, he will push until your third way breaks into the two he's already chosen. Which way will you pick, then?"

After the healer's, I'd wanted to hold him like this again, so warm and alive against me. So close that I could feel his heartbeat. This couldn't be the last time.

"I don't want you to be a soldier," I told him. "That's another thing I'd never be able to forgive myself for."

"Not a soldier, then," Cor murmured. He ran a hand through my hair, brushing the back of my neck with gentle fingers. I had never been aware of how many nerves I had beneath my skin. "I'm good at a lot of things, *dacha*. I can find a place elsewhere. As long as you're there in the morning."

I tilted my face up to his, reading the truth of it in his golden eyes, the confident smile on his lips. But Cor had never been abandoned by his family before.

"I would rather find a way for you to stay here," I said. "You're loved, here. You've enjoyed these last few days. Don't pretend you haven't."

"I have," he agreed easily. "More than any other days I've spent among my kin in years. But the difference wasn't my House."

"I'll make it work," I said. I had to. I couldn't let Cor go and I couldn't let him lose his House.

Cor was still nodding when I pulled his face down to mine and pressed my lips to his. He made a small, soft sound against my mouth and pulled me closer. In that moment, it felt like we must have both been imaginary, dreamed up just for each other. Two halves of a whole brought back together after too long.

We'd admitted our ignorance to each other before, but we were clever students. Cor's mouth teased mine, full of promises. These ones, I could meet. We explored each other's smiles and tastes and I learned exactly where to nibble on Cor's lower lip to make him gasp.

When I drew back, intending to try a line of kisses down the tempting angle of his jaw, Cor cupped my cheeks in his hands, holding me in place. We were both breathless and, at some point, Cor had leaned back against the door to his sitting room. It was likely the only thing keeping us upright.

He pressed a kiss to my forehead. "Any more of this, and we'll never get to the *denet* before sundown."

"Right." That dumped some cold water down my spine. I stepped back, missing his warmth as soon as his arms dropped away. "Maybe...maybe I should dress up a bit more. I don't have to answer him until tomorrow."

Cor straightened, pulling his rumpled tunic into order. He still wore the casual clothes he'd had in the courtyard. I'd changed back to my regular clothes, but that just meant jeans and a nice-ish pink shirt I'd bought with Rose. Terribly casual in a Thurei House.

"I think the clothes will matter less than your words," Cor said. He glanced away, his orange lashes hiding his lovely eyes. "Give him your answer today. There's no reason to spin it out any further, if you've decided."

Cor wanted an answer, in other words. And he wouldn't be sure of it until he heard me tell his father.

"All right," I said, running my hands through my hair to smooth it back out. "Then let's go talk to the *denet*."

Cor caught my hand, bringing it to his lips for a kiss. "My brave one."

I hoped at least one of us believed it.

CHAPTER THIRTY-ONE

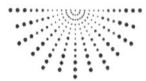

I expected us to find the *denet* in a grand chamber like the dining room the Pareshols had used when Cor and I had visited, but instead, Cor led me into a smaller chamber on the ground floor. Of course, the *denet* didn't expect my answer today, and "smaller" still meant several times larger than my entire apartment and expensively furnished and decorated, but still.

A dozen or so formally-dressed Thureis sat in clusters of chairs arranged to allow for separate conversations. A handful glanced up at us as we entered and their gazes snagged on me, the only human in the House. Probably ever. I forced my spine straighter.

"I have a matter for the hearing of *Denet* Temarel," I said in Kuyene, repeating the phrase Cor had given me in the hallway. Everyone turned to look at us and the low conversations fell silent. I recognized a couple as instructors from the training courtyard.

The *denet* beckoned us from about halfway down the room. The two Thureis speaking who'd been sitting with him rose to join other groups.

Cor bowed precisely when we reached his father. Too human, I did not.

"We request a private moment," Cor said. "If you can spare one."

The *denet* did not invite us to sit. Leaning back against the velvet chair cushions, he lifted both cobalt brows. "I believe this is a House matter, not a private one. Do you have an answer for me, Kjelgaard?"

We might as well have been alone, for the depth of the silence. I could pretend.

"I do, *Denet*." I forced my voice level and clear. "I have no desire to cost Coraven his place in this House, but—"

"Then you reject him," the *denet* said, slicing across my sentence before I could get the rest of it out.

"No," I said. Beside me, Cor had gone still, lips pressed together in a white line. "I will never ask Coraven to break this vow or any other. His choices are his own and I cherish the gift he's given me. But I can't do that by taking him from his kin. You have my sincere gratitude for any losses the House has taken on my behalf. I'll mend it however I can, just—please, let Coraven stay in his House."

Though the *denet* still leaned back, one elbow resting comfortably on the arm of the chair, he reminded me less of a man at ease than a coiled snake. "Coraven?"

"I follow my *dacha*, as always," Cor said. Of the three of us, I thought his calm came closest to genuine.

"There is nothing you're capable of mending, offworlder," the *denet* snapped, flicking my plea from his fingers like trash. "You meet my son's loyalty with selfishness at every turn. You've blinded him to reason and honor and you've proved yourself every bit as obstinate as he is. If you refuse to release him, the House doors will be barred to you both."

Cor looked to me as if the *denet* had never spoken. He held out his hand to me, the gesture clear.

He intended to leave.

I could hear faint murmurs behind us, but I couldn't turn around. I'd watched Cor bow often enough, but I knew I'd never be as graceful at it. I did it anyway, aiming to convey deep respect.

"I'm sorry, *Denet* Temarel, for any harm I've caused your son. I didn't have the strength to keep myself safe on my own world for years, and I'm forever in debt to Coraven and your House for the risks he took to defend me. I know I can't make it right. But a friend of mine came just today with evidence that the Shevern Scholars have set Hunters on our trail. Coraven is in danger. Please don't drive him away from his kin who might protect him."

The muttering from the other Temarels grew louder. The *denet's* gaze swept the room behind us, as sharp as shards of glass, and it fell silent once more.

"What do you think you've been doing all of these years, if not exactly that? It didn't bother you then and it doesn't move you to action now. Your character is clear." The *denet* pushed himself to his feet, tall enough to loom over me, but as straight as a blade. "Coraven, you've disgraced your name and shamed your kin. I judge you unworthy to bear the name Temarel. The doors are barred to you as of dawn tomorrow." His lip curled in a sneer. "See if a human House might take you."

"Wait—" I started, but the *denet* turned away from us both.

"It's done, Katen," Cor whispered in English, reaching for my hand. This time, I let him take it.

The couple of Thurei I recognized from the training yard glanced up as we passed, but even they said nothing as we left.

"I'm sorry, Coran," I managed, hurrying to keep up with Cor as he strode back down the hallway.

Cor hadn't released my hand, and now he lifted it to kiss my knuckles. "There's nothing for you to be sorry for. You were fierce and brave. Truly, there was never a third path to take."

"But now..." I trailed off, my mind churning with all of the repercussions. A part of me—a big part—had believed it wouldn't come to this, even after the *denet's* threats.

"But now many things. I know." Cor slowed to a stop, searching my face. He brushed a thumb lightly along my cheekbone, wiping at a tear. "Be fierce a little while longer, *dacha*. Until we reach my rooms and then we'll talk. Will that do?"

Despite the way his father had treated him, Cor still didn't want to make a scene in the hallway. I nodded, trying not to count the hours he had left before those rooms wouldn't be his any longer.

Even in the sprawling House Temarel, it only took a couple of minutes to reach Cor's room again. As soon as he'd closed the door, he pulled me into his arms. I hugged him tightly, burying my face against the curve of his neck.

The rasp of someone clearing their throat made us both jump.

"Do you still need me here?" Shom asked from where she sat at the table, a small book lying open in front of her.

"Yes," I said, pulling away from Cor reluctantly. He followed me to the table and pulled another chair close beside mine. "I just got Cor kicked out of his House and we still have to deal with the Hirach."

Shom's eyebrows nearly disappeared beneath her black hair as she looked over at Cor. "You're Houseless?"

His hand tightened on mine, belying his calm. "When did my service ever please the *denet*, truly? It's done. Tharkesh is the next stone to deal with. I don't need to worry about the other side of the river yet."

Shom glared at me, but Cor flicked his free hand.

"Katen couldn't have done any more than she did. He'd made up his mind. She offered apology, House debt. She even bowed." He gave me a glimmer of a smile then. Teasing, so my bow must have looked worse than I'd thought.

The fact that he could tease at the moment loosened a little of the tightness in my chest.

"Do you even know what House debt is?" Shom asked, skeptical.

I sighed. "It doesn't matter. Whatever it is, I would do it. If there was anything I could do to let Cor stay, I'd do it. But the *denet* wanted me to refuse...his vow." Of course Shom knew what it was. The conversations we'd had made much more sense rearranged around that central truth. "I didn't want him to get kicked out."

Shom's expression softened, just a little. "I'll speak with my *tol*. At the least, you can stay there while you make arrangements."

"My thanks." Cor inclined his head.

"Not as a soldier," I said. "You've fought enough."

He kissed my hand without taking his gaze off of Shom and added, "But I'm not offering my service as a soldier."

"Understood," she said, rolling her eyes. "It looks distinctly as if I'm done here." Shom gathered up her book and pushed her chair back. "I hope to see you both later."

"Me, too," I said, and then she faded away, slipping her way home.

Cor turned a little in his chair so he could face me more fully. The late afternoon sunlight pouring through his window caught his orange lashes and made them glow.

"I still think the Hirach is likely to find us soon on his own, if we stop trying to avoid him," Cor said. "But after what Shom told us, we have another option to get this done as quickly as possible."

My medical leave would run out tomorrow. The worker's comp doctor, however he made sense of what he saw on the follow-up visits, assured me that my back was healing just fine. After that, as Rose put it, I'd need to get back to real life. I couldn't spend every night waiting for monsters to find me.

"All right, shoot," I said.

"We can Summon him. Tharkesh os Chigaf, Finder of the Akevad. Choose a place and time of our own. We can have this done when we're ready for it to be done. What do you think?"

We had Tharkesh's full name. That would allow us to send him a Summons.

"Telling someone who's hunting us exactly where we'll be and when...is that a good idea?"

Cor rippled his fingers across the back of my hand. His touch tingled against my skin, like static electricity coiled inside us both.

"Not generally," he admitted. "But there is status at stake in trophy hunts like this one. The Hirach must act with honor, or what counts for it among his kind. There may be more Hunters than we'd like, but even if they try to overwhelm us, with your skill, numbers aren't a problem."

He'd called me brave. Maybe I could live up to it. "Let's send for him. Get this over with."

Cor nodded in approval. "What ground do you choose? Which world?"

"The beach you showed me," I said. Cor's brows rose, so I explained. "I want to put my nightmares to rest where they started."

I didn't mean the Hunter. I'd seen him first at Scholars' Hall. I meant the place I'd first been made to disbelieve.

He knew me. "You can see the lights of Bayshore from there."

Maybe his nightmares had started there, too.

"I'll meet you at dawn," he continued. "And we can go from there."

I nodded. By dawn, Cor would have to be out of his rooms, anyway. "Coran, where do we go from here?"

Cor leaned forward and pressed his lips to mine, his kiss tender and sweet. Short, too, as he leaned back too soon.

"The Hirach is first," he murmured. "Stone by stone, we'll find our way across. I promise."

I traced a bright orange brow with my fingertip, framing his cat-like eyes. For all his projected confidence, he'd just lost everything. Maybe he didn't know the way forward, either.

"I'll see you at dawn," I whispered, no longer able to ignore the tug of sunset.

Cor tilted his forehead against mine. "Until dawn."

I slipped back across the gap, hoping there would be other stones past this one.

CHAPTER THIRTY-TWO

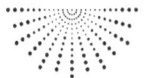

Issai was right. I ruined everything I touched in Kuyen, even when I tried to do the right thing. Even when I had considered Cor a symptom of illness, I'd never wanted him to lose everything.

I'd better be worth it. And we'd better not die.

I dragged myself out of bed hours later, after a restless muddle of memory and drowse, dream and worry. No matter how much I would need the rest tonight, it was clear I wasn't going to get any. There were a few hours left before sunset. If we were wrong and calling the Hirach to us turned out to be a fatal idea, these hours might be my last. There were things I wanted to do before facing an enemy that could kill me.

The next stones Coran had talked about could be dealt with tomorrow. Tonight I couldn't think past this single step, and the possibility that I might not survive it.

If someone had asked me what I would do with twenty-four hours left to live, I wouldn't have mentioned my parents. In the middle of this less hypothetical situation, I wanted to speak to them, in case I didn't get another chance. Though I'd been checking in with them every day to let them know I was all right, it had quickly devolved to short texts. We hadn't been close for years, but seeing Coran and his *denet*, I knew things could have been worse. They hadn't believed me, but they loved me and had tried to do what they thought would make things better.

Calling them up to say, "Just in case something happens to me..." would just cause panic. Ditto for calling Rose. I settled for writing letters. I left them on my table. Someone would find them, if things didn't work out like we hoped.

Then I did the other little things I could think of to inch the sun down toward the horizon. When my apartment was tidy, my bills paid, and I could invent nothing else to keep me busy, I settled back at the table. I'd found the hair comb Coran had given me on my bookshelf. I turned the carved comb over in my hands, running my fingers over the satiny smooth wood, tracing the shapes of birds in flight.

I could wear it tomorrow. I left it on my nightstand.

When I went back out into the living room, Cor was just shifting across the gap from Kuyen, becoming more present and solid right before my eyes. He wore a mottled gray-and-tan outfit like tight coveralls, or maybe a scuba suit. It covered him from ankle to wrist to throat, fitted to his slim form but not constricting, thick without being heavy. He carried a bundle of similar material under his arm. His vibrant hair and bright eyes almost glowed in contrast.

Cor smiled, just as brilliant. "Good morning, Kate. Or evening."

As if we weren't about to go fight monsters.

"Hello, Coran." My voice didn't come out nearly as smooth. I closed the gap between us in a couple of steps and Cor shifted the bundle under his arm so we could kiss.

Once I got my breath back, I asked, "Where did you decide to go?"

"Shom spoke will her *tol*, and I have a place to stay there, for now."

And after that? But instead, I asked, "Did you sleep okay?"

"I can sleep all I like tomorrow." The heat in his gaze promised more than sleep, but the next kiss he gave me was a quick brush of his lips against my cheek. He moved back slightly to offer me the bundle of clothing. "Seretun gifted us armor. It'll give us some protection, just in case. It should fit."

The armsmaster had offered this to Cor even after he'd been kicked out? The bundle was heavier than I'd expected. When I took it to my bedroom and tried it on, the material didn't feel like cloth, nor quite like leather. The texture felt strange under my fingers, almost pebbly. Thick, but supple, it had enough give to fit me like a second skin without hampering my movement at all. Seretun must have gotten measurements from whoever had tailored my training clothes.

When I was reasonably sure I had all the lacings and buckles done up correctly, I took a deep breath and went back out to Cor.

"Good," he said, looking me up and down. "Is it comfortable?"

I shrugged. "Considering the circumstances, sure."

"Good," he repeated, and I realized he wasn't quite as calm as he tried to sound. He brushed a lock of my hair behind my ear. "We shouldn't leave your hair loose, *dacha*."

"Okay."

His nimble fingers worked quickly, weaving a braid and coiling it into a neat, tight bun. The tips of his fingers rested at the nape of my neck, a tiny touch that simmered against my skin.

"Let me slip us across to my side," Cor offered, "and you can bring us back to the beach and we'll send our Summons."

"All right." I found his hand with mine and tucked my face against his neck.

"We'll come back to this, *dacha*," he promised. "Are you ready?"

No. "Yes."

CHAPTER THIRTY-THREE

Cor slipped us back to the training arena where Shom had shown me how to use my skill. It made a decent slip anchor, since he was banned from his home. I pushed the thought away and pulled us back to Earth.

The air cooled, the scent shifting to the salty tang of the sea. When I opened my eyes, we stood on the beach near the edge of the bluffs, with the sweeping expanse of the ocean off to our left, painted silver in the light of a three-quarter moon. Above us, the sky was dusted with a glitter of stars.

I scanned the dark border of trees along the cliff edge, my skin prickling with apprehension, as if the Hirach might somehow be here waiting for us.

"Give me a moment to send this," Cor said, pulling a pre-folded Summons from a pocket at his hip. "Remember how Shom taught you to hide your *jeira*? You can bring it out now. Let yourself be bright."

While Cor took care of sending his challenge out, I concentrated on my *jeira* as Shom had coached me, letting the walls of the 'room' fade away. Cor nodded and held out his hand. "Perfect. Will you walk with me, Katen?"

Hand in hand, we walked along the edge of the high tide line that wound along a few feet from the edge of the bluff. He told me stories in an attempt to distract me, but my nerves tangled too tightly, and most of his words rolled past unheard. When I didn't relax or make any sounds of listening, he fell silent. I tightened my grip on his hand and he squeezed back, and that was conversation enough for the moment. We walked on, my eyes straying again toward the sinking moon suspended in the great darkness.

"I don't often find prey that's willing to stand and fight." The voice behind us grated like steel against stone. We whirled and Cor called his *zaret* to hand. The Hirach stood silhouetted against the bright sand, his cloak billowing in the wind off the sea.

More shadows resolved themselves as four more of the Hunters, ranged behind him.

"You've been trailing us like scavengers." Cor's familiar voice darkened with threat and he made a brief scan of our surroundings. "But I'm still disappointed to see you hunt like cowards. Such a pack for the two of us. I thought your kind had more pride."

"Coraven Temarel, the Hunterslayer himself, and the very human he's been guarding since he called blade to hand. Your deaths will make me legend." Tharkesh laughed, a sound that made me shiver. He stalked toward us. "I see why you guarded her, Hunterslayer. For all her *jeira*, she's a frightened thing that hides in her burrow. I was told she'd be the bigger danger. So much for the wisdom of weaklings."

The other hunters fanned out, creating a semicircle that pinned us near the wall of the bluff. Cor elbowed me in the ribs, a grade-schooler's trick made chilling by the gleam of teeth and claws.

"I can't," I whispered. Cor was too real beside me, as real as the sand beneath my boots. Or the Hunters in front of us. I couldn't disbelieve the predator away. He was real and we were going to die tonight.

Cor spread his arms with a flourish worthy of a circus ringleader. "Come, Hunter. Let's measure my edge against your teeth and see whose name is legend in the scrapheap you call a home."

He angled in front of me, his steps measured and confident, giving me time to focus. I backed away, my feet almost tangling in a pile of dried kelp. The Hiraches didn't seem to be paying much attention to me. I struggled to find the certainty I'd been practicing, to believe this couldn't possibly be happening when it so clearly was.

"Concentrate, Katen," Coran urged in English. "Five is a lot, even for me."

The Hunters charged. I heard claws ring off Coran's blade as Tharkesh closed with him. The nearest two followed him, circling the pair, but Cor's movements came flicker-fast. I had no time to notice more.

The other two Hunters came for me.

The nearest one lunged toward me and I hit the ground rolling, sensing the swipe of his claws above my head. I scrambled to find my feet in the sand and flung myself aside, plowing into the looming shadow-shape of the other Hunter. His claws scraped across my hip, but the armor held. I ducked out from under the Hirach's clinging, snagging cloak. I tripped, my foot caught on driftwood or a rock, and the Hunter's next blow missed my chest, catching my side instead. I felt the armor give with a rip and pain burned in the wake of the claws.

"Clumsy human. Unworthy prey." The one on the left spoke in Kuyene. He wanted me to understand his insult. "But the Thurei..."

"That one belongs to Tharkesh," snarled the other, but his packmate turned away. The other three Hunters still clustered around the whirling, dodging Cor, who was managing to hold them at bay. How long could that last?

"No!" *Center, concentrate!* I leaped for the cloth trailing behind the departing Hirach, yanking him with me as I dodged a halfhearted swipe of the other Hunter's claws.

The tiger I had by the tail stumbled off-balance, then recovered as neatly as a cat. I now had his full attention. Loud as I could, I shouted in his face, "You're not even real!"

With a snarl, they both charged, inhumanly fast. They'd been playing with me, I realized, my heart in my throat.

I leaped through the space between them and a blow tumbled me aside, claws blunted by the armor. The pair whirled in deadly tandem and gathered to leap again as I struggled to find my footing. I pressed my hand to my side, warm with blood, and braced for impact, for tearing, as they closed again.

I ducked, twisted, felt claws graze along the nape of my neck. I jerked away, caught against a sudden, gagging pressure on my throat. I thrashed, hands scrabbling at my neck. In that distraction, the other Hunter bore me down. A stripe of pain burned across my throat, but I could breathe again. Broad hands snatched at my arms, claws digging into my skin through the armor.

He hauled me around to face his leader. One Hunter sprawled, motionless, on the sand. The other two flanked Cor, harrying him from both sides, but their claws seemed to only find his blade as he dodged and spun to counter. But he didn't have the space to attack, and now the other Hunter who had been after me headed to join his packmates.

I twisted and kicked, but my captor hardly noticed. He roared something in a broken-gravel language I couldn't understand.

Cor's head whipped up and the moment of distraction cost him. One of the Hunters struck at him. Cor dodged by diving out from between two of them, but not quickly enough. The blow sent him tumbling to the sand. The Hunter lunged to take advantage, but the other one snarled orders at him. Tharkesh.

Tharkesh laughed, harsh and snarling. "You lost, whelp. Shall we rip out her throat while you watch?"

No. No, they're not even...

Cor had regained his feet by now, the remaining two Hunters stalking around to flank him again, waiting on the signal to strike from their leader. They didn't get it. Cor launched himself at Tharkesh with a yell.

Kate, they are not even...

The monster braced to meet him with gleaming claws, the other two crouching to spring.

I couldn't let this happen.

...real.

I twisted again in my captor's grasp and this time, it melted away. The Hunter howled as his hands dissolved. I ducked, willing him gone, tangling in the trailing edge of his cloak for a moment before it disappeared.

He wasn't real. Not anymore.

The Hunters ahead of me crashed together, Cor's slight figure lost among them.

"No!" I sprinted forward. "Coran!"

The Hunters dissolved in a flare of searing disbelief, their forms peeling away to reveal Cor.

Too late.

His legs buckled and he slumped to the ground, his arms curling about his belly. All around him, blood soaked into the sand. The front of his armor was a shredded ruin, his belly clawed open underneath.

For one stuttering heartbeat, I couldn't make sense of the scene. My lungs, my throat, my voice all worked on their own to fill the night air with a scream of denial. This couldn't happen. Not to Coran. Not because of me.

He needed a healer. Havro. I crouched over him, gathered him as closely as I could, pressed my cheek against his. The single, sharp breath he took gave me hope.

I wrenched us across the gap with all my strength. Night sky blinked into the bright, sunlit white of the healer's, salt and blood to the living scent of Havro's collection of plants.

"Help! Havro, please! Help!" I didn't even know what language I yelled, but the healer appeared, pressing a thick bundle of towel over Cor's abdomen to hold him together, one tawny hand tight over Cor's wrist.

There were others, a moment later, talking to each other, talking to me, picking up Cor to take him away.

"No!" I lurched after him, hardly able to see for the tears, my limbs refusing to obey me like they should have. "Wait, Coran!"

Someone caught my arms and I struggled, wanting him *gone*, but no, I couldn't do that here. I wrapped myself around my skill, my heart, the aching sobs I couldn't release, while my mind spun around Hunters and blood and had Coran been breathing when they'd taken him away?

"Katherine." Birasef crouched next to me on the floor, his hands tight on my arms. "You have to calm yourself."

I blinked at him and it came back to me in a rush. This wasn't Cor's House anymore. His father had kicked him out. Was that why they'd taken him away?

"Where is he?" I demanded, grabbing the front of Birasef's tunic. "Are they throwing him out? He's dying."

"No, no. Havro would never." Birasef looked horrified. "He's being healed, don't worry."

"It's too late." I pressed my knuckles to my lips to keep from crying, but my hand was covered in blood and gritty with sand.

"No, it's not too late," Birasef said, but he sounded uncertain himself. He looked up and another Lewrit knelt down beside us, setting her hand on my shoulder. "Katherine, you're hurt. Go with Rumel, she'll take care of you."

"Kjelgaard, allow me to tend to you," the Lewrit said, lightly touching the ripped armor on my side, and the slashes beneath it. Pain seared through me, but I didn't care. Not now.

I kept my eyes locked on Birasef. "The *denet* kicked him out. Havro's not healing him. Where did they take him, Bir? Please."

"He's being treated," Birasef began, but Rumel interrupted.

"We serve the House, but we're not of it. Not in this. We're healers first." She pulled my arms from Birasef's grasp gently. "We will see you both well if it's in our power to do so, Kjelgaard. Come, let me take care of you."

Birasef added, "Cor will kill me if I let you sit here injured while you wait for him. You know he will."

I gave up and let Rumel help me to a cot.

CHAPTER THIRTY-FOUR

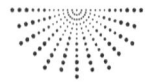

I opened my eyes to stare at a white ceiling. Calm spread over dark, jagged places inside me, too thin to keep the shadows from bleeding through.

Hunters. Claws. Blood. Cor, crumpling to the sand.

I bolted upright, my heart racing. I sat on a cot in a small, white-walled room, alone. *Healer's. I'm at the healer's.*

And Cor is here, somewhere, too.

Unless I'd gotten him killed.

I forced down the tears and got up. I still wore the armor, though the ripped spot over my side had been trimmed away to make a neat oval hole. The skin beneath was unmarked, just a little tender when I pressed on it.

When I walked out of the door, I ended up back in the entry atrium. I didn't see either Lewrit healer, but Birasef was working his way down a line of potted plants rotating each pot a quarter turn.

Maybe I was dreaming.

"Excuse me," I said, the words coming out ragged.

"Good, you're up." Birasef abandoned the plants and hurried over. He gave me a shallow bow, back to some semblance of Thurei formality. Before I could ask, he added, "Havro and Rumel are still with Cor. A wound that severe will take time."

I wrapped my arms around myself. After all, everything else had fallen apart. "Where is he?"

Cor had waited with me, when I'd been healed the first time. I needed to be there.

"He's here. Havro will tell us as soon as he's finished." Birasef cleared his throat. "I can come tell you, as soon as he's done."

"Why? I'll be here. I need to be here." I tried to hang on to the last shreds of the calm from the healing, but panic coiled around behind my ribs. "Just tell me where he is. He'll want me there."

"I know he would." Birasef lifted his hands in a placating gesture. "But the healers need to concentrate. You can't go see him now. And... Kate, you're not allowed to be here. You're healed now."

Despite using the shorter version of my name, he didn't mean the closeness he implied. He'd tricked me into getting healed so he could make me leave. I forced the hurt down, where it knotted together with the others, making it harder to breathe.

I scrubbed a hand over my eyes, wiping them dry. "Why are you talking to me, then, Temarel? Why are you even here?"

"Cor told the armsmaster what your plan was for the Hirach and Seretun sent me to Havro to do chores and wait, just in case. He can't be here himself. Havro invited his sister to visit, so that...well, there are two of you." Birasef didn't answer with anger, though I thought I had offended him. It didn't make me feel better. Nothing would. "The *denet* had banned you both. I wish I could do more, but I don't have Cor's edge, to do battle with the *denet*."

He didn't want me here, either. I just ruined everything.

"Fine," I said, my voice breaking over the word. "I'll get out of here. But make sure Coran's okay."

"Kate," Birasef said, his voice level, but his gaze gone hard. "I'll tell you as soon as I can when Cor's healed, but you're the one who needs to make sure he's well."

Of course I was. I was his *dacha*. He wasn't even Birasef's kin anymore, and he'd already done all he could.

"Thanks for your help," I said because I didn't know what else to offer. I reached for my side of the gap between worlds and pulled, letting Birasef and the healer's atrium dissolve before I fell apart.

The dark, cramped space of my apartment solidified around me and I stumbled into my bathroom. I stripped off the armor, my shaky fingers clumsy on the buckles and laces.

Seretun's gift. Would I even see him again, the man who'd taught Cor how to save my life?

I couldn't stop and think about whether I'd get to see Cor. Havro had to save him.

Rumel had cleaned the area around my wound and wiped the worst of the sand and blood off my clothes and skin, but more sluiced off under the needles of hot water in the shower. I scrubbed and scrubbed, trying to get every trace of the horror off, until my skin hurt and the heat and fatigue combined to make me dizzy.

When I toweled off the foggy mirror, I noticed the raw, red stripe across my throat. Like other scrapes and bruises, it was too minor for the healer's attention. This one had come from the cord I'd used for Cor's token. It must have gotten pulled off during the fight.

If he left House Temarel while I was stuck here during the daytime, I wouldn't be able to find him.

It'll be okay, I told myself. *It has to be.*

Cor and I had promised each other a tomorrow, even if I couldn't imagine what that looked like yet.

CHAPTER THIRTY-FIVE

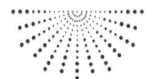

The next day marked the end of my medical leave. Sleep or no sleep, I couldn't miss work.

I got to work half an hour late. Rose took one look at me and told me to go back home.

"You're not ready to be back yet. I thought you said you were healing up okay."

"It's not that." I started gathering up some finished prints so I wouldn't have to look at her. At least I'd covered up the welt on my throat with makeup. No other evidence of the fight showed. "My back is fine."

The monsters had gotten Coran instead.

I could feel her watching me. When I didn't turn around, she said, "You've been acting weird since the attack, not answering half my calls, not wanting to talk. When I finally do get a hold of you, you're trying to sleep at all hours of the day." She rested a hand lightly on my shoulder. "Maybe you need more time."

It sounded great, but I didn't have more time. I'd used up all the medical leave and I didn't have vacation leave. Dropping shifts would mean less on my paycheck.

"I'm still a bit rattled, I guess," I admitted. "But I don't think hiding out in my apartment will help with that."

Not during the daytime, anyway.

"If you want to talk about it, I'm here to listen," Rose offered.

"Thanks," I said. "And I'm sorry for being such a flake over the last couple of weeks."

She gave me an understanding smile. "Forgiven, but don't let it happen again. Anyway, if you don't want to talk about how you're coping, let's talk about how you're feeling." She drew the last word out. "How's your guy?"

I dropped the stack of magnet blanks I'd been shelving. "Coran?"

"Is that his name?" Rose came over to help me pick them up.

"Um…" Not that I'd have to worry about it, but I could just imagine the look on Cor's face if a bunch of human strangers knew him by the most intimate version of his name. Even if they never saw him. Plus, it couldn't hurt to have something that sounded normal. Human. "It's Corey."

"Have you been letting him visit you, at least?" She lifted an eyebrow and I guessed I wasn't out of the woods yet as far as disappearing on her over the last few days.

"Yeah, we've been spending some time together." All those hours working on my skill in the courtyard, watching him tutor Fos. Learning how Cor liked to kiss.

"Why don't you tell me about him? You look happier when you're thinking about him."

"Oh, um." What could I say about Cor? He could fight with a magic sword and craft illusions just to make me smile? I'd gotten him kicked out of his House and almost killed? "He's a pretty great guy, that's all."

That brought back the concerned look again. "Okay, okay, I'll leave you alone."

I didn't have any topics safe for talking about, so I stayed silent and let her work on the list of online orders.

That set the tone for my entire shift. My mind spun in circles over Hunters on the beach, Cor getting carried away at the healer's, the terrible certainty in his *denet*'s face as he'd banned Cor from the House. I misprinted three posters. I gave the wrong change or sent it clattering over the counter through nerveless fingers. Every time I moved, it seemed I knocked something over or stubbed my toes.

When Eviana and Frank came in to take over for the afternoon, I grabbed my bag and caught up with Rose on her way to the door.

"Hey, thanks for trying to help distract me," I said. "Sorry I've been so..."

She patted my shoulder. "I understand. You've been through a lot lately. You ask Troy, though, and he'll tell you it's hard for me not to meddle."

"I appreciate it. It's nice to know you care."

"It's more than just me. Everyone's been asking about you. One of these days you feel like getting out and doing something, you should let me know." Her grin tilted toward suggestive. "That's assuming that you're not super busy with your dude."

If only. My cheeks heated up. I reached for my bike lock, loathing the thought of a long ride home and the lonely wait for sunset.

"Actually," I said, "what are you doing the rest of today? I'd like to have some company."

Rose's eyes lit up. "Depends on how much company you want. While you were out, Logan's show opened at Gallery Twelve and we were going to get dinner to celebrate. Also totally cool for me to take a rain check on it if you want to hang with just the two of us. Whatever you like."

"What time is dinner?" The absolute last thing I wanted was to sit and brood in my empty apartment while I waited for the sun to set. Being around a bunch of Rose's friends chatting and teasing each other and having a good time would distract me, at least.

"Five-thirty. Tell me you have a date later!"

I hoped that I'd be hearing from Birasef as soon as the sun went down. "I just don't want to be out too late. I'm pretty tired."

"Hey, I can drive you home whenever you want, no worries."

I knew she would, but even that would mean waiting the length of the car ride before I could slip back to Kuyen.

Rose caught my hesitation. "Look, how about this? We'll go to that diner by your house. Then, if you need to go home, I can take you or it's just a couple of blocks if you don't want me to drive you. But seriously, I don't mind at all."

"You don't have to change restaurants," I protested, but she already had her phone out, sending a text.

"It's done." She shrugged and the gesture managed to convey triumph. "You don't have to come if you don't want to, but we'll be just down the street and you're definitely welcome."

I managed to laugh. I hadn't thought that would be possible today. "You're the best bully I've ever met."

"It's not bullying if you like it." She pointed to my bike. "Throw that in the back and let me drive you home."

When we got to the apartment, I hurried to the table and snatched up the letters I'd written the night before. I'd been in too much of a hurry this morning. With a jolt, I remembered I had a pile of bloody, not-quite-leather armor in my bathroom. I bolted to the bathroom and wrapped the mess up in a towel to stash in my laundry basket.

Rose lifted a brow but sat down without asking about any of it. Instead, she told me a little about the show while I debated what to wear.

"It's not like we're going somewhere fancy," she finally said when I came out to ask for another opinion. "And it's just us. You don't have to impress us. What you've got on is fine."

I'd upgraded my usual jeans and T-shirt for a slightly nicer pair of black jeans and a ruffly pink blouse she'd picked out on our shopping trip. I wanted Cor's eyes to light up when he saw me.

I wanted Cor to see me. He had to be okay.

"I just want to look nice," I said, too seriously. "You said that looking good is feeling good, right?"

"You do look good, Katherine. This is like the sixth outfit you've put on. They all look fine." She studied me. She herself looked perfect, but she was tiny and gorgeous, so of course she did. "You could always invite Corey, Man of Mystery."

My heart thudded, thrown a step off its beat. "Maybe another night."

"You'll have to trot him out sometime, I insist," Rose said, her benevolent bully smile on display.

"Maybe sometime," I said, escaping to the bathroom to do my hair. Whether or not Rose would see Cor didn't have much to do with me. I pulled my hair back into a loose twist and seated the hair comb in it.

Rose nodded with approval when I stepped out. "If looking good is feeling good, you're on fire."

At the diner, we waited for Rose's friends a couple of tables away from where I'd seen Coran that first night, weeks ago. It felt like a lifetime, and so much of it wasted. I should have believed him.

I should have been someone he could trust to hear the truth.

Troy and the others trickled in and they dragged a line of tables together to accommodate us all.

Rose hadn't lied. Her crew seemed happy to see me. Chloe had even brought me chocolates.

"It's the best way to feel better," she said, handing them over.

"Hey, how's your back?" Eric asked.

Right. I tried to smile. "Good, thanks."

Logan leaned over from his end of the table. "Did they catch that guy?"

I blinked away the memory of Hunters' bodies dissolving away, revealing Cor. I cleared my throat. "I don't think so. Hey, congratulations on your show. How's that going?"

Not the subtlest segue, but the conversation shifted away from me, giving me a moment to steady my breath. I tried to smile and join in now and then, but my thoughts stayed a world away. I nibbled at the food, my stomach all gone to nerves. I kept glancing at the windows, watching the sun turn orange, sinking low in the sky.

When the sun touched the roofs of the houses, I excused myself, declining Rose's offer of a ride.

As the sun dipped the rest of the way below the horizon, I paced my tiny living room, unable to sit down.

When the Summons finally materialized before me, I snatched it out of the air. I got it unfolded before I even reached the chair to sit down.

A glance at the end of the note confirmed that Birasef had written it, but he'd written in haste, making his Kuyene script even harder to read.

Havro has finished healing Cor and says his body is healthy, the injury mended. The damage that remains is beyond his reach. Cor still sleeps at the healer's and will not wake. The denet *has forbidden your presence, but if Cor needs anyone, it's you. Don't tell the* denet *I told you.*

The *denet* forbade my presence? Something uncoiled inside me, furious and unstoppable. He wasn't *my denet.*

Birasef hadn't told me which room to find Cor in, so I slipped across to the healer's entry room. Havro sat in an armchair, close to his shelves of plants. Birasef paced, just like I'd been doing a minute ago.

They both glanced up as I arrived, then looked at each other, Havro surprised, Birasef guilty. The Thurei glanced away first, rippling his fingers in a slight shrug.

The healer stood, pulling himself out of the chair like an old man. In a soft voice, he said, "It's good you've come. Coraven has retreated too far within himself for me to reach and he won't answer his kin, either." Havro closed his eyes briefly before adding, "But he may listen to you."

"Just tell me what I need to do," I said, without hesitation. "Where is he?"

"Here." The Lewrit led me to one of the closed doors. "With his *denet.*"

I took a deep breath and opened the door.

Coran lay motionless on a narrow bed, pale even against the white of his clothes, the blanket, the room.

Denet Temarel stood up from a chair beside the bed, stepping in front of me before I could even reach for Cor.

"I forbade you to be here," he snapped, glaring past me out the open door. Fatigue lined his face, but pride still kept his posture straight. "You're an intruder. Haven't you done enough?"

"*Denet*," Havro said behind me. I stepped out of his way, my attention all for Cor. "She may be able to help your son."

"He's not my son," the *denet* said, the disdain in his tone credible, except that I'd found him sitting at Cor's bedside at dawn. "Are you responsible for her presence? I can hire another healer. Your blatant disobedience is a disgrace."

"I came because Coran's here," I cut in. "He put his care into my keeping. No one has to call me to his side."

It wasn't a lie, though I remained glad Birasef had written to me. I would have been here to look for him anyway, as soon as the sun rose.

"You did this to him. He would be well if not for you." The *denet*'s tone was icy. "Birasef, remove this trespasser from the House."

Cor's cousin stepped up to the doorway, reluctant.

Havro didn't move out of his way. "*Denet*, let me see if she can reach him."

I pressed my hands together so I wouldn't curl them into fists. "Please. I'm his *dacha*."

"Well, he certainly never listened to me." *Denet* Temarel looked down at Cor, then back at the healer. "Do whatever you wish. It means nothing to me."

Havro stepped out of the *denet*'s way as he strode out of the room. The *denet* barked at Birasef to follow him and then the healer shut the door behind them both.

"He will have you removed," Havro said. "But he'll give us a little time, I think."

"How am I supposed to reach him?" I asked.

"When I healed you, the mending happened in your body, not your mind," Havro said, guiding me to the chair pulled up close to Cor's bedside. "But you felt a little of my presence in your mind, didn't you? You were frightened."

"Yes," I said. I remembered hiding away from him as best as I could. The healer at House Pareshol, too, had been in my head.

"I've healed Coraven's body. The wound was grave, and he lost a lot of blood. If you had brought him any later, he would not have survived. But he should have woken by now so that he can eat and replenish the energy his body has used in healing. When I reach for his mind, he is hiding too deeply to hear my call."

I laid my hand over Cor's where it rested beside him. His skin felt too cool. "What if he doesn't hear me?"

Havro's dark eyes held mine. "He will soon weaken as his energy fails. There's nothing else I can do for him."

The thought of someone else in my head still made me shiver, but it didn't matter. "Please, show me what to do."

"I'll try to bring you close enough for him to hear you." Havro placed one hand on my forehead and the other on Cor's. "I can't hold you there for long, so please be quick. Make sure he listens."

CHAPTER THIRTY-SIX

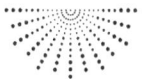

I closed my eyes, but the blackness behind my lids vanished a moment later. Havro strode into the center of my mind like it was a room with an open door. Instinctively, I started to fight it, but then I pushed the fear away.

Cor needed me. I had to make this work.

Havro tipped me out like a box. All the files marked 'Katherine' or 'Kate' or 'Katie' or 'Katen' splayed across the floor in a confetti of moments. Shom showing me a better way to build pillow forts, a whiff of my dad's aftershave. The flare of sunburn the summer we'd gone to Disneyland. Mom's hands on mine, helping me roll cookie dough. The healer sifted through the pieces, searching, searching.

The memories slid past one another, far too many to look through each one.

It would take too long for Havro to search on his own. I pushed forward, reaching for the healer's presence. I called up the pattern that held all of my memories of Cor together: the unwavering core of his honor, the breadth of his generosity, the sparks of his humor. And his love, as constant as sunlight.

There. Bayshore.

The fluorescent lights and stark walls of the building's interior flickered around me for a moment and then disappeared. In their place, Bayshore's grounds stretched before me. The blocky white buildings and institutional landscaping looked desolate in the cold patches of electric floodlights. Fog and the glow of downtown San Jose turned the night sky into a flat, gray smear. This place looked depressing enough in the daylight. Nighttime only made it worse.

I'd never seen the grounds this way, from outside the ward, at night. Havro must have slipped me from my memory to Cor's memory somehow.

Close enough for him to hear me.

I ran down the path to the psych ward, calling his name. Nothing.

Coran would be here somewhere. He had to be. I refused to accept the possibility that he might have been out of reach. That he wouldn't return with me, if I came to find him.

I circled the building, peering around shrubs. When I found my old window, I saw a younger me, sleeping the deep sleep of the sedated. My roommate slept in the opposite bed, but there was no sign of Coran.

I went back around to the front. The automatic doors slid open, but the night security guard didn't look up when I walked in. In the real hospital, the doors behind him would have been locked, but here, they opened when I leaned on the handle. I walked the halls, ignored by the night nurses, who brushed past me on their own errands. *Is this what it felt like for him?*

I couldn't ask him. He wasn't there.

He'd mentioned roofs a time or two, so I climbed the stairs to the emergency roof access. Like the ward doors below, it opened easily, soundless despite dire warnings of alarms. Up here, wind whipped over the flat roof, chilling me to the bone. Coran's long, leather House coat must have been useful, if he spent any time up here.

But he wasn't here now. I went around the edge of the roof, in case I'd somehow missed him below. The grounds spread below me, a patchwork of lawn and other hospital buildings, netted with concrete pathways. Beyond, the city to the north and east.

West of the building, in the direction of the ocean, the roof of the building somehow overlooked the beach, regardless of true distance, as if I stood right on the edge of the bluffs rather than the edge of the roof.

Movement on the moonlit sand caught my attention. Figures below dashed and circled.

Not the two of us and five Hunters who had fought on the beach last night. Just three figures.

Me, backing away. Two Hunters, closing in. The scene unfolded before me like a play as I stood on the roof, a captive audience far too far away to change any of it. The Hunters closed in on the retreating figure of me and caught her, taunting and cruel. I was too far away to help, too slow to get there in time to save her. A failure, all of my skill with the *zaret* counted for nothing, in the end. The Hiraches let me loose to run again, toying with their prey.

No, the zaret *is Coran's skill.* I spun in place, looking for him. I could feel him, his fear a tang in my mouth, an itch in my hands for a blade I wouldn't even know how to use, but I stood alone on a cold, empty roof.

"Coran! Please, I need you!"

Down on the beach, the Hunters caught Kate again and laughed.

"Coraven Temarel!" The yell scraped in my throat. Could I go hoarse in a dream? If he couldn't hear me call him, it didn't matter. All I could hear were the snarls and gasps coming from the Hiraches and their prey.

If I couldn't fix anything else, I could fix that. I turned to the struggling trio and focused on my skill. The fight dissolved, leaving the beach empty in the moonlight, and me out of ideas.

"I'm sorry I didn't learn sooner," I whispered. If I had, none of this would have happened.

"*Are* you sorry?" a familiar voice asked. Coran stood beside me, the wind ruffling his bright hair and tugging at his long coat. I flung my arms around him and buried my face against his chest. He tipped my chin up. "Would you rather we'd never met each other?"

Would it have made his life easier? Yes. Would it have made mine easier? Yes. Could I bear the thought of it? "No."

"Then stop saying *sorry*." He bent his head down and kissed me.

The kisses we'd shared until now had been delighted and curious and surprised—but still tentative somehow, half-afraid of pushing too far or asking too much.

This kiss wasn't. This kiss was passion and hunger and years of waiting distilled into a single moment. His lips were soft on mine, but demanding, pulling something up from inside me like a secret I'd never said out loud.

When I could breathe again the two of us stood on the beach under the moonlight. Coran smiled down at me. His hands had snuck under the hem of my shirt, resting on the bare skin above my hips. It was hard to think straight, but there was something I had to remember.

"You need to wake up," I said, curling my fingers in the fabric of his tunic. "I'm here to tell you that."

"No, *dacha*. I always dream of you," he whispered against my temple. He set a line of kisses across my brow. "If I wake up, I'll wake up alone."

I leaned into him. It felt so good to feel him alive, to feel his arms around me and press my face into the curve of his neck. I could feel his heartbeat through every inch of me. I could stay just like this. *No, there's no time. Wait until it's real.* I pushed against his chest. "I'll be there. Don't worry. I'm not going away anytime soon."

Coran's expression darkened, his easy confidence bleeding away. "But they got you, Katen. The Hunters caught you, I saw it. If I wake, you'll be gone."

"No!" I shook him, shook us both, since I still stood in the circle of his arms. "You saved me. We saved each other. They almost got us both, but we beat them, Coran. We won. Please, wake up. I'll be there when you do, I promise."

"You always promise that," he said softly, with a wistful smile. "But you never are."

Cor opened his eyes. He looked dazzled, like he might still be dreaming. I sat in a chair beside his cot, clutching his hand. Havro massaged his temples, like he had a migraine coming on.

"I told you I'd be here when you woke up." I traced the line of Cor's cheekbone. Alive. Alive and well and beloved.

"You promised," he agreed, his voice wondering and soft.

The healer patted my shoulder. "She came for you as soon as she could. As much as I hate to say it, I recommend you leave soon. Katherine, he'll need food and sleep. See that you take care of him."

"I will," I said. "And thank you."

"My thanks, Havro," Cor added as the healer let himself out. Cor pushed himself up to sit against the headboard and winced at the movement.

"Does it still hurt?" I asked.

He flicked his fingers. At some point, they'd removed Cor's ruined armor and replaced it with a simple white tunic and pants. He pulled up the hem of the tunic. New, pale skin covered a wide swath of his stomach. "I imagine it will be tender for some time."

"I'll have to be careful with you, then." I set my hand on his chest, well above his healed injury, where I could feel his heart racing. "Let me help you up."

Not that Cor needed my help. He used his arm around my shoulders as an excuse to pull me closer once we were both standing. While the area around his wound might have been tender, the rest of him worked just fine.

I kissed his cheek before stepping back. "You heard Havro, we need to go. I'm sorry."

"Stop apologizing." He touched my lips, a simple gesture for quiet that shifted into him tracing the shape of my smile.

"Coran." I caught his hand. "You just got healed. You need food and then sleep, but we need to leave. We...can't stay here."

"I know a place that has food made from books and I believe it has a bed." He grinned, eyes bright, before settling his expression into more serious lines. "I know we have a hundred things to figure out still, *dacha*. But for today, you were here when I woke up. And you will be tomorrow. Won't you?"

"I promise." At least a hundred things. But those stepping stones lay in the future and we'd find our way over them together. I threaded my fingers through his. "Come on, Coran. Let me take you home."

THANK YOU FOR READING!

Please consider leaving a review. I would love to read your feedback.
To connect on social media, find me at:
Instagram: Dana Ardis (@danaluki)
Twitter: Dana Ardis (@ZooLuki)
Facebook: Dana Ardis

AUTHOR'S NOTE

This book exists because I have good mental health care. After a long struggle, I finally got an accurate diagnosis for my bipolar disorder. With the help of my doctor, I found the right medication that worked for me. I found a therapist who listened to me and taught me to pay better attention to what I was thinking and how I was feeling.

It all helped, but it still took a lot of time and effort to adjust to the fact that my brain works a little differently from most people's. It's hard to feel like you can't trust what's in your own head.

I wrote Kate's story in the middle of processing all of that, filtered through the lens of fantasy. The journey she makes to trust her own decisions, face her fears, and find love holds a great deal of meaning for me, but fiction is a separate world from the real one.

For those of us who live on this world full-time, I encourage you to take the best possible care with your mental health and well-being. If you're struggling, please reach out to your doctor or a trusted friend or family member. There are resources out there that can help you. You're not alone.

ABOUT THE AUTHOR

Dana Ardis grew up surrounded by books and decided she likes it that way, pursuing a career in public libraries. Now she writes her own books, creating the rich worlds and vibrant characters that tugged at her imagination as a child.

In addition to writing, she loves art, board games, travel, and anything to do with dogs.